I0572782

THE FINAL VERDICT

THE FINAL VERDICT

ERIC HALSTEAD

STEELE AND CURRY
PUBLISHING

Copyright @ 2025 by Eric Halstead
All rights reserved. No part of this book may be reproduced in any manner
whatsoever without written permission except in the case of brief quotations
embodied in critical articles and reviews.
First Printing, 2025

Dedication

To the men and women who put their uniform on every day and decide to put their country above all else, both at home and abroad.

Contents

Dedication   v

One   Man on a Noose   4

Two   Iron and Stone   17

Three   A Tear in the Seam   30

Four   The Deployment   42

Five   Camp Eagle   65

Six   Rules of Engagement   85

Seven   Highway to Hell   100

Eight   Market Day   115

Nine   The Arms of a Friend   132

Ten   All Left Behind   146

Eleven   Speak no Evil   162

Twelve   Back Against the Wall   175

Thirteen   Frozen Hell   196

Fourteen   Half a Truth   215

Fifteen   The Defense   231

Sixteen   To Failure   247

Seventeen   The Devil Works for NATO   262

Eighteen   Far Away   281

Nineteen   Closer to Home   292

Twenty	Dust in the Wind	308
Twenty One	Return Fire	326
Twenty Two	Across Borders	338
Twenty Three	Bullet for my Brother	364
	Epilogue	377
	About the Author	381

From the Author

I want to start out by saying thank you for taking the time to read *The Final Verdict*. This book has been a work in progress for many years and had been set idle for just as long.

Although this is a work of fiction, there are situations similar to this that our men and women in uniform go through every day. Sometimes, rules get blurry in the heat of the fight. Sometimes, things are not as clear as we would like them to be. Sometimes, the system is just flat out broken, and it takes someone with the courage to fight to be able to fix it.

When I first started writing this, it was a way to deal with injuries sustained in the military and cope with what was to come. As a child, I had always dreamed of being in the Army, and once I was in, I could not imagine life without it. After sustaining injuries, it became apparent that I was going to have to continue on in life without the military, that is where this book, and the entire series of *Shane Alexander* comes from.

There are a number of people that I need to thank, and I know I will miss some, for those I forget, I am sorry. It does not make your contribution to my life any less meaningful.

First, I want to thank my publishing team. I know it's been a lot of work going through the book and making sure that it is authentic, but still an easy read. You have made something that I have wanted to do for a very long time a reality, and I cannot thank you enough.

Next, I want to thank my mom, Mary. I know that you question the decisions you made many years ago when you decided to put me up for adoption. You made a very hard decision that you felt was the best for me. Without that decision, I would not be the person I am. Since we have connected, you have supported me in everything I have done and even let me bounce some crazy ideas off of you. Thank you for your support and for showing me the love of a mother.

I also need to thank my father-in-law, Boyd. I wish I had done this while you were still with us. You always supported me in everything I did.

I remember when I found my biological mother. I think you were more excited about it than I was. All the support you gave Shannon and I and the words of encouragement when times were hard. When it felt like there was no hope, you made sure we kept fighting for what was right. I know I've told you this before, but you really were like the father I never had. We all miss you every day.

Finally, I need to thank my wife, Shannon, my daughter, Lexi, and my bonus girls, Allie, Jill, and Payton. You have all made me a better person in one way or another; without all of you, I wouldn't be the person I am. Thank you, and I love you all.

And to my grandson, Braxton (thank God, it was a boy!). Braxton, you bring such joy to all of us and make our lives so interesting yet *so complete*. I can't wait to see what the world has in store for you.

Preface

CLASSIFIED MISSION BRIEF

REF: OPERATION LAST VERDICT

ACCESS LEVEL: ECHO SIX – EYES ONLY

DATE: [REDACTED]

SUBJECT: AFTER-ACTION REVIEW – NONSTANDARD ENGAGEMENT / FRIENDLY FORCE INCIDENT

The following account has been compiled from testimony, field reports, tribunal transcripts, and unredacted operational records.

It concerns one soldier, one firefight, and one decision made in less than five seconds—under pressure, no simulation could recreate.

Allegiance, memory, and truth fracture when rounds leave the barrel.

- Read with discretion.
-
- Draw your own conclusions.

One

Man on a Noose

A hush had fallen over the courtroom. The air smelled of old varnish and faintly of brass polish, but neither could mask the stench of sweat and fear that had settled in the room.

It was spring in North Carolina, 1998, of our era. The heavy, humid air outside had been locked out by the regimented sterility of Fort Bragg's military courtroom. The dim fluorescent lighting cast a glow over the mahogany panels and the neatly pressed uniforms of those in attendance.

At the front of the courtroom, Brigadier General Louis Nolan, the Fort Bragg Judge Advocate, sat tall behind the raised bench. His clean-shaven square jaw was clenched so hard it was a miracle it had not shattered. His uniform, crisp and adorned with his rank insignia, only added to the steel in his eyes. He had presided over dozens of court-martial and had seen soldiers, both old and young, rise and fall.

Each case was its tragedy.

Everyone had their own crimes to pay for.

And if there was one thing they all had in common, it was that the law made exception for none.

To his right, a jury of non-commissioned officers sat in silence, their expressions carefully measured. Some of them had spent their careers leading men like Specialist Shane Alexander into the field. Today, they would decide his fate.

At the defense table, Shane Alexander stood rigidly beside his attorney, Major William Davis. The young Specialist had barely moved since entering the courtroom that morning. His lean, athletic frame was locked into a posture of attention, though his fists remained clenched at his sides, nails biting into his palms. His dress uniform—a deep green Class A with neatly pinned ribbons—was flawless. Every inch of fabric pressed, every brass button polished, but none of it would matter, for today's inspection was something else entirely.

His face, once youthful and full of life, had been drained of all color. Fair skin looking almost ghostly. His dark brown hair was clipped short in regulation style, his sharp features betraying nothing, but his eyes—gray like an overcast sky—were set ahead, unblinking.

Behind him, his parents, Tim and Mary Alexander, sat on the cold wooden bench. Tim, a man who had built his life with his hands, set his mouth so hard that the muscle in his cheek twitched. His work-worn fingers, thick from years of labor, rested on his knees, white-knuckled.

Mary sat beside him, her back unnaturally straight, as though her spine alone was holding her together. Her hands, small and delicate, twisted the edge of a white handkerchief in her lap, a futile attempt to contain the trembling that threatened to overtake her. She had dressed with care that morning—a soft blue dress, simple pearl earrings—but none of it mattered now. The only thing she saw was her son, standing alone before the judgment of the military he had idolized since childhood.

Across the room, the prosecution table remained impassive. Captain Raymond Lindstrom, a man known for his unshakable demeanor, sat with his hands folded neatly before him. His uniform, as immaculate as the others, bore the Combat Infantryman Badge and an assortment of ribbons—each a silent proof of a career forged in discipline and adherence to military law.

Silence stretched across the room, thick and suffocating. Then, at last, Brigadier General Nolan spoke.

"Ladies and gentlemen of the jury, have you reached a verdict?" His gaze swept over the seated officers before settling on the ranking juror, Sergeant Bassey.

The Sergeant, a seasoned soldier with broad shoulders and the stern countenance of a man who had seen too much, stood with the rigid discipline which came from having spent years in uniform. His eyes flicked momentarily to Shane, then back to the Judge.

"We have, Your Honor," he said, his voice steady.

As the words left his mouth, the weight of inevitability settled over the room like a crushing force.

Tim and Mary Alexander did not move. They only stared at their son.

Mary's lips parted slightly, but no sound came out. Tim, usually a man of few words, sat frozen, his weathered hands pressing into the wooden bench as if anchoring himself in place.

Shane had always wanted to be a soldier. From the time he was a boy, he had spoken of service, of duty, of making a difference. It was all he had ever dreamed of.

And now, the Army was about to cast him aside.

Brigadier General Nolan let the silence hang for a moment longer before his voice rang out again, steady as ever.

"The defendant will rise."

Major Davis shifted first, adjusting the papers in front of him before standing, his movements calm, practiced. Shane followed; his limbs stiff as though he were held together by sheer force of will alone.

Across the aisle, a reporter from the Fayetteville Observer scribbled furiously into his notebook, barely looking up as he documented the moment. The gallery was packed—other soldiers, members of the press, a few civilians who had come to witness the trial's conclusion. Some leaned forward slightly, as if being closer might reveal some unspoken truth in the young soldier's expression.

Judge Nolan's voice cut through the room, sharp as a blade.

"What say you?"

Sergeant Bassey's fingers tightened around the charge sheet in his hands. He did not hesitate as he read, his voice unwavering, though the words themselves seemed to shake the very foundation of the room.

"On the charge of violation of Article 118, we find Specialist Alexander guilty."

A breath caught somewhere in the courtroom.

Murder.

Shane's lips twitched into a scowl; his brows furrowed despite his attempts to keep any sort of feelings from showing.

His father exhaled slowly, his fingers tightening around his knee.

"On the charge of violating Article 92, we find Specialist Alexander guilty."

Failure to obey a lawful order.

Mary's lips trembled. The handkerchief in her hands was twisted beyond recognition.

"On the charge of violating Article 135, we find Specialist Alexander guilty."

Bringing discredit upon the service.

The silence that followed was absolute.

For a moment, the courtroom itself seemed to exhale, the finality of the words settling like a lead weight on every pair of shoulders present. The air seemed thicker, heavier.

Shane did not move. His face remained unreadable, though his fingers curled into a fist so tight that his nails pressed against the flesh of his palm.

Across the room, Captain Lindstrom didn't so much as blink. He had expected nothing less.

Mary's breath finally left her in a sharp, involuntary sob. The sound, though small, was deafening in the quiet. She pressed her fingers to her lips, her shoulders shaking. Tim shifted, his arm moving just slightly as though to reach for her, but he didn't. His gaze remained locked on his son.

Judge Nolan let the silence settle before his voice, steady as ever, cut through it.

"Have you reached a sentence?"

Sergeant Bassey looked down at the final paper in his hands.

"We have, Your Honor."

Shane swallowed for the first time since the verdict had been read. It was a small movement, barely noticeable, but his throat worked once before he set his jaw again.

Sergeant Bassey's voice did not falter.

"We, the jury, in unanimous agreement, recommend a sentence of forty-three years in confinement, reduction in rank to E-1, forfeiture of all pay and allowances, and a dishonorable discharge."

A murmur rippled through the spectators, a mixture of quiet gasps and shifting bodies. Even those who had expected a harsh sentence could not help but react.

Tim Alexander inhaled sharply. His fingers flexed as though he had been struck, his broad chest rising and falling in controlled, measured breaths. Something to make sure he wouldn't hyperventilate.

Mary shook her head slightly, tears slipping from the corners of her eyes.

Shane did not move. His expression remained impassive; his posture stiff as ever.

Judge Nolan's gaze remained on him for a moment before he gave a single nod.

"So be it."

Then, his voice hardened.

"Security, remove the defendant."

The courtroom erupted into movement.

Mary let out a choked sob.

Tim didn't move. His knuckles were white.

The world had gone silent.

The voices in the courtroom—the shuffling of feet, the hushed murmurs, the shifting of bodies—felt distant, like echoes bouncing through water. Shane still stood motionless. The handcuffs were cold, their weight unfamiliar yet absolute. They were no longer hypothetical. No longer a threat looming in the distance. They were real, clamped around his wrists, marking him not as a soldier but as a prisoner.

Forty-three years.

The number might as well have been smashed against the inside of his skull. It felt impossible, a punishment so disproportionate it defied reason. Forty-three years. He'd be sixty-five before he saw the outside world again—an old man, his life wasted in a cell. No career. No redemption. Just time. Endless, cruel time.

It wasn't supposed to end like this.

He had done his job. Followed orders. And yet, here he was, stripped of everything. His rank, his pay, his future. His very identity.

Through the storm raging in his mind, he barely registered Judge Nolan speaking. The Brigadier General's voice remained firm, professional, detached—like he wasn't sending a man to rot behind bars. Like he hadn't just erased Shane Alexander from the Army's books.

Dishonorable discharge. That stung almost more than the prison sentence. He could stomach the time—hell, soldiers were trained to endure. To push through pain, to suffer in silence. But the *dishonorable discharge*? That was a mark he could never erase.

He'd spent his entire life wanting to be a soldier. Dreaming of the uniform, of service, of purpose. He had given everything to the Army. Bled for it. And in return, it had turned its back on him.

Somewhere behind him, his mother was crying.

Shane kept his gaze forward.

Don't look back.

If he looked at her, if he met his father's eyes, he might shatter. And right now, he needed to hold the line. The same way he had in the field. The same way he had in every mission, every goddamn moment leading up to this.

He squared his shoulders, inhaled sharply and continued to stare ahead...even if what lay behind those eyes was miles away from this godforsaken place. His heart pounded, heavy and steady, like a drum in a march for the departed.

The MPs flanked him now, one on either side. He could feel their presence, the shift of their boots on the courtroom floor. They weren't rough with him, but they didn't need to be. The cuffs did all the talking.

Judge Nolan's voice rang out one final time. "This court is dismissed."

A murmur of movement swept through the room—benches creaked; boots scuffed against polished tile. Somewhere, someone whispered. Shane caught snippets of words— "forty-three years"— "dishonorable"— "murderer."

He forced himself to breathe.

Murderer.

His throat tightened, a flash of white-hot anger searing through him. He wasn't a murderer.

The thought coiled inside him like a fist ready to swing. He wanted to shout, to throw the whole damn courtroom into chaos. Wanted to grab the nearest officer and ram his head into the wall, demand to know how the hell they expected a soldier to do his job if they were going to call it murder afterward.

He'd been trained for war. Trained to act. To neutralize threats. That was the mission. That had always been the mission. But when the dust settled, when the bodies were counted, suddenly everyone wanted to pretend it was something else.

Bullshit.

He had done his duty.

The rage burned in his chest, but it had nowhere to go. His hands were bound, his voice stolen by the weight of the verdict. He could scream, fight, demand justice—but it wouldn't matter. The decision had been made.

Shane gritted his teeth as the MPs moved him forward. The courtroom blurred around him, but he kept his steps steady. Left. Right. Left. Right. He wouldn't let them see him fumble. Wouldn't give them the satisfaction.

He felt a hundred of them shamelessly eyeballing him as he was led toward the side door. Some gazes were filled with pity, some with indifference, some with an odd kind of satisfaction. The kind one gets watching two people rip the third to shreds.

And then there were the eyes he wouldn't look at. The ones that mattered most.

His mother. His father.

He was aware of his mother's shaking hands, knew his father's face was so stiff, he'd probably forgotten to breathe. But he didn't turn. *Couldn't.*

Because if he did, he might see the truth in their eyes—the silent heartbreak, the helplessness, the quiet understanding that their son, their soldier, was being taken from them. And he couldn't bear it.

He had been a soldier first. Before anything else. And now, they were stripping even that from him.

The MPs finally guided him through the doorway, the heavy wooden door clicking shut behind him, sealing him off from the life he had known.

The hallway was cold. Dim. The air smelled faintly of disinfectant, and the walls were a dull shade of beige that reminded him of barracks he would never see again.

Shane swallowed hard.

Forty-three years.

Goddamn.

His boots echoed against the linoleum as they led him down the hall. The weight of the cuffs bit into his wrists, constantly reminding him that he wasn't just walking—he was being taken. Escorted. Processed like an inmate.

His breath came slow and steady, but inside, his mind was anything but calm.

What the hell had just happened?

One moment, he was a protector. Someone who'd vowed to serve his country. To be the pillar his nation needed for the road to progress. A Specialist in the United States Army.

The next, he was a convict.

A no-good, treacherous criminal. A single reading, and just like that, everything he had built, everything he had given, was gone.

He thought of the men he had served with. The ones who knew what it was really like out there. The ones who wouldn't have hesitated to pull the trigger in his place. Would they have been convicted too? Or had he just been the unlucky bastard they decided to make an example of?

He thought of his father. The quiet, steady man who had always been there, even when words failed them both. *What was he supposed to say to him now?*

And his mother—his sweet, patient mother—who had always prayed for his safety. What had she prayed for today? Mercy? Justice? A miracle?

None had come.

The MPs took a sharp left, guiding him toward a steel-barred holding cell at the end of the corridor. The sight of it sent a fresh wave of nausea rolling through him.

This was real.

This was happening.

And there wasn't a damn thing he could do about it.

Shane inhaled sharply as they reached the cell. One of the MPs reached for his keys, the metal jingling as he unlocked the door.

Shane took a slow breath, stepping forward when prompted. He didn't resist. Didn't speak. Didn't acknowledge the finality of the moment as the gate slid shut behind him.

He stared at the gray walls, at the thin mattress bolted to the metal frame, at the tiny window set high in the concrete.

Forty-three years.

God help him.

Two

Iron and Stone

Shane stepped off the transport bus into a wall of heat so thick it felt like stepping into an oven. Kansas summer didn't play around. The air was still, heavy with the scent of hot asphalt, sweat, and something faintly metallic—like old blood and rust.

The gates of the United States Disciplinary Barracks at Fort Leavenworth loomed ahead, taller than they had any right to be, crowned with razor wire that gleamed under the midday sun. Thick stone walls, old as hell but solid as ever, wrapped around the facility like a fortress. The place wasn't just a prison; it was a goddamn relic. The Castle, they called it.

Behind him, the other prisoners shuffled off the bus, the chains on their ankles clinking softly like wind chimes from hell. Nobody talked. The heat sucked the words right out of the air, and besides, what was there to say? Everyone here had already lost.

Shane squared his shoulders, keeping his posture straight. They could strip him of his rank, his uniform, his name—hell, they already had. But they weren't getting his spine.

A group of guards in crisp khaki uniforms stood waiting, hands on their belts, eyes sharp. They weren't like the MPs he was used to. These men weren't part of his world anymore. They were here to make sure he understood that.

"Move."

The order was barked, short, and clipped.

Shane walked.

Processing took hours.

First, they took his name. Gave him a number. 45287. That was him now. Just five digits sewn onto a jumpsuit.

Then came the paperwork, fingerprints, the medical exam. He stood still as they photographed him—front, side, back—like an animal being cataloged.

When they handed him his new uniform, it was stiff, uncomfortable. Faded brown, like everything else in this place. He pulled it on, the fabric rough against his skin, nothing like the crisp military fatigues he had once taken pride in.

He caught his reflection in a scratched-up mirror as they buzzed his hair down to regulation length. The sight made his stomach tighten. The beard he'd been forced to shave off, the empty stare in his own eyes—he barely recognized the man looking back at him.

They weren't just locking him up. They were erasing him.

By the time they led him out onto the main yard, the sun was beginning to sink behind the stone walls, casting long shadows across the compound. The place was massive—concrete buildings stacked like lifeless gray tombstones. The yard itself was a stretch of hard-packed dirt, ringed by high fences and guard towers. No grass, no trees. Just heat and dust and the quiet hum of a prison running like a well-oiled machine.

The first thing he noticed was how orderly everything was. This wasn't some civilian pen filled with junkies and gangbangers stabbing each other over cigarettes. This was military.

Everyone walked in formation. No talking out of turn. No slouching. Every move had purpose, drilled into them by the same institution that had trained them to be soldiers in the first place. And now, they were prisoners.

He followed the guard through the main corridor, the heavy steel doors clanking shut behind them. The air inside smelled like sweat and disinfectant, the same institutional stink he had known in every barracks he'd ever slept in.

He passed row after row of identical cells—men standing at attention for evening count, backs straight, eyes forward. Some glanced at him, sizing him up. Others didn't bother. Everyone here had seen fresh meat before.

Finally, they stopped in front of his new home.

Cell 14, Block C.

The door slid open with a metallic groan.

"In," the guard ordered.

Shane stepped inside.

The cell was a tight fit—eight feet long, six feet wide. Just enough space for a cot, a metal toilet, and a tiny desk bolted to the wall. No privacy, no comforts. He had seen smaller rooms in forward operating bases overseas, but at least there, he could step outside without a leash.

The door slammed shut behind him, the sound final.

He was in.

***

Day One hit like a boot to the ribs.

0430 wake-up. Military discipline never died in a place like this. When the lights flicked on, Shane was already sitting up, boots laced, back straight. Old habits.

Mess hall was silent. No talking, no laughing. Just trays slamming down, metal spoons scraping against cheap food. The eggs were rubber, the toast was cold, but he ate without complaint.

Work detail followed. Laundry duty. Scrubbing uniforms for men who used to wear real ones. The irony wasn't lost on him.

Lunch. Count. More work. More silence.

And then came yard time.

That's where things got interesting.

Shane had spent years in military units where a man's reputation was everything. Here? Same rules applied. Just different stakes.

The first lesson came fast.

He was leaning against the fence, soaking in the Kansas heat, when a voice cut through the air.

'You're the one that shot that kid, right?"

Shane turned.

The guy staring at him was big. Built like a linebacker, arms covered in faded ink from his old unit. His face was lined, eyes full of something unreadable. Not hostility. Not yet.

Shane met his gaze, steady. 'What's it to you?"

The man smirked, taking a slow step forward. "Just wondering how a soldier ends up a murderer."

There it was. The challenge. The test.

A dozen eyes locked on them from across the yard. Some waiting to see if Shane would fold. Some waiting to see if there'd be blood.

Shane's eyes widened, but he kept his voice calm. "You ever clear a room, Marine?"

The guy's expression didn't change. "Yeah."

"You ever hesitate?"

Silence.

Shane took a step closer, just enough for his words to land heavy. "Neither did I."

The man studied him for a long moment, then gave a slow nod. Not approval. Not friendship. Just understanding.

The tension bled away, and the moment passed.

Nevertheless, weeks turned into months.

Prison life settled into a brutal, mind-numbing rhythm.

At 0430, Shane sat on the edge of his cot, elbows resting on his knees, staring at the gray concrete floor of his cell. The air inside was thick—stale, heavy with the faint stench of sweat and disinfectant. The place never felt clean, no matter how many times the guards made them scrub it down. The walls, cold and unyielding, had long absorbed the weight of shattered dreams and dead ambitions.

A hard clang echoed through the corridor—someone shutting a steel door too hard. Somewhere down the block, an argument flared up, voices sharp and ragged, followed by the bark of a guard telling them to shut the hell up.

Shane barely blinked.

Around oh-five hundred, they let the animals out. The yard was already boiling under the Kansas summer sun, heat waves shimmering off the concrete. The smell of dust and hot metal hung in the air, mixing with the sweat of men who had long given up on anything resembling dignity.

They lined up in rows, heads forward, shoulders squared. Some still carried themselves like soldiers, backs straight, trying to hold onto something of their past. Others had given up completely—slouched shoulders, dead eyes, men who had surrendered to the machine.

Shane stood in the middle, silent.

Roll call. Names became numbers. Men became statistics.

They moved through the motions—marching to the chow hall, eating in silence, keeping their heads down. Some of the lifers talked, the ones who had been here long enough to carve out a place. They ran gambling rings, traded contraband, held their own strange kind of power. Shane ignored them.

He ignored everything.

Half an hour later was when the worms needed feeding. Shane sat at a corner table, away from the clusters of men who had formed their own groups. Some stuck together by branch—former Army with Army, Marines with Marines. Others grouped up by race or gangs.

Shane stayed alone.

He ate quietly—plastic fork scraping against the cheap plastic tray. The food was the same every day: some kind of pale, rubbery meat, watery vegetables, bread that felt like eating a sponge. It didn't matter. He wasn't here to enjoy anything.

From the next table over, he could hear some of the other guys talking.

"Another goddamn class?" One of them snorted. "You really think that's gonna get you outta here any faster?"

"Gotta do something," another said. "Ain't gonna rot in here like the rest of you."

A third one chuckled. "Hate to break it to you, man, but we all rotting. Just at different speeds."

Shane tuned them out.

Programs, therapy, reintegration courses. They pushed all that hard here. Some guys went to classes, worked prison jobs, tried to rebuild something. The ones with shorter sentences played along, hoping for good behavior points. The ones in for life just did whatever they had to do to keep their heads above water.

Around 1745, the sun dipped lower, but the heat still clung to the concrete.

Shane stood near the edge of the yard, arms crossed, watching the basketball game in the center. The usual players were out—big guys, loud guys, the ones who had something to prove. A fight had nearly broken out earlier, but it fizzled out when the guards shot a warning glare from the towers above.

Shane never spoke, simply stood in a corner and stared at the concrete.

When it was finally 2000, the lights went out.

He lay on his cot, staring at the ceiling.

The nights were worse.

During the day, he could keep moving, keep his focus on the routines. But at night, when the cell block went quiet, when the guards did their rounds and the only sound was the occasional snore or the rustling of a restless body, that's when the memories came creeping back.

He could still feel the weight of the trigger against his finger.

He shut his eyes, but the images were waiting for him.

Some guys talked about regrets. About choices. About how they wished they'd done things differently. Shane didn't wish that. He knew he had done what he was trained to do. He had followed orders. He had protected his men.

So why the hell was he in here?

The anger boiled up, tight in his chest. But it had nowhere to go. It never did. He let out a slow breath and turned onto his side, facing the wall.

Nothing new ever happened. No phone calls. No letters. His parents had stopped visiting after the first month; he'd refused to engage with them. His mother's tears were too much to bear, his father's silence worse.

The world outside kept moving. His old unit was still out there, still training, still deploying. His name was forgotten, buried beneath newer headlines, newer scandals.

Here, inside these walls, Shane had no future. No past.

Just now.

And *now* was a stone box lined with iron.

Some days, the anger burned so hot he felt like it might consume him. Other days, he felt nothing at all.

That was the dangerous part.

Because when you stop feeling, you stop fighting. And once you stop fighting...You're just another number in the system. One with five digits to be exact.

***

The smell hit first—gunpowder, burnt flesh, wet earth. It was the kind of stench that burrowed into a man's skin, clung to his clothes, made a home in his lungs. It was always damp here. Even when the sun broke through the low-hanging clouds, it felt like the mud swallowed the light whole.

Shane moved fast, his boots sinking into the ruined ground with every step. The air cracked with gunfire, sharp, unforgiving. A familiar chorus. He barely registered it anymore.

Ahead, a collapsed shack smoldered, its roof a charred skeleton. The smoke curled thick into the air, blending with the cold mist that hung over the valley.

Movement.

To his right—thirty meters out, just past a row of rusted-out cars. Someone darted between the wreckage, too fast for him to get a clean ID. Civilian? Combatant? He didn't have the luxury of hesitation.

He raised his rifle.

"Soldier! Hold fire!" Sergeant Laughlin's voice cut through the chaos. "It's a kid!"

The words barely had time to register before Shane saw him—thin, ragged, covered in soot. A boy, maybe ten, clutching something against his chest, eyes wild. He looked right at Shane, lips moving, but the noise swallowed the words whole.

Shane's finger was already tightening on the trigger.

Then he saw it—the cord running up the boy's sleeve. The weight of something beneath his tattered jacket.

A vest.

The kid took a step forward.

Shane fired.

A flash of light. A deafening roar.

The world shattered.

Shane blinked.

The echoes of the explosion faded into the low murmur of prison noise. The stink of Bosnia—smoke, blood, damp rot—was gone, replaced by the sterile, chemical bite of the USDB.

His fingers dug into the rough fabric of his prison-issued pants; his knuckles white. He exhaled slowly, but the weight in his chest didn't lift.

Same dream. Same memory. *Always the same ending.*

Outside his cell, boots scuffed against the concrete floor. A guard.

"Four-five-two-eight-seven."

Shane didn't move. They didn't call him by name anymore. He wasn't Specialist Alexander. He wasn't a soldier. He wasn't even a person, just another goddamn number.

The guard rapped a knuckle against the bars. "You got a visitor."

Shane frowned. His parents had stopped coming months ago. There was no one left.

"Not family," the guard added, as if reading his mind. "Some civilian lawyer. Michael Chisholm."

Shane didn't answer. He just stared at the wall, scowling.

A lawyer. What the hell did a lawyer want with him?

The guard shifted, clearly impatient. "You wanna see him or not?"

Shane closed his eyes.

Bosnia was still there, waiting for him. Every time he shut his eyes, every time he let his mind drift, he was back in that valley. Back in the mud, back in the smoke, back in the moment where it all unraveled.

But now, for the first time in a long time... someone was offering him something.

A chance. A reason to care.

He let out a slow breath.

"Yeah," he said finally. "I'll see him."

Three

A Tear in the Seam

The visitor's room at Fort Leavenworth was a sterile, functional space designed less for comfort and more for control. Cinder block walls, painted a dull off-white, enclosed the room like a forgotten basement, the kind where conversations were meant to *die.* The air smelled of cheap disinfectant and old coffee, a scent that clung to the linoleum floor and the metal chairs bolted to the ground.

A long Plexiglas partition stretched across the middle of the room, dividing inmates from visitors. No warm embraces, no reassuring handshakes—just reinforced glass, thick enough to remind you that whatever life you once had was on the other side. A black phone was mounted on either side of the barrier, the only link between two worlds that would never touch.

Shane was marched in, his wrists cuffed to a chain at his waist, his ankles shackled just tight enough to limit his strides. He'd stopped noticing the weight of the restraints weeks ago. They were just part of him now, the same way his inmate number had replaced his name, the same way his reflection in the scratched metal mirror of his cell barely looked like the soldier he used to be.

Two guards escorted him, one in front, one behind. Standard procedure. Nobody got left alone with a convicted murderer, even if he was just another uniform in a sea of forgotten men.

"Sit," one of the guards ordered, voice flat.

Shane lowered himself onto the chair, the metal cold even through his prison jumpsuit. He hadn't asked for a visitor. His parents had stopped coming after the sentencing, unable to look at him without breaking down. Most of his friends had disappeared the moment the conviction came down. He didn't blame them. Nobody wanted to be associated with the guy who got thrown in the brig for murder.

So, whoever the hell this was, it wasn't a friendly face.

He looked across the glass.

The man sitting on the other side wasn't military, but he carried himself like he'd been in the game before. And he probably had. It wasn't uncommon for officers to demand or bring in their own personal lawyers instead of state-appointed ones. His posture was too sharp, his shoulders squared like someone who still had discipline in his bones. Mid-to-late thirties, short dark hair neatly combed, sharp jawline just beginning to show hints of age. He was clean-shaven, but not in a way that screamed high-priced law firm—more like he did it out of habit. His suit was good quality, well-fitted, but not flashy. This wasn't a man who cared about impressing people with money—*he cared about being taken seriously.*

Shane picked up the phone. The man did the same.

"Shane Alexander," the man said, nodding once like he was confirming it for himself. His voice was steady, direct. "I'm *Mike* Chisholm."

Shane didn't respond. He just stared, waiting.

Chisholm exhaled, resting an arm on the table. "I know you didn't request this meeting, but I need you to hear me out."

Shane glanced at the guards posted along the back wall, their hands resting near their batons. He turned back to Chisholm, glaring.

"I already had a lawyer," he said, voice low. "Didn't do me much good."

Chisholm's expression didn't change. If anything, there was a flicker of understanding in his eyes.

"Yeah," he said. "I read the transcripts. That's why I'm here."

Shane narrowed his eyes. "Why?"

"Because I work with military clients, and *your* trial was a goddamn mess."

That got Shane's attention.

Chisholm leaned forward slightly, lowering his voice just enough to keep the conversation from carrying to the guards.

"I reviewed every piece of testimony, every motion, every ruling Judge Nolan made," he said. "Your court-appointed attorney? Useless. The prosecution ran circles around him, and he didn't push back on half the things he should have. He let evidence get entered without challenge and let witnesses go unchecked. And that's before we get to the real problem."

Shane stayed silent, but his grip on the receiver tightened. Chisholm leaned forward again, adjusting the way he sat like this conversation wasn't something he could afford to rush.

"Like I said, I've been through your entire trial transcript," Chisholm began, his tone matter-of-fact. "Every page. Every exchange between you and the prosecution. Every single question that was asked of you. And let me tell you something, Alexander, the issues are glaring."

Shane stiffened. "Issues?" he repeated, a small sneer pulling at his lips. "What the hell are you talking about? The trial's done. They found me guilty. What's the point now?"

Chisholm held up a hand, his face calm but his eyes intent on Shane. "The trial's not as solid as you think. You were railroaded, plain and simple. And that's not just me talking. You don't get sent to Leavenworth for *nothing*—especially when there's clear evidence of procedural errors that could've had a massive impact on the outcome."

Shane shifted uncomfortably, eyes lowering to set at the floor. Chisholm knew that look. The look of a man who hadn't just lost his life, he'd lost his spirit too.

Shane's eyes darted up, and he stared at him skeptically. "What kind of 'errors' are we talking about?"

Chisholm leaned back, folding his arms across his chest. "First off, the whole jury selection process was a disaster. Do you remember who was on your jury?"

Shane blinked. "I... I don't know. I wasn't paying attention to that."

"Exactly." Chisholm's eyes were sharp now, his voice taking on a slight edge. "But your court-appointed lawyer sure as hell should've been. He didn't bother to challenge any of the jurors who had biases. Hell, a few of them had direct military connections, and one was even married to someone in a high-ranking government position." He shook his head. "That's a major conflict of interest, Alexander. A lawyer with half a brain would've raised hell about that, but yours didn't. And that's not all. There were questions about whether the prosecution had misrepresented your actions. They've got a history of playing fast and loose with facts, but your attorney didn't bother to challenge any of that either."

Shane frowned. "But they read the charges, didn't they? I mean, it was all laid out in front of me, right? The court heard it all."

Chisholm exhaled sharply. "Yeah, but here's the thing, Alexander. The trial record is also full of inconsistencies. When your testimony was read back to you, you were asked leading questions—questions designed to make you say what they wanted you to. They controlled the narrative from the beginning."

Shane was quiet, taking it in.

"Take the part where they asked about the shooting," Chisholm continued, voice dropping just enough to convey the weight of what he was about to say. "Your defense attorney didn't ask a single follow-up question when they started twisting your words about what happened right before you shot. The prosecution was quick to suggest that you acted with premeditation, but there was no question about whether you were in a heightened state of fear, no challenge to the way they framed the events surrounding the incident."

Shane shifted, a knot of discomfort tightening in his chest. "I already told them what happened."

"And they took it at face value," Chisholm said, his voice getting quieter. "But they didn't ask the right questions. They never addressed the evidence of the ambush or the fact that there was a lot of confusion about the events leading up to the shooting."

Shane rubbed a hand over his face. "So... what? No one gave a real rat's ass about it?"

"Pretty much." Chisholm's gaze softened a little, though his tone remained firm. "The prosecution had evidence that contradicted the charges against you—testimony from soldiers who were there, records that showed there was no clear line of sight to the target at the time of the shooting—but none of it was presented. And do you know why?"

Shane looked up, suspicion creeping into his thoughts. "Why?"

Chisholm paused for a beat, his gaze steady and sharp. "Because it didn't fit their story. It didn't help them build the case they needed to convict you."

Shane stared at him, disbelief settling in his chest. "You're saying they hid stuff from my defense?"

Chisholm nodded. "Exactly. It's right there in the record. And your defense attorney didn't pick up on it, didn't push for the right subpoenas to get the evidence out in the open."

Shane felt the heat building up, but he kept his temper in check. "So what, they just let me take the fall for it all? Let me rot in here for something I didn't do?"

Chisholm's face darkened slightly, but his voice remained calm. "That's exactly what they did. And your attorney was so focused on just getting the trial over with that he didn't notice the loopholes in the case. And now, you're paying for it."

Shane gritted his teeth, trying his hardest to keep himself from slamming the receiver and cutting the line. "You said that they wanna keep me in; I don't know how the fuck *you're* gonna get me out if they got the damn keys."

Chisholm didn't answer him straight away; instead, he inhaled deeply and continued. "Your unit's engagement in Bosnia was never properly classified as a combat operation." His voice was softer than before, and he lowered his eyes for a brief moment, understanding the need to let the boy breathe. "That means the rules of engagement weren't clear-cut. And yet, you were tried as if they were. The prosecution framed it like you executed a civilian in cold blood, but they ignored the chain of command, the intel reports, and the context of the firefight leading up to it. None of that was adequately presented. That's malpractice."

Shane looked like he was about to break someone's bones with his bare hands. He'd sat through that trial, listened to men in pressed uniforms dissect his actions, and twist his decisions until he barely recognized them. He'd been painted as reckless, as someone who had crossed the line between soldier and killer. But he hadn't. He knew he hadn't.

"I see," he muttered, his voice edged with doubt.

"Think about it, Alexander." Chisholm met his eyes. "I'm telling ya, there's a chance we can appeal."

Shane exhaled sharply, shaking his head. "And why the hell do you care?"

For the first time, Chisholm hesitated. Just a beat. Then, he leaned back slightly, expression unreadable.

"Because I've seen good men go down for bad reasons," he said. "And I've seen what happens when no one gives a damn to fix it."

Something about the way he said it made Shane pause.

This wasn't just a job to him.

It would've been easy to write Chisholm off as another lawyer looking for a headline—a pro bono case to boost his reputation. But the way he spoke, the way he laid it all out without sugarcoating a damn thing, made Shane reconsider.

He studied the man for a long moment. "So what's your angle?"

"You ask the same thing over and over, boy," Chisholm smirked faintly. "My angle is getting you out of here. I'm really gonna need you to cooperate with me here. You up for that?"

Shane didn't answer right away.

He glanced around the room, at the guards watching him like he was just another inmate, at the reflection of himself in the Plexiglas—**the man in the brown jumpsuit, the inmate number stitched across his chest where his name used to be.**

If Chisholm was right, if there was even a chance that the trial had been rigged from the start, then the last three months had been for nothing.

He met Chisholm's gaze.

"Alright," he said. "Let's hear it."

The metal chair beneath Shane felt harder than it had ten minutes ago. Maybe because now, he was bracing against it. Across the Plexiglas, Chisholm sat forward slightly, phone pressed to his ear, eyes locked onto Shane with the kind of persistence that made it clear he wasn't going anywhere.

"I need the whole story," Chisholm added. "Not the one they wrote in the trial record—the real one."

Shane didn't answer.

Chisholm waited for a beat. Then, when Shane still said nothing, he sighed. "Look, I know you've spent months keeping your mouth shut. You think it doesn't matter what you say because they already decided you were guilty before you ever set foot in that courtroom." He held Shane's gaze. "And I get it. But if you want a shot at getting out of here," he paused. Controlling his voice once more, he swallowed before adding, "I would suggest that you reconsider your silence."

Shane scoffed, shaking his head. "There's nothing to talk about."

Chisholm tilted his head slightly. "Bullshit." The sharpness in his tone was back. The guy spoke like a damn CO.

Shane sucked his teeth, furrowing his brows.

The lawyer leaned in just a fraction, lowering his voice. "You don't get sent to Leavenworth for 'nothing.' You don't get thrown under the bus, stripped of your career, and locked in a cell because of 'nothing.'" He sat back again, giving Shane space to react. "You're a soldier, goddammit. You were there; you got eyes. You lived it. And whatever happened in Bosnia didn't just occur on the shooting day. So go on, boy, tell me the whole thing right from the very beginning."

Shane's fingers curled into fists in his lap, the heavy cuffs shifting against his wrists. "I already told my story."

"No, you gave testimony," Chisholm countered. "Testimony you were coached into giving by an incompetent lawyer who was more interested in keeping the trial moving than actually defending you." His voice remained even, but his words hit like a slap. "I read that transcript. *And you know what I see?* A guy answering questions like he's been told to stick to a script. A guy who's holding back."

Shane exhaled sharply, looking away. Chisholm let the silence stretch. When he spoke again, his voice was calm but insistent.

"I get it. You don't want to go back there. Bosnia. The trial. None of it. But we can't fix this if you don't give me something to work with."

Shane's whole face stiffened. The last thing he wanted was to go back there. He'd spent three months in this prison trying to force it all into a locked box in the back of his head, burying it under the routine—wake up, chow, work detail, count, lockdown, repeat. He kept his head down. Didn't engage. Didn't let himself dwell.

Now, this guy wanted him to drag it all back out.

He shook his head. "There's nothing to fix."

Chisholm exhaled sharply. "Alexander—"

"I shot him," Shane snapped, his voice low but sharp as a blade. "I pulled the goddamn trigger. *That's it.* That's the whole story."

Chisholm didn't even blink. "No, it's not."

Shane looked away again, his pulse pounding in his ears.

"I ain't blind, boy. Men don't put on that damn uniform all 'protecting the people' and lose that spark in their eyes for nothing." The lawyer studied him for a moment. Then, voice quiet but edged with steel, he said, "You're still protecting someone, aren't you?"

Shane's head snapped back to him, his glare sharp enough to cut. Chisholm just nodded to himself like he'd confirmed something. "Yeah. That's what I thought."

Shane felt his pulse hammering against his skin. His gut tightened.

"You think you're doing the right thing," Chisholm went on. "Taking the fall. Keeping quiet. But let me tell you how this ends if you don't talk." He gestured vaguely at the room. "You spend the next four decades in here, and the people who actually screwed you walk away clean. Is that what you want?"

Shane looked away again, staring at the floor, shoulders rigid. There was a time when he would've fought back, argued, told Chisholm he didn't know what the hell he was talking about. But the truth was, Chisholm wasn't wrong. Not entirely, at least. And that made this worse. Any sane person would agree; if there was even a sliver of a chance that he hadn't deserved to be here—if there was even a chance that he'd been set up to take the hit for something bigger—then that meant he'd let them win by keeping his mouth shut.

"I know what you're doing," Chisholm repeated, voice quieter now. "You think if you don't say it out loud, it won't be real. But it's already real, Alexander. The only difference is whether you rot in here for it or whether you fight back."

Shane's fingers flexed against his cuffs. His breath felt heavier. Chisholm waited, watching him carefully. Finally, after a long beat of silence, Shane exhaled sharply. He shifted in his chair, then rolled his shoulders back like he was bracing for impact. His voice, when he finally spoke, was quiet.

"You wanna hear it?" He met Chisholm's eyes. "Fine." He inhaled sharply, closing his eyes briefly before exhaling through his nose. Then, after a pause, he said the words that would pull them both into the past.

"It started long before the day of the shooting. It started when we *landed* in Bosnia in '97."

Four

The Deployment

The barracks smelled like old boot leather and cheap aftershave. A couple of bunk beds, a footlocker shoved against the wall, and a wooden desk covered in crumpled MRE wrappers made up Shane and Loran's little slice of Fort Bragg, North Carolina. It wasn't much, but after almost two years in the Army, it was home.

Shane sat on the bottom bunk, rolling a cigarette between his fingers. He hadn't lit it yet—just something to do with his hands. Loran stood by the desk, pulling off his BDU top and tossing it onto the chair. The briefing had barely ended an hour ago, and their heads were still spinning.

"Bosnia," Loran said, dragging the word out like he was still trying to wrap his head around it. "Man, you believe that shit?"

Shane smirked. "Ain't exactly what I pictured when I signed up. Thought we'd be drinking margaritas in the Gulf or something. Now we're goin' to freeze our asses off in the Balkans."

Loran let out a sharp laugh. "Hell, I don't even know where the Balkans are."

Shane pointed to the laminated world map taped to the wall. "Over there. Europe. Kinda."

Loran leaned in, squinting at the tiny letters. "Damn, we really are goin' to the ass-end of nowhere."

The excitement and nerves settled between them like a thick cloud. This was it—their first real mission. Up until now, it had been training exercises, endless drills, and the occasional field op that barely felt like the real thing. But this? This was different.

"They said we're flyin' out in two weeks," Shane muttered, flicking his unlit cigarette against his knee. "You catch everything in the briefing?"

Loran scoffed. "Man, I was tryin' not to fall asleep. But yeah, peace-keeping and all that jazz. We're supposed to keep those crazy bastards from killin' each other."

"Yeah." Shane leaned back against the wall, staring at the ceiling. "They gave us the rundown—Operation Joint Guard. NATO's been over there since '95, and now it's our turn to take over from the IFOR guys. We're goin' in with the 1st Armored, mostly runnin' patrols outta Tuzla."

Loran snorted. "Patrols, huh? That's a nice way of sayin' 'drive around and pray you don't hit a landmine.'"

Shane chuckled, but there wasn't much humor in it. The captain hadn't sugarcoated it—theres were still plenty of landmines left over from the war. And snipers. And paramilitary groups who weren't too happy about NATO babysitting their country.

"They said we gotta enforce the Dayton Peace Accords," Shane continued, running through the briefing in his head. "Means makin' sure the Serbs, Croats, and Bosniaks stick to their sides, don't start no trouble. If they do, we step in."

Loran flopped down on his bed, hands behind his head. "Step in, huh? Ain't we supposed to be peacekeepers?"

Shane shrugged. "Peacekeepers with M16s. Rules of engagement say we can return fire if we're threatened. We're not goin' in guns blazin', but if shit hits the fan, we hold our ground."

Loran sighed, staring at the ceiling. "Man, I just don't wanna get stuck doin' some bullshit checkpoint duty the whole time."

"Better than gettin' shot at."

"Maybe." Loran grinned. "But checkpoints sound boring as hell. You think we'll see any action?"

Shane hesitated. The truth was, he didn't know what to expect. Bosnia wasn't an active warzone anymore, but that didn't mean it was safe.

"Maybe," he admitted. "Intel says most of the big players agreed to the peace deal, but there's still rogue militias out there. Serbian para-militaries, Croat hardliners, warlords who don't wanna give up their power. If we run into them, it won't be pretty."

Loran whistled low. "Shit, man. And here I was thinkin' we'd be throwin' sandbags, handin' out food to orphans, maybe see some exotic ankles."

Shane smirked. "We'll probably do that too, but I think you got that confused with Afghanistan."

Loran grinned. "Really? Okay, big shot, tell me; where the fuck's Afghanistan?" He gestured to the map.

Shane rolled his eyes. "It's gotta be *somewhere*." He shifted forward, resting his arms on his knees. "Could be worse. We're not infantry. We're not front line."

Loran snorted. "Yeah, tell that to the guys who got ambushed last month."

Shane didn't have a response for that. Because it was true. Everyone knew Bosnia wasn't supposed to be an active combat deployment, but anyone who actually paid attention to the situation knew that didn't mean shit.

"Peacekeeping mission," Shane muttered, the phrase tasting bitter.

"Right," Loran said, deadpan. "Because everyone over there is *real* peaceful."

They sat in silence for a bit, the weight of it all settling in. Two twenty-year-old kids from Oklahoma were about to ship out to a place they'd barely heard of six months ago.

"You talk to your mom yet?" Shane asked.

Loran exhaled hard. "Nah. I will, though. She's gonna lose her damn mind."

Shane nodded. He'd called his own folks earlier. His dad had just grunted like it was no big deal. His mom had said she was proud but made him promise to write.

Loran finally sighed, shoving the lighter into his pocket. "Gonna hit the showers." He pushed himself up and stretched, rolling his shoulders like he was shaking off a bad feeling. "You comin'?"

"Nah. I'll go later."

Loran nodded, grabbed his towel, and headed out the door, leaving Shane alone with his thoughts.

He let out a slow breath, staring down at his hands. Three years in the Army, and it all came down to this. He thought back to the briefing, the way the CO had laid it all out—what their unit's role would be, the risks, the reality of the mission. He leaned forward, elbows on his knees, rolling the cigarette between his fingers again. *Bosnia.* The word just refused to feel real.

SFOR. Stabilization Force. That's what they were being sent in for. Bosnia was still a mess after the Dayton Accords were signed in late '95. NATO had already sent in the first wave—**IFOR, the Implementation Force**—to enforce the ceasefire between the Serbs, Croats, and Bosniaks. Now, the job of SFOR was to keep things from falling apart again. They were supposed to ensure compliance with the peace agreements, monitor demilitarization, and assist with rebuilding efforts.

But none of that changed the fact that Bosnia was still a war-torn wreck. Landmines were everywhere. Ethnic tensions were still high.

And even though NATO had declared the mission a success so far, there were plenty of stories floating around—stories about ambushes, sniper attacks, and locals who still saw American soldiers as enemies.

Their unit, part of the 1st Infantry Division—the Big Red One—was being sent to **Tuzla.** *Their job?* Patrol routes, escort supply convoys, and keep an eye on designated checkpoints. Basically, make sure nobody started shooting again.

Shane exhaled and leaned back in his chair, closing his eyes for just a second.

Peacekeeping. *Right.*

This wasn't training anymore. This was the real thing.

And ready or not, they were going.

***

The summer heat was thick and heavy, the kind that made the air shimmer over the baseball field. Cicadas droned in the distance, their song stretching long and lazy over the Oklahoma afternoon. Shane sat back on the splintered wooden bleachers, one boot propped up against the bench in front of him, arms draped over the seat behind him. The sweat on his T-shirt stuck to his back, but he barely noticed. He was used to it.

Loran, sitting beside him, had his arms resting on his knees, eyes scanning the field—not for the game, but for the girls walking past the chain-link fence.

"Damn," he muttered, whistling low under his breath as a group of them wandered by, laughing about something. "That one in the white tank? I swear to God, man. She looked right at me."

Shane didn't even glance up. "She ain't lookin' at you."

"You're blind, Alexander." Loran leaned back, smirking. "'Course, can't blame her. It's hard *not* to look."

Shane shook his head. "You got it hard for a new girl every damn day."

Loran scoffed. "Nah, man, I'm just showin' appreciation. World's full of beauty, and I'm just a man tryin' to respect it."

Shane snorted. "That what you call it?"

Loran grinned. "Hey, if it works, it works."

They fell into silence, watching as the team on the field wrapped up practice. A few players lingered, tossing a ball back and forth, the sound of leather meeting leather sharp against the slow churn of cicadas. The scoreboard's peeling paint caught the last of the sunlight; the numbers faded from too many summers. Beyond the outfield fence, the Del City skyline—*if you could call it that*—stretched out toward the horizon, a mix of old gas stations, mom-and-pop diners, and the ever-present hum of the highway.

"You really think you'll be a soldier someday?" Loran asked, voice quieter now. "I mean…you kept talkin' about it when them folks from the Infantry school came with applications last week."

Shane turned his head, watching him. His friend's curly brown hair was damp with sweat; his cheeks smudged with dirt from messing around earlier. His fingers idly traced patterns in the dust on the bench beside him.

"Yeah."

Loran glanced at him. "You sure?"

Shane nodded. "Always been sure."

Loran was quiet for a long time before he said, "Guess that means I'll be one too."

Shane frowned slightly. "You don't have to."

Loran just shrugged. "Yeah, I do. That's the only way I'll get to see Nashville."

They sat there in silence, the weight of those words settling between them. Then, without warning, Loran smacked Shane's arm hard enough to make him grunt. "C'mon, we gotta get home before your mom freaks out."

Shane groaned, rubbing his arm. "Jesus, Tay, you got hands like a goddamn bear."

Loran snickered. "Yeah, well, maybe if you actually did some push-ups, you wouldn't be so soft."

"I ain't soft," Shane protested, standing up.

"Mm-hmm. Keep tellin' yourself that."

They hopped off the bleachers and started walking back, their pace slow, unhurried. The air smelled like cut grass and sunbaked dirt, the way it always did in late summer.

"Think we'll ever get outta here?" Loran asked suddenly.

Shane glanced at him. "Yeah."

Loran kicked a rock down the sidewalk. "How do you know?"

Shane shrugged. "Just do."

Loran was quiet for a moment, then muttered, "Hope you're right."

Shane clapped him on the shoulder. "You know I am."

Loran scoffed but didn't pull away.

By the time they reached the road leading back to Shane's house, the sun was beginning to sink, painting the sky in streaks of gold and orange. The town was quiet, the way it always was in the evenings, with only the distant hum of a truck engine and the faint barking of a dog somewhere in the distance.

Loran bumped his shoulder against Shane's as they walked. "Race you back."

Shane smirked. "You'll lose."

"Hell, I will."

And with that, they took off sprinting, laughter trailing behind them like dust in the wind. As they disappeared from view, the dust did indeed swirl while the winds carried it away. Far, far away, where the seasons had changed and where time's wheel had spun longer than the boys would care to admit.

****

"MOVE YOUR ASS, PRIVATE!"

Shane's legs burned like fire as he pushed himself up the last stretch of the obstacle course, breath coming in sharp, ragged gulps. His muscles screamed in protest, sweat dripping down his back and soaking through the standard-issue gray Army PT shirt. He reached up, fingers scraping for purchase on the wooden ledge, and with one last grunt, he heaved himself over. The second his boots hit the platform, he rolled onto his back, sucking in air like it was the first he'd ever breathed.

A second later, Loran landed beside him with a loud thud, his own breath coming in ragged gasps. He flopped onto his side, chest heaving.

"Holy shit," Loran wheezed, rolling onto his back. "We're insane."

Shane grinned despite the exhaustion, propping himself up on one elbow. "Come on, Tay. Don't tell me you're already tapped out."

Loran turned his head and shot him a glare, blue eyes narrowed. His face was flushed from exertion, beads of sweat rolling down from his buzzed brown hair. His normally pale complexion had deepened into a sunburned red over the last few weeks of relentless training, and dirt smudged across his jaw and forehead.

"Go fuck yourself, Alexander."

Shane laughed, and Loran, after a second of pretending to be pissed, cracked a grin. They barely had a moment to breathe before the drill sergeant's voice cut through the air like a whip.

"YOU THINK THIS IS BREAK TIME? GET OFF YOUR DAMN ASSES AND MOVE!"

The two scrambled to their feet, Shane nearly tripping over himself in the process. Loran groaned but took off running again, muttering under his breath, "Jesus, this guy's got a hard-on for making us suffer."

The next obstacle was the rope climb, and by this point in training, they had it down to muscle memory. Shane jumped first, wrapping his legs around the thick rope and pulling himself up, hand over hand. Loran was right behind him, his lean frame making him quicker at climbing than most of the bulkier guys in their unit.

Shane reached the top first, touching the beam, and looked down to see Loran smirking up at him. "Didn't think you had it in you, country boy."

"Shut up, Tay," Shane said, but he was grinning as he climbed back down.

By the time they were done with the course, they were both drenched in sweat, their gray shirts darkened and clinging to their backs. They collapsed onto the dirt near the other recruits, panting, barely able to sit upright.

Loran yanked his shirt away from his chest. "Man, I swear, I'm gonna die out here."

Shane chuckled, stretching his legs out. "Nah, you'll survive."

Loran rolled his eyes. "Yeah, barely."

They didn't have long to sit before their drill sergeant, Sergeant Hanley, stomped over, his boots kicking up dust. "On your feet, ladies! You're not done yet."

A collective groan rippled through the group, but no one dared say anything loud enough for Hanley to hear. Shane and Loran exchanged a look, then hauled themselves up, ignoring the ache in their muscles.

The next part of the day was hand-to-hand combat training, something Shane had been looking forward to. They lined up in pairs, fists up, and got to work. Shane ended up sparring with a guy from New Jersey named Vance, while Loran got stuck with a broad-shouldered recruit from Texas who looked like he'd been lifting weights since birth.

Shane dodged a swing from Vance, ducking low before driving his shoulder into the guy's chest. They grappled for a moment before Shane managed to sweep his leg under Vance's and send him sprawling onto the mat.

Nearby, Loran wasn't faring as well.

Shane turned in time to see Loran hit the ground hard, letting out a grunt as the big Texan knocked him flat on his back.

"Damn, Tay," Shane called out. "You gonna let him do you like that?"

Loran glared up at him. "Eat shit, Shane."

Shane snickered but helped him up once the drill was over.

By the end of the day, every part of Shane's body ached, and he was sure his legs would give out at any moment. The sun had started to dip, painting the sky in deep orange, and all the recruits shuffled toward the barracks, some limping, some groaning, all exhausted.

Loran walked beside him, stretching out his arm. "Well, that sucked."

Shane smirked. "What, gettin' your ass handed to you?"

Loran shot him a look. "Watch it, Alexander, or I'm shoving your face in the mud next time we're on the course."

"Jesus, at least *try* pulling yourself into the 90's," Shane just laughed, clapping a hand on Loran's shoulder. "C'mon, man, chow hall's callin' our names."

As they walked, Shane took a moment to glance at Loran. He looked the same as always—tall and wiry, built more for speed than brute strength, his brown hair looked glossy under the harsh camp sun. His face was lean, his nose slightly crooked from a baseball accident when they were kids. His uniform, like Shane's, was drenched in sweat and dust, but despite all of it, he still had that smirk on his face, the one that had been there since they were kids.

Shane shook his head. If nothing else, at least they were going through this hell together.

***

Shane woke up with a stiff neck, blinking against the dim glow of the hallway light filtering in through the door. He shifted in his chair, stretching out the tight muscles in his back. Across the room, Loran lay on his bed, curled on his side, facing the wall. They weren't kids anymore. This wasn't the country. There were no toy guns, no Ma trying to get you to Sunday church, no farm work, no playing in the mud. Nah, he was back where he'd dreamed of being. Somehow, back then, this dream felt a lot brighter than pale walls, strict meal times, and very real bullet wounds.

Shane stared at him for a long moment, a lump forming in his throat.

Loran never wanted this. He never dreamed about the Army the way Shane had. He never spent his childhood memorizing old war stories, watching every documentary he could find. The only reason Loran had signed up was because Shane did.

And now they were going to Bosnia together. Shane ran a hand over his face, swallowing hard.

This is my fault.

***

The walls were lined with maps of Bosnia-Herzegovina, red and blue markers tracing routes, supply zones, and conflict areas. Shane sat with Loran and the rest of their unit, arms crossed, boots planted firmly on the tile floor. The overhead fluorescent lights buzzed as Captain Holloway, a broad-shouldered man with a permanent scowl, tapped a long pointer against a map tacked to the board.

"Alright, listen up, maggots. As y'all know, we're deploying as part of Operation Joint Guard, continuing the NATO mission under the Dayton Peace Accords. Now, Bosnia ain't an active warzone anymore, but don't let that fool you. This place is still a powder keg. You got Bosniaks, Croats, and Serbs all livin' side by side, and a whole lotta folks still ain't happy about it. There are minefields, rogue paramilitary groups, and civilians who see us as either saviors or invaders, dependin' on who you ask."

Shane shifted in his seat, absorbing every word. He wasn't scared, not exactly, but the weight of it settled deep in his chest.

"Ya'll be stationed in Tuzla," Holloway continued, pointing to a northern region of Bosnia. "We're responsible for stability operations—security patrols, convoy escorts, keeping an eye on the local police and military to make sure nobody starts trouble. Rules of engagement are strict. We are *not* here to fight a war. We're here to keep the peace. You do *not* fire unless absolutely necessary. If you see something suspicious, you report it. You do *not* go cowboy on me. Got it?"

A chorus of "Yes, sir" rippled through the room.

"Good. Gear up, pack smart, and say your goodbyes. Wheels up in forty-eight hours."

Back in their barracks, Shane sat on the edge of his bunk, staring at the rotary phone on the small desk beside him. The dim light from the desk lamp cast long shadows against the wall. Loran was across the room, flipping through a magazine, boots kicked up on his footlocker.

"You callin' your folks?" Loran asked without looking up.

"Yeah," Shane muttered. He rubbed the back of his neck before picking up the receiver and dialing home.

The line rang twice before his mom answered.

"Shane! Baby, oh my Lord, I was hopin' you'd call."

Shane smiled, leaning back against the wall. "Hey, Mama. How y'all doin'?"

"Oh, we're alright. Your daddy's out back fixin' the fence again—storm knocked it down last week. You eatin' enough? You takin' care of yourself?"

"Yes, ma'am," Shane said, chuckling. "Army feeds us just fine. Ain't starvin' yet."

She sighed, but he could hear the smile in her voice. "Where are they sendin' you, Shane? When do you leave?"

He hesitated, debating whether to soften the truth. "Bosnia. We leave in a couple days."

Silence. Then a quiet, worried, "Oh."

"Mama, it ain't as bad as you're thinkin'," Shane said quickly. "The war's over. We're just goin' in to make sure things stay quiet. It's peace-keeping, not fightin'."

"Shane..."

He closed his eyes, resting his head against the wall. "Mama, I promise I'll be alright."

Her voice wavered. "I just... I just don't want you gettin' caught up in somethin' dangerous. We been seein' things on the news—"

"Ain't like that," Shane interrupted gently. "They make it sound worse than it is. Most of the fightin's done. We're just keepin' folks from startin' trouble again."

A long pause. Then, "You sure?"

"Yes, ma'am."

He heard her sigh, then shuffle the phone. A second later, his father's deep voice rumbled through the line.

"Shane?"

"Dad."

"You ready?"

Shane exhaled. "Yeah."

"You nervous?"

He hesitated for half a second. "No, sir."

His father grunted. "Good. You keep your head on straight, listen to your CO, and watch out for your men. That's your job now."

"Yes, sir."

"Don't take any unnecessary risks. You ain't gotta prove nothin' to nobody."

Shane felt his throat tighten. His father wasn't the type to say "I love you" outright, but this was as close as it got.

"I know, Dad."

A beat of silence passed, and then his father cleared his throat. "Alright. I'll let your mama back on."

Another shuffle, and his mother's voice returned, softer now. "You write to us when you can, alright?"

"I will."

"And you come home safe, Shane Alexander. You hear me?"

"Yes, ma'am."

"Love you, baby."

"Love you too, Mama."

He hung up slowly, staring at the phone for a long moment before sighing and rubbing his hands over his face.

Across the room, Loran finally looked up from his magazine. "You good?"

Shane scoffed, shaking his head. "You ever try lyin' to your mama and makin' her believe it?"

Loran smirked. "Every damn day growin' up."

Shane huffed a laugh. "Yeah, well... she didn't buy it, but she let me have it anyway."

Loran set the magazine down. "They worried?"

"Of course, they're worried. Mama's actin' like I'm marchin' straight into hell."

Loran nodded, picking at a loose thread on his uniform. "Yeah. My folks were the same way."

Shane glanced at him. "What'd you tell 'em?"

Loran shrugged. "Told 'em I'd be fine."

"And they believed you?"

"Hell no." Loran grinned. "But what else am I supposed to say? 'Hey, Mom, I might step on a landmine or get shot by some pissed-off militia guy?' Nah. Better to just let 'em think we're gonna be babysittin' some checkpoint all day."

Shane let out a low chuckle. "Yeah. Guess so."

A comfortable silence settled between them before Loran stretched and stood up. "I'm hittin' the showers. You comin'?"

"Nah," Shane said, leaning back in his chair. "Gonna sit here a bit."

Loran nodded, grabbing his towel. "Don't fall asleep sittin' up again. You snore like a goddamn chainsaw."

Shane smirked, watching as Loran disappeared into the hall.

The room felt quieter now, almost too still. Shane exhaled, staring at his boots.

He was excited—this was what he'd trained for. But deep down, beneath the bravado, he knew there were things no amount of training could prepare them for.

He leaned back, arms crossed behind his head. In two days, they'd be halfway across the world.

And all he could do now was wait.

Two days felt like two seconds. Shane wasn't sure he'd ever felt time move that fast. It never did during training, and it sure as hell never did whenever he was on course.

The hum of the C-130's engines thrummed beneath their boots as Shane and Loran stepped onto the plane, rucksacks slung over their shoulders, packed tight with gear—and, as their sergeant had insisted, extra socks.

Inside, the rest of their unit was already settling in. Some sprawled across the webbing seats, others stood around talking, their voices carrying over the roar of the aircraft. The mood was a mix of excitement, nerves, and cocky bravado.

"Man, I can't *wait* to test out the new M4s in the field," Martinez said, rubbing his hands together. "Been stuck with that damn M16A2 too long."

"Yeah, because the peacekeeping mission's totally gonna give you a reason to shoot," Brown scoffed.

"Hey, you never know," Martinez shot back. "Could get into some shit."

"Better hope not," Dawson muttered, strapping himself in. "I'd rather be bored than get shot at."

A couple of the guys nodded in agreement, but Tanner—loud, always-talking Tanner—grinned as he leaned back against the webbing. "Man, I ain't worried about none of that. I'm in it for them tan honeys."

Shane closed his eyes, already regretting where this conversation was going.

"Tan girls?" McBride frowned.

"Yeah, man, you know—exotic," Tanner said, waggling his eyebrows. "Dark eyes, dark hair, real soft-spoken. Always in those big sheets."

Martinez snorted. "You dumbass. You think Bosnia's full of Arabs?"

"Isn't it?" Tanner asked, genuinely confused.

McBride groaned. "Jesus Christ, no."

"But, like... it's in the Middle East, right?" Tanner said. "Near Iraq and shit?"

Shane rubbed his temples.

"Bosnia is *not* in the Middle East, you absolute fucking idiot," Brown said. "It's in Europe."

Tanner squinted. "Wait—so, like, Afghanistan?"

"I think so," Dawson muttered.

"Oh, fuck, no!" McBride groaned.

"Man, I don't fucking know, alright? All them places blend together," Tanner huffed. "Bosnia, Pakistan, Ukraine, fuckin' Kuwait—same shit."

"You just named four places that got *nothing* to do with each other," McBride said, exasperated.

"Well, whatever," Tanner said, waving them off. "Still bet they got some fine-ass women over there."

Martinez shook his head. "You're a goddamn lost cause, man."

The argument kept going, bouncing between who knew what about Bosnia, the war, and whether the food was gonna be any good. Some guys stayed quiet, just listening, lost in their own thoughts. A couple stared at the floor, hands folded in their laps, the reality of deployment finally settling in.

Loran had been in on the ribbing, laughing right along with the others, but then his attention slid sideways. He turned to Shane, a knowing smirk tugging at the corner of his mouth.

"So," he said, just loud enough for Shane to hear, "you bring extra socks?"

Shane snorted, shaking his head. "Man, fuck you."

Loran chuckled, leaning back against the bulkhead. "Just sayin', Sarge drilled it into our heads for a reason."

Shane sighed, patting his rucksack. "Yeah, I got the damn socks."

"Good," Loran said, smirk still in place. "Wouldn't want your ass bitchin' about blisters halfway through deployment."

Shane rolled his eyes, but he grinned anyway.

The engines roared louder, the aircraft shuddering as the last of the guys strapped in. A few of them crossed themselves; others adjusted their gear. Tanner muttered something about finally getting some shut-eye.

Shane exhaled, tightening his straps. Loran nudged his shoulder, nodding toward the open cargo ramp as it began to close.

"Guess this is it," Loran said.

Shane nodded. "Yeah."

The ramp sealed shut, locking them in.

And with that, they were off.

Five

Camp Eagle

Camp Eagle, Sarajevo – January 1997

The transport plane's engines whined as it descended, its massive body shuddering against the cold Balkan air. The deep hum of the C-130 Hercules had long since become a background noise, but as the aircraft tilted slightly on approach, Shane felt a knot of unease tighten in his gut. He wasn't alone—around him, the rest of the unit sat in silence, bracing themselves for what lay ahead.

Through the small porthole windows, the snow-covered mountains stretched out beneath them, jagged and vast, swallowing everything in their presence. The land below was a patchwork of white and gray, a ghostly landscape of skeletal trees, abandoned villages, and narrow, winding roads that cut through the hills like scars. From up here, it was easy to imagine Bosnia as just another winter-struck country. But even at this altitude, the war's presence was unmistakable—burned-out buildings, craters where homes had once stood, and the faint, eerie remnants of trenches and fortifications that now sat empty.

A jolt ran through the plane as it hit the tarmac. Shane gripped his rucksack tighter, fingers digging into the fabric. The ramp lowered, and the cold rushed in like a living thing, slicing through the lingering warmth of the aircraft's interior.

"Alright, move!" The sergeant's voice rang out.

Boots hit the steel ramp in rapid succession, the unit filing out into the open. The first breath Shane took was sharp and dry, the air heavy with the scent of burning wood and fuel.

Camp Eagle sat sprawled out before them—a mix of pre-fabricated barracks, towering floodlights, and rows of sandbagged fortifications. Some buildings were simple metal-frame structures with tarped roofs; others were sturdier, converted warehouses and old barracks left behind by previous forces. Razor wire snaked along the perimeter, and in the distance, armored vehicles sat parked in neat formations, their dark green bodies standing in contrast to the white ground.

The base itself felt like a strange halfway point between order and chaos. Some parts were neat, almost clinical—rows of tents, Quonset huts, and storage containers lined up with military precision. Others bore the weight of recent occupation, hastily assembled bunkers, makeshift guard towers, and walls riddled with bullet holes. Signs, written in both English and Serbo-Croatian, were posted around: **"DANGER: MINES," "AUTHORIZED PERSONNEL ONLY," "NO PHOTOGRAPHY."**

The mountains loomed in the background, steep and watchful. Shane had read about the geography of Bosnia before deployment, but seeing it now, standing beneath those peaks, he understood why the war had been so brutal. This was a sniper's paradise.

They moved toward the central processing area, boots crunching over ice-packed gravel. Soldiers milled about in groups, some lugging gear, others warming their hands over metal barrels filled with burning scrap wood. A few locals in civilian clothing—contractors, translators—hurried between buildings with their heads down, eyes wary.

"Welcome to the vacation resort," one of the older soldiers muttered, adjusting his pack.

Someone snorted. "Yeah, real fucking cozy."

Shane exhaled, watching his breath cloud in the air.

***

Inside one of the warehouses, the air was warmer but carried a heavy, oily scent—gunmetal, grease, and the faint bite of burnt powder. Rows of tables stretched across the space, each covered in meticulously laid-out weapons, ammunition cases, and stacks of paperwork.

The line moved quickly. Soldiers stepped forward, received their assigned weapons, and moved aside to check them over. Shane stood with his hands shoved into his pockets, rolling his shoulders to shake off the stiffness. He already knew what he was supposed to get—an M16A2 rifle, same as he'd trained with, same as the one he'd carried stateside. The routine was familiar, expected.

Then his name was called.

He stepped forward, signing the form, then reached out instinctively for the weapon the armorer slid across the table. His fingers hesitated as he looked down. It wasn't an M16.

Instead, the weapon was larger, bulkier. A long, perforated barrel extended out in front, ending in a thick flash suppressor. The body was matte black with thick polymer grips, and a long belt of disintegrating-link ammunition sat coiled beside it like a sleeping snake. The **M249 Squad Automatic Weapon**—the SAW.

Shane blinked, a cold weight settling in his stomach.

"You sure?" he asked, looking up.

The armorer, a stocky sergeant with a clipboard, barely glanced at him. "That's what's assigned to you."

Shane ran a hand over the receiver, feeling the weight of it. He knew the M249. He'd seen it, handled it during training, even fired it a few times—but he wasn't trained to carry it. He wasn't supposed to be the guy running a light machine gun in the field.

"Thought I was gettin' an M16," he said, trying to keep his voice steady.

"Things change." The sergeant shrugged. "Congratulations, you're the SAW gunner now."

Shane exhaled slowly. The M249 was a beast—twenty-two pounds unloaded, nearly thirty with a full drum. It could spit out 5.56 rounds at almost 800 rounds per minute, and while that made it a hell of a weapon for suppressing fire, it also meant he'd be lugging a heavy son of a bitch through the mountains, up and down icy roads, through god-knows-what terrain.

And worst of all—he wasn't confident with it.

He picked it up, feeling the weight settle across his arms. The balance was different, heavier toward the front. The collapsible bipod folded neatly beneath the barrel, but even without it deployed, the gun felt long and unwieldy compared to an M16. His fingers curled around the pistol grip as he brought it up slightly, feeling the unfamiliar heft in his hands.

Someone clapped a hand on his shoulder. "Sucks, doesn't it?"

Shane turned to see one of the other guys grinning at him—a corporal with a scar running down the side of his jaw.

"You get used to it," the corporal said. "Or you don't."

Shane forced a smirk. "Encouraging."

The corporal chuckled. "Just don't forget to keep the fuckin' bolt clean, or you'll be carrying a thirty-pound paperweight."

Shane nodded absently, but his mind was already racing. He needed to practice. Needed to get comfortable fast. Because if things went sideways out here, he'd be the one laying down covering fire for his unit—and the last thing he wanted was to be the weak link.

He stepped aside, moving to a quieter corner of the warehouse. He set the weapon down, popped open the feed tray, and ran his fingers over the metal, checking for any rough spots or fouling. The belt-fed system was different from the magazines he was used to, and he reminded himself to keep an eye on the links—one jam at the wrong time could mean the difference between covering his squad or leaving them exposed.

As he worked, a few other soldiers passed by, some shooting him looks of sympathy, others amusement. Loran strolled up last, hands stuffed into his pockets, smirking like he'd just won a bet.

"They gave your scrawny ass a SAW?" he asked, grinning.

Shane didn't look up. "Shut the hell up, Tay."

Loran chuckled, leaning against a crate. "Hey, I'm just sayin'. I'd have thought they'd give you somethin' lighter. Like maybe a sharp stick."

Shane huffed, shaking his head. "You see what you got yet?"

Loran pulled his own weapon up slightly—a standard M16A2. "Got exactly what I wanted. Can't all be so lucky, huh?"

Shane shot him a dry look before turning back to his weapon. He ran his fingers over the sights, checking alignment, getting a feel for the grip, the trigger. The weight of it was still foreign, still wrong. But he didn't have a choice.

Loran watched him for a moment, then smirked. "You brought extra socks, right?"

"You asked when we were leaving," Shane snorted, finally cracking a small grin. "Yeah. Figured I'd need 'em."

"I know, just bein' helpful," Loran nodded approvingly. "Good. Can't have you bitchin' about cold feet while you're gettin' us all killed."

"You've said *that* before too, you dickwad." Shane exhaled, looking down at the M249 one last time. He still wasn't sure about it. Still felt the doubt pressing against his ribs.

But he'd figure it out. He had to.

***

The morning air hung heavy the very next day. It's cold, damp chill settled into the bones of every soldier gathered at the makeshift range outside Camp Eagle. A low ceiling of gray clouds pressed down on the valley, threatening snow, but for now, the air remained dry. Shane stood near the firing line, his breath curling in the frigid air as he adjusted his gloves, shifting his grip on the M249's polymer handguard.

The weapon still felt unnatural in his hands, heavier and more unwieldy than the M16 he'd trained on. His fingers instinctively searched for the comfort of a standard rifle grip, but there was none. The SAW was a different beast entirely, designed not for precision but for sustained firepower, laying down rounds in bursts meant to suppress and dominate.

Across from him, Staff Sergeant Steven Laughlin watched with the same unreadable expression he always wore, arms crossed over his plate carrier. At 34, Laughlin had been through multiple deployments, his face lined with the kind of experience that only came from years spent in the field. He wasn't the kind to hand out praise, nor was he one to ignore weaknesses. Right now, Shane was the weak link.

"Alright, Alexander," Laughlin finally spoke, his voice even, unhurried. "Show me what you've learned."

Shane nodded, dropping to one knee as he moved through the steps. His mind went into checklist mode, ticking off each action like a drill instructor was screaming over his shoulder.

Step One: Conduct a function check.

With practiced movements, he locked the charging handle to the rear, feeling the weight of the bolt slide back against its spring tension. He visually inspected the chamber—clear. He released the bolt and dry-fired once, listening for the crisp metallic snap of the firing pin releasing. No sluggishness, no stick in the trigger pull.

Laughlin gave a small nod. "Alright. Load up."

Shane grabbed a belt of 5.56mm linked rounds, the brass casings catching what little light broke through the clouds. He placed them carefully onto the feed tray, ensuring the lead round sat properly in the groove before closing the feed cover with a firm *clack.*

Step Two: Confirm the seating.

He racked the charging handle back, letting the bolt strip the first round into the chamber. Then, taking a breath, he settled into firing position.

Step Three: Find stability.

Shane flattened his body against the frozen ground, elbows digging into the packed dirt as he adjusted his grip. The SAW's bipod, already deployed, pressed firmly into the earth, giving the weapon much-needed stability. He widened his stance slightly, feet angled outward to absorb the recoil, just as the training manuals had instructed.

"You're sitting too high," Laughlin said coolly. "Get that stock deep into your shoulder. You're firing a light machine gun, not a goddamn hunting rifle."

Shane gritted his teeth and adjusted, pulling the stock tighter against his shoulder pocket. He could already feel the strain building in his arms from controlling the front-heavy weapon, but he ignored it.

Step Four: Sight alignment and trigger control.

The iron sights were simple but effective—a standard peep sight and post. Shane centered the target, a silhouette cutout sitting a hundred meters downrange, and settled his breathing.

"Short bursts," Laughlin reminded him. "Three to five rounds. Keep control."

Shane pressed the trigger, and the M249 bucked against his shoulder with rapid, mechanical violence. The burst was over in an instant, a sharp *rat-tat-tat* cutting through the cold air. The muzzle climbed slightly, but the bipod kept it from veering wildly off course. He paused, corrected, and fired another burst.

Brass casings clattered against the ground beside him. The spent links—now just empty skeletons of the belt—spilled from the side of the receiver.

"Not bad," Laughlin muttered. "Again."

Shane continued, working through several more bursts, adjusting his posture between each. His shoulder burned from the repeated impact, but he pushed through, focusing on keeping the weapon steady.

By the time the belt ran dry, his fingers were stiff from the cold, and his muscles ached from holding the weapon in place. He sat up, exhaling hard.

Laughlin crouched beside him, eyes scanning the target through his binoculars. "You're grouping a little wide, but it's manageable. Your first shots are on target, but you're losing control on the tail end of each burst. That's your grip."

Shane nodded, shaking feeling back into his fingers. "Yeah. Feels like I'm fighting the weight every time."

"You are." Laughlin sat back on his heels. "It's front-heavy. You've got to counterbalance it with your stance; keep that bipod locked in. Don't muscle the gun—let it work for you."

Shane wiped the sweat from his brow despite the cold. "I'll keep working on it."

"You better." Laughlin's tone was firm but not unkind. He stood and nodded toward the weapon. "Alright, clear it and reload. We're running another belt."

Shane sighed but didn't argue. He went through the clearing drill with precision—pulling back the charging handle, opening the feed tray, confirming the chamber was empty, and then dry-firing one last time before moving to reload. It was going to be something he'd have to work on over the span of a few days at least.

***

The perimeter of the base was lined with razor wire, guard towers cutting stark silhouettes against the gray sky. The place was functional—built for utility, not comfort. Snow had crusted over the roads, turning to slush where boots and heavy vehicles churned through it. The air smelled of diesel, damp earth, and the lingering scent of burning wood from the makeshift fire pits scattered across the camp.

Shane Alexander kept to himself. He wasn't rude about it, never dismissive, never outright ignoring anyone, but he wasn't the kind of guy to strike up casual conversation. He answered when spoken to, nodded when necessary, and kept his head down. If it weren't for Loran, he might've seemed downright unapproachable.

Loran, on the other hand, talked to damn near everyone. The guy had a way of slipping into conversations like he'd always been part of them, grinning, cracking jokes, making small talk with a mix of genuine curiosity and effortless ease. When they ate in the mess tent, Loran drifted between tables, catching up on stories, learning names, soaking up the camaraderie like it fueled him. Shane sat with him, but he always waited until the moment was right—until Loran settled back in next to him, a little quieter, a little less surrounded—before he spoke.

"Man, you ain't gotta be so sneaky about talking to me," Loran teased one night, stirring a steaming cup of instant coffee. "It ain't like folks are gonna bite you."

Shane smirked. "I like to pick my moments."

Loran laughed, shaking his head. "You're somethin' else, bud."

At night or even after the rotations had ended when the cold had settled in deep, and there wasn't much else to do, the guys who'd been in Bosnia longer would sit around in clusters, swapping stories, passing the time. Shane never joined in, but he listened. He always listened.

The ones who'd been there for months—some since the first NATO forces rolled in—spoke of Bosnia with the kind of hardened bluntness that came from seeing too much.

"This place ain't like Iraq or Afghanistan," said Staff Sergeant Walker, a stocky, no-bullshit Texan who spoke as every word cost him effort. "You ain't fightin' nobody. You're just stuck here, watchin' people who still hate each other pretend to play nice."

Corporal Hayes, a wiry guy with a permanent scowl, nodded. "Yeah, 'cause they *have* to. If we weren't here? Shit. They'd be right back at it. You go out there, past the checkpoints, and you see it. The way they look at each other. Like they're just waitin'."

They talked about the local population—how some of them were grateful, but plenty weren't. How the war might've been officially over, but it sure as hell didn't feel like it.

"Had this old man come up to me last week," said Private Medina, rubbing his gloved hands together. "Kept thanking me in broken English. Said his whole family got killed back in '92. Just him left now. Guy was shakin' so bad; I thought he was gonna pass out right there."

Hayes scoffed. "Yeah, but then you get the ones who spit at the ground when you walk past. Ain't no love lost here. Some of 'em lost everything, some of 'em lost power, and some just lost the war. All they see is us keepin' 'em from finishing what they started."

Walker let out a low breath, nodding. "We ain't heroes to everybody, that's for damn sure."

And then there were the landmines. That was the thing that made Shane's stomach twist when they talked about it—the sheer, ever-present danger of what lay hidden beneath the soil.

"Had a kid lose his damn leg last month," said Specialist Devers, shaking his head. "Little Bosnian boy couldn't've been older than ten. Stepped off the road to pick up somethin' and—" He made a quick, sharp motion with his hands, mimicking an explosion. "Gone. Just like that. You see the way his mama screamed, you don't forget that shit."

There were nods all around. No one had anything to add to that.

Shane stared at the fire, absorbing every word, letting it sink deep. He never showed it, never let anything cross his face, but it stayed with him, settling in the back of his mind like a weight he hadn't figured out how to carry yet.

Not all the stories were bleak, though. Some were ridiculous, stupid in the way only soldiers could appreciate.

Walker, who had been leaning back against a crate, took a long sip of his coffee and let out a grunt. "Y'know, I got a buddy back in Houston—an old boy named Jimmy—did a tour in Iraq a few years back. Lost a damn leg. Came home, brought himself a wife."

Loran raised a brow. *"Brought?"*

Walker smirked. "Yeah, man. Met her there. One of them Iraqi girls. Swear to God. Said 'fuck it, I need someone to take care of my ass,' and two months later, she's there in his house, cookin' breakfast like she's been there her whole damn life."

There were chuckles around the circle.

"No shit," Medina said. "And that worked out for him?"

"Hell yeah, it did," Walker drawled, shaking his head. "Man's happier than a pig in shit. Ain't gotta do a damn thing. She handles the house, the bills, even fixes his prosthetic when somethin' goes wrong. Says losin' that leg was the best thing that ever happened to him."

Loran was grinning. "Damn, maybe I oughta step on a mine, then."

Walker let out a barking laugh. "Shit, son, if you did, you'd probably just end up with a hospital bill and a lifetime of regrets. Jimmy just got lucky."

The mood lifted for a moment, the shared amusement a brief reprieve from the heavier conversations of the night. But as the laughter faded, the silence that followed carried the same weight as before.

"Still," Walker mused, staring into the fire. "He's got a simple life now. Ain't much, but it's his. Bet he sleeps a hell of a lot better than we do."

No one disagreed with that.

Shane never jumped into these talks, never offered up his own thoughts or stories. But he was there. He listened.

He watched how the older guys spoke, the way their eyes flickered between humor and something heavier, something more settled. They weren't broken, not by any means, but there was a part of them that seemed resigned to what they were doing here. Like they'd expected something different, something simpler, and ended up with... this.

It wasn't fear. It wasn't regret. It was just reality.

And Shane sat with it, letting it muddle deep in his gut. He wasn't sure what kind of soldier he'd be by the time he left this place. He only knew he wouldn't be the same one who had arrived.

Afterward, that same evening, after the rest of the squad had finished their training rotations, Shane remained at the range. The sun had set, and the temperature had plummeted even further, but he wasn't leaving until he was sure he could operate the M249 without hesitation.

Laughlin, to his credit, had stuck around. Though he didn't say it outright, Shane suspected the squad leader was keeping an eye on him, making sure he didn't burn himself out or make mistakes in exhaustion.

This time, Shane worked through different malfunction drills.

Failure to Fire: He simulated a misfire, waiting for the mandatory seconds before clearing the round. Pull the charging handle back, observe the chamber, release, fire.

Failure to Feed: A jammed belt was trickier. He had to manually pull the links out, reseat them, and rack the charging handle again.

Failure to Extract: If a spent casing got stuck, he practiced manually clearing it with a knife tip, keeping his hands away from the chamber.

By the time he worked through the last cycle, his fingers were raw from handling cold metal. But there was a certain satisfaction in knowing he was getting faster, smoother.

Laughlin finally nodded, seemingly satisfied. "Not bad, Alexander."

Shane exhaled, feeling the cold settle into his bones. "Appreciate it, Sergeant."

Laughlin glanced around, then lowered his voice. "Look, I get it—you didn't sign up to be a SAW gunner. But the squad needs one, and right now, that's you. So you learn this weapon inside and out, make it second nature. If you hesitate in the field, you're not just screwing yourself—you're screwing everyone."

Shane met his gaze. "I won't hesitate."

Laughlin studied him for a long moment before nodding. "Good. Now pack it up—we've got an early start tomorrow."

Shane shouldered the heavy weapon, feeling its weight settle against him. It still didn't feel all that natural. But it *was* getting there.

***

A week later, they were given the instructions for which they'd traveled an ocean for. The night was cold, but everyone already knew that. It wasn't new.

Sergeant John Fitzpatrick stood tall near the edge of the campfire circle. His posture was straight, the flicker of the flames reflecting in his hard eyes. He was a man who didn't speak much, but when he did, everyone listened. His salt-and-pepper hair and the rough lines of his face told stories of battles fought. How years spent in the military had worn him down but never broken him. Someone who'd sunk, yet never sank.

"Alright, listen up," Fitzpatrick's voice cut through the murmur of conversation, pulling everyone's attention like a magnet. The night grew quieter, the usual background chatter falling away as the soldiers turned to face their platoon sergeant. "We'll be receiving our first mission briefing tomorrow morning, 0800 sharp. You're gonna want to get a good night's rest and be ready to move out fast. This ain't some training exercise; this is the real deal. So, get your gear squared away and your heads right. Tomorrow could get interesting."

The campfire crackled in the silence that followed. The men exchanged glances. For most, this was their first taste of real combat after months of training, and it was starting to feel more and more like the prelude to something they couldn't quite see coming.

Shane stood a few feet away from the group, his focus locked on his new weapon, the M249, which he had spent hours getting to know over the past few days. The cold, steel body of the machine gun rested across his knees as he knelt on the ground, a clean rag in one hand and a bottle of oil in the other. His hands moved over the weapon with something bordering obsession, making sure every moving part was free of dirt, dust, or debris.

It wasn't that Shane was a perfectionist. He just knew that a clean weapon was the difference between life and death, especially when you were going to be carrying it into the unknown. Every click of the bolt, every twist of the cleaning rod, was another step in his preparation for whatever lay ahead.

The sound of Fitzpatrick's boots crunching in the snow brought Shane's attention back to the present. The platoon sergeant's silhouette was framed by the light of the fire, his face unreadable as he approached. Fitzpatrick didn't say anything at first; he just watched Shane clean the weapon, his eyes assessing, weighing.

"You'll be alright with that thing?" Fitzpatrick finally asked, his voice low and steady.

"I've been working with it the past week, sir." Shane was respectful, but the man could sense that he wasn't fully convinced of himself yet. "I'll get it right, Sergeant."

Fitzpatrick grunted, the sound almost like approval. "Good. You've got a lot to learn about that weapon. Take it seriously. Don't let your guard down."

Shane nodded, but he didn't speak. He didn't need to. He knew exactly what Fitzpatrick was getting at. The M249 had a rate of fire that could chew through a line of enemies in seconds, but if you weren't careful with it, it could turn on you just as quickly.

The platoon sergeant turned to walk away, but not before he threw one last glance over his shoulder. "Get some sleep, Alexander. Tomorrow, we start earning our pay."

Shane didn't respond, but he wasn't offended. It was the kind of comment that didn't require a reply. Fitzpatrick was the kind of guy who said what he meant, and he'd already said more than enough for Shane to know where he stood.

As the sounds of the camp grew quieter, Shane continued working on his weapon. The oil was smeared on the barrel, glinting faintly in the firelight. His hands were steady, almost mechanical, as he reassembled the M249 piece by piece. Each click and clank of the parts felt oddly reassuring, like the gun was becoming an extension of his own body. He didn't have time to be afraid of it. There was no room for fear when the stakes were this high.

Once the weapon was clean and ready, Shane sat back on his heels, wiping his hands on the rag before tucking it into his pocket. He glanced over at the other soldiers, still gathered around the campfire. Loran was talking animatedly with Walker, his voice loud and carefree, as usual. Some of the others had already started to retreat to their tents, eager to get a little rest before the mission briefing in the morning.

He stayed where he was, his mind a whirlwind of thoughts and half-formed concerns. The sounds of his comrades' laughter and chatter seemed distant, even though they were only a few yards away. He was mentally preparing for whatever lay ahead, running through scenarios in his head. The usual; *what if I fuck up and get myself killed?* kind of standard questions. His thoughts were interrupted by the sound of Loran's voice calling his name. Shane didn't respond at first, but he could feel Loran's eyes on him. He looked up briefly, meeting Loran's gaze.

"What?" Shane called.

Loran grinned, the firelight dancing on his face. "You gonna just sit there all night, or are you gonna get some sleep like the rest of us?"

Shane gave him a small, tight smile. "I'm good. Just got some things to think about."

Loran's smile faded a little, but he didn't press. "Well, if you change your mind, you know where to find me." He gave Shane a brief nod and wandered off toward his tent.

Shane watched him go, then turned his focus back to the rifle in his hands. His mind was already on the briefing tomorrow. On the mission ahead. On everything that could go wrong and everything that might go right.

The night stretched on, the cold creeping deeper, but Shane didn't move. He was ready, in his own way. Whatever came next, he would face it head-on, just like he always had.

After a while, he stood up, stretched his stiff legs, and made his way to his tent. The sounds of the camp faded behind him, replaced by the steady, rhythmic sound of his own breathing. He crawled into his sleeping bag, his mind still racing with thoughts of the mission and the weapon by his side. But somewhere in the back of his mind, there was a quiet voice telling him that tomorrow would be the start of something far bigger than any of them had prepared for.

And whatever it was, Shane knew that he was ready.

Six

Rules of Engagement

The cold morning air bit at the soldiers' faces as they filed into the briefing tent at Camp Eagle. Their boots crunched against the frozen ground, steam rising from their breaths as they huddled inside, shaking off the chill. The makeshift space smelled of damp canvas, stale coffee, and the ever-present scent of gun oil that seemed to cling to everything. A kerosene heater in the corner hummed softly, doing little against the winter bite.

Captain Mitchell stood near the front, his uniform crisp despite the conditions, his face calm but serious. Beside him, Sergeant Fitzpatrick had the look of a man who had been up since before dawn, his sharp eyes scanning the room, assessing each soldier as they took their seats on the wooden benches. He carried his usual air of no-nonsense authority, the kind that came from years of service in places most men wouldn't want to set foot in.

Once the last man sat, Mitchell cleared his throat. "Alright, listen up. We've got our first official assignment. We're moving out tomorrow morning to Kiseljak." He tapped a stick against a large laminated map pinned to a board beside him, the jagged borders and winding roads of Bosnia and Herzegovina stark in the dim light. "It's about an hour's drive from here, and our job is straightforward: market security."

A few soldiers shifted in their seats. Market security didn't sound like the kind of job men carrying M16s were sent for, but nobody voiced their thoughts—yet.

Fitzpatrick stepped forward, rubbing a rough hand over his stubbled jaw. "Now, before any of you start thinking this is some fuckin' cakewalk, let me set you straight," he growled, his voice edged with experience. "This ain't some county fair we're watching over. This market is a goddamn powder keg. Croats and Bosniaks both use it, and that means tension. You'll see civvies going about their business, trying to live their lives, but make no mistake—one wrong move, one bad look at the wrong person, and shit can go sideways fast."

Mitchell gave him a nod before turning back to the map. "Our presence is meant to keep things stable. Make sure no fights break out, no weapons get flashed, and no one decides to settle an old score with a grenade."

Fitzpatrick let out a dry chuckle, void of humor. "And speaking of grenades, let's go over the damn Rules of Engagement before any of you get ideas." He reached for his notebook, flipping it open before looking up at the unit. "These rules ain't suggestions. They ain't guidelines. They are the law for this mission, and if you break 'em, I guarantee you'll wish you hadn't."

He held up a finger. "Rule one: No offensive operations unless specifically ordered. That means you don't start shit. You don't go clearing buildings; you don't chase down 'suspicious-looking' assholes just 'cause your gut tells you to. This ain't 'Nam, and it sure as hell ain't the Gulf. If you shoot first, you better be prepared to answer for it."

"Rule two," he continued, raising another finger. "Use the minimum force necessary. That means if you can handle a situation with words, you do it. You don't go waving your rifle around like a goddamn cowboy. You see a fight? Break it up with your presence first. Escalation is a last resort."

"Rule three: Your weapon is your last fuckin' option. That M16 you're carrying? That SAW? That Beretta on your hip? They are not your problem solvers. If you pull that trigger, you be damn sure you had no other choice because there will be an investigation, and no one—" he let that word hang in the air, his gaze sweeping across the room, "—is covering your ass if you can't justify it."

He exhaled sharply, shifting his weight. "Rule four: No retaliation. I don't care if some asshole spits in your face calls your mother a whore, or throws a rock at you. You don't shoot back just because you're pissed off. We are here to keep the peace, not make more graves."

A few soldiers nodded slowly, understanding settling in.

Fitzpatrick tapped the side of his boot with the edge of his notebook. "And rule five, pay real close attention to this one: If the other guy stops shooting, you stop shooting. Period. I don't care if he just tried to light you up a second ago—if he drops his weapon, you do the same. No executions, no revenge. We are here as peacekeepers. Act like it."

Silence hung in the air, the weight of the words pressing down on the group. Shane sat near the back, absorbing every syllable. He didn't show it—his expression remained impassive, hands resting on his thighs—but he took in every detail, every rule, every warning. He had heard some of this before, but hearing it from Fitzpatrick, from a man who had lived it, made it all the more real.

One of the younger privates, Jansen, raised a tentative hand. "Sergeant, uh… have we done this kinda thing before? Peacekeeping, I mean?"

Fitzpatrick smirked. "Oh, hell yeah," he said, crossing his arms. "You think Bosnia's the first time Uncle Sam's played referee? Let me give you a history lesson, kid."

He started ticking off on his fingers. "Somalia. '93. You've heard of Black Hawk Down, right? That was a peacekeeping mission before it went to hell. We went in to deliver food to keep the warlords from carving up the civilians. Ended up getting dragged into a goddamn street war. Lesson learned? You can't trust every 'ceasefire' you hear."

He ticked off another finger. "Haiti. '94. We rolled in, supposed to make sure their government didn't collapse. Another shitshow. Rebels, coups, street gangs, all of it. We walked a thin line, and let me tell you, when people are desperate, they don't give a damn about peacekeepers."

He gave the room a sharp look. "So why's it important here? Because this place is barely holding together. The war just ended, and you got people who still wanna kill each other. They don't see peacekeepers. They see obstacles. Some will be grateful, sure. But others? They'd rather you weren't here."

The room remained quiet, the reality settling in. This wasn't going to be like training. Shane sat with his hands clasped together, staring at the map where Kiseljak had been circled in red. The market. Their first assignment. It sounded simple enough—until Fitzpatrick cleared his throat and stepped back up, his expression even grimmer than before.

"Now," he started, arms crossed, "We got credible intel that Bosnian Serb extremists might be planning an attack on that market."

That got everyone's attention. A few heads lifted.

Fitzpatrick nodded. "Yeah. That's right. Told you idiots this ain't just a damn babysitting job. The Croats and the Bosniaks both use that market. You know who doesn't? The Serbs. And some of 'em still got a score to settle. Our job is to make sure nobody gets a chance to do that."

He turned and jabbed a finger at the map, dragging it across the different regions. "For those of you who still don't quite get what the hell's goin' on here, let's break it down real simple. *Bosnia's a goddamn mess.* That part's been said so many times I'm sure you're hearin' it in your sleep. And that's good," he shook his head. "You got three main groups: Bosniaks—Muslims—who made up most of the population before the war. Then you got Croats—Catholics—who got their own reasons for hating the Serbs. And then you got the Bosnian Serbs—Orthodox Christians—who think Bosnia should've been part of Serbia from the start. Mix 'em all together, throw in a few centuries of bad blood, and you get one of the nastiest wars since World War II."

He took a step forward, voice lowering slightly. "The Dayton Peace Accords put a stop to the fighting—on paper. But just 'cause a treaty got signed doesn't mean these people stopped wanting to kill each other. The Serbs were on the losing end when NATO started dropping bombs on 'em in '95, and some of them still want payback. That's where we come in."

He scanned the room, letting that sink in.

"You see a Bosniak? He lost family to Serb death squads. You see a Serb? He thinks NATO screwed his country over. You see a Croat? He's just waiting for his chance to make Bosnia part of Croatia." He smirked. "Same assholes, different flags. And you, gentlemen? You're stepping right into the middle of it."

A few soldiers exchanged uneasy glances. Shane kept his face unreadable, but his mind was already picking apart the reality of what they were walking into. The rules Fitzpatrick had drilled into them earlier made sense in a textbook. But in the field? Against extremists looking for an excuse to turn a crowded marketplace into a bloodbath? He had a hard time seeing how "minimum force necessary" was gonna hold up when the shooting started.

Fitzpatrick let the tension hang for a moment before he exhaled sharply and crossed his arms again.

"And since we're talkin' about rules, let me make one more thing crystal fuckin' clear," he added, his tone shifting. "The weapon between your legs? Yeah, that's got rules too."

A few guys chuckled, but Fitzpatrick's glare shut them up fast.

"This ain't back home," he said. "I don't care how pretty some girl looks at you; keep your goddamn eyes and hands to yourself. You get chummy with the wrong woman; you're askin' for trouble. *Especially with the Bosniaks.* Fuckers wouldn't waste a second tryna cut eyes out for the name of 'honor.' You think they'll take kindly to you idiots sniffing around their women? Think again."

His eyes swept the room before he added, voice hard as iron, "And before any of you get dumb ideas in your heads—you don't gotta be brown to be dangerous."

A few of the younger guys looked confused. Fitzpatrick scoffed.

"Yeah, I know how some of you think. You hear 'Muslim,' you picture some Arab dude in a turban. Maybe some lady with her eyes peepin' out from a damn tablecloth. Well, that ain't what you're gonna see here. These Bosniaks look like any other European. Blonde hair, blue eyes, all that shit. And guess what? The cold's got *everyone's* heads covered, so now, you can't tell them apart from a Croat or a Serb just by lookin' at 'em."

Mitchell glanced at his watch, then nodded at Fitzpatrick. "Wrap it up, Sergeant."

Fitzpatrick nodded and looked over the group one last time. "You all got your orders. We leave at 0600. Get your gear ready, and get some sleep. And remember—tomorrow, we ain't playing soldier. We're keeping people alive. Don't fuck it up."

With that, the meeting ended, and the soldiers began filing out, murmuring among themselves. Clipboards passed from hand to hand as the squad leaders began sorting names and finalizing team assignments. Shane stood near the back, watching as men gathered into their units, double-checking gear and exchanging murmured conversations about the briefing.

Staff Sergeant Steven Laughlin, their squad leader, strode into the center of the room, his clipboard in hand. He didn't waste time.

"Alright, listen up, ladies," he said, voice carrying over the noise. "You're gonna be running security in four-man teams. You stick together, you move together, and you don't fuckin' wander. If shit goes sideways, the guy next to you is all you've got, so you'd better know him as well as your own damn shadow."

Shane's name was called early.

"Alexander," Laughlin said, nodding at him. "You're with Taylor, Wilson, and Rodriguez. I'll be running your fire team."

Shane exhaled through his nose. He wasn't surprised. Loran was the only guy he really spoke to, even if he preferred to keep those conversations out of earshot of the others.

Loran grinned as he stepped up beside him, nudging him slightly with his elbow. "Guess you're stuck with me, bud."

Specialist Wilson, a tall, wiry guy with an easygoing face, joined them next. "Well, shit," he muttered, looking over the group. "I was hopin' for a team with at least one ugly bastard to make me look better. Guess I'm outta luck."

Private Rodriguez, the youngest of the group, snorted. "That's real fuckin' tragic, man," he said, shaking his head. "I'll light a candle for you."

"Don't worry," Loran chimed in, "You'll make sure no girl even looks in our direction. Easier mission, you know?"

Laughlin ignored them, already moving down his checklist. "You all got your gear squared away?"

"Yes, Sergeant," they answered in near unison.

"Good. We roll out at 0600. I want weapons clean, ammo prepped, and every single one of you squared away before then. No last-minute bullshit. If you're missing something, fix it now. We're not stepping off until I'm damn sure every one of you is ready."

He gave them all a hard look, then moved on to the next team.

Loran exhaled and adjusted his helmet. "Well," he said, clapping his hands together, "It's not Nashville, but we did get out, huh?"

Shane simply nodded. He stared at his kit, replaying everything he'd heard tonight.

***

The barracks room was dimly lit, the small overhead light casting a muted glow over the cinderblock walls and standard-issue furniture. Wilson's bed was unmade, his duffel tossed haphazardly at the foot of it. Across the room, his roommate was out cold, the slow, steady rhythm of his breathing blending into the background noise of the base—occasional footsteps in the hall, distant murmurs of other soldiers killing time before morning.

Loran had been the mastermind behind this little gathering. He had shown up with a grin, a six-pack of cheap beer tucked under one arm, and an air of casual confidence like he was walking into a neighborhood bar rather than a barracks room in Bosnia.

"Thought we could use a little… team bonding," he had said, nudging Shane in the ribs as he popped the first can open.

Shane had given him a look but hadn't refused when Loran shoved a beer into his hand. He wasn't much of a drinker, never had been, but declining would have made him stand out even more than he already did. So he sat, can in hand, letting the others fill the silence.

Wilson took the first swig and smacked his lips. "Goddamn, this tastes like watered-down piss."

Rodriguez snorted. "You'd know what that tastes like, huh?"

"Hey, man, you grow up in a house with five older brothers, you end up drinkin' a lot of questionable shit." Wilson leaned back against his pillow, stretching his legs out. "One time, my brother Trey poured me a glass of what I thought was sweet tea. Turns out it was straight-up tobacco spit."

Rodriguez gagged. "Fuckin' nasty, bro."

"Yeah," Wilson agreed. "You ever had the taste of Red Man and backwash sit in your mouth for a whole hour? I swear, my tongue still remembers that trauma."

Loran chuckled, taking a sip of his own beer before setting it on the nightstand beside him. "You got a whole crew back home then, huh?"

Wilson nodded. "Texas born and raised, man. Whole family's still down in Beaumont. Bunch of blue-collar sons' a bitches, working oil fields and construction. I was the first dumbass to sign up for this gig, though."

Rodriguez shook his head. "Nah, man, not dumb. You just got out. That's smart."

Wilson shrugged. "I mean, yeah, but... shit, sometimes I think about what I'd be doin' if I'd just stayed. Workin' sixteen-hour shifts, drinking on the weekends, maybe knockin' up some girl from down the street. My oldest brother's got three kids already, and he ain't even thirty yet. But at least he gets to be home, y'know? See his family, eat home-cooked meals, sleep in his own damn bed."

That quieted the conversation for a second. The barracks walls felt thinner, and the distance from home was what Rodriguez felt.

Loran, always the one to fill silences, leaned forward, elbow resting on his knee. "So what about you, Rodriguez? You got family back home?"

Rodriguez gave a half-smile. "Yeah. I mean, not a big one. Just me, my mom, and my little sister. California, San Diego area. Mom works two jobs, and my sister, well, she's a smart kid. She wants to go to college, so I'm trying to send money back whenever I can. She's got it in her head she wants to be a lawyer."

Wilson raised his can in a mock toast. "Good for her, man. Someone in the family's gotta be the rich one."

Rodriguez huffed a laugh. "That's the plan."

Loran, ever the social butterfly, grinned and took another sip. "You boys ever play sports?"

Wilson shook his head. "Nah, I was too busy workin' after school. But Trey—same asshole who tricked me into drinkin' dip spit—he played football. Big ol' linebacker. Got a scholarship and everything, but then he blew out his knee in his second year. So now he just gets drunk and talks about what could've been."

Rodriguez smirked. "Man, that's every guy who played sports in high school."

Loran laughed, then turned to Shane, giving him a nudge. "Shane here was a wrestler."

Shane, who had been quietly nursing his beer, shot Loran a look. It wasn't exactly a secret, but it wasn't something he volunteered either.

Wilson raised a brow. "No shit? You one of those guys who could pick somebody up and slam 'em?"

Shane exhaled, shaking his head slightly. "I wasn't a heavyweight."

"Still," Rodriguez said, tilting his head. "You any good?"

Shane hesitated. He had been, once. State champ his senior year. But what did it matter now?

Loran, of course, answered for him. "Man, he was a beast. Used to take guys down like it was nothing."

Shane gave a half-shrug. "It was a long time ago."

"Yeah, but you don't forget that kind of stuff," Loran said. "Bet you could still throw one of us around if you wanted to."

Wilson grinned. "Let's not test that theory, huh?"

They laughed, and for a moment, it almost felt normal. Just a few guys sitting around, shooting the shit.

Rodriguez swirled his can, watching the liquid inside. "You miss it?"

Shane thought about that for a second. Did he? He missed the feeling of being good at something. Of having control, knowing exactly what to do and when. But that was high school, a whole different world from where they were now.

"Sometimes," he admitted.

That seemed to be enough for them.

Loran stretched, exhaling as he leaned back. "Man, I swear, if I wasn't in the Army, I'd probably be coaching little league somewhere."

Wilson chuckled. "Yeah? You one of those guys who peaked in high school?"

Loran grinned. "Nah, I just like baseball. Played shortstop all four years. Thought about college ball, but... well, here I am."

"Here we all are," Rodriguez murmured.

The mood shifted again, the weight of reality settling in.

Wilson exhaled. "You ever wonder what we'll be doing five, ten years from now?"

Rodriguez scoffed. "Man, I'm just trying to get through tomorrow."

Loran smirked. "That's the spirit."

Wilson tapped the side of his can, thoughtful. "I dunno. Sometimes I think about just goin' home, findin' a girl, settlin' down. Livin' the simple life."

Rodriguez arched a brow. "You? Settling down?"

Wilson grinned. "Hell yeah, why not? Some backyard BBQs, couple kids runnin' around, drinkin' beer on the porch with my brothers. That don't sound too bad, does it?"

"Nah," Rodriguez admitted. "It don't."

The conversation slowed, the quiet moments stretching a little longer. Shane sat there, absorbing it all, listening more than he spoke—like always.

Eventually, Wilson yawned. "Alright, I'm tapping out. Some of us actually like to sleep before a mission."

Loran rolled his eyes. "Yeah, yeah." He stood, grabbing the empty cans. "Guess I'll get rid of the evidence."

Rodriguez pushed himself up. "I'm out too. Catch you guys in the morning."

Shane stayed a little longer, watching as Loran tossed the last can in the trash.

Loran looked at him, tilting his head slightly. "You good?"

Shane nodded.

Loran gave a small smirk. "Y'know, one of these days, Alexander, you're gonna have to talk more."

Shane exhaled, standing up. "Maybe."

Loran chuckled. "I'll take that as progress."

And with that, the night was over.

Tomorrow, the real work began.

Seven

Highway to Hell

The convoy rolled out of Camp Eagle at dawn, the sky still bruised with the last remnants of night. Frost clung to the earth, and the air carried a sharp bite, cutting through the exhaust fumes curling from the Humvees as they rumbled forward. The M1025 Humvee rattled over the rough road, its heavy tires kicking up slush and mud as the convoy pressed deeper into Bosnia's winter-stricken countryside. Shane sat in the backseat, shoulders stiff, his rifle wedged between his legs. A chill seeped through the metal floor of the vehicle, but nobody seemed to notice. It had taken only a few days, and they were all used to it; just another layer of discomfort on top of everything else. The glass beside his face was cold.

They formed a staggered column winding through Bosnia's scarred countryside. The road—a patchwork of cracked blacktop, frozen mud, and packed-down snow—snaked through valleys where the land still bore the wounds of war. Charred skeletons of buildings stood like silent sentinels. Their windows were hollowed out, their walls riddled with bullet scars. Some had collapsed entirely, nothing but piles of rubble, while others bore the signs of hasty repairs—plastic sheets where roofs had caved in, tarps stretched over shattered walls.

Loran sat beside him, crammed in with Wilson opposite him, who was massaging his temples, nodding along to something Rodriguez was saying up front. The vehicle hummed with the murmurs of soldiers, a mix of bullshit, half-truths, and real talk meant to pass the time.

"Alright, listen up," Staff Sergeant Laughlin called out from the front passenger seat, his voice sharp but not unkind. "We're about an hour out from Kiseljak. Since I doubt most of you took the time to read any of the briefings, I'm gonna give you the basics now so you don't go making an ass of yourselves first thing."

"Aw, c'mon, Sarge, we'd never do that," Loran said, barely keeping a straight face.

Laughlin didn't even turn around. "Taylor, if anyone's gonna step on their dick today, it's you."

That got a few laughs, but the sergeant pressed on. "Alright, Kiseljak's a small town, couple thousand people. You'll see a mix of folks trying to get back to normal and those who still got a grudge to settle. Most of 'em will just go about their day and keep their heads down. You'll get some who'll test you—nothing crazy, just seeing what they can get away with. And then you got the ones who'll smile at you one day and put a bullet in your back the next."

That sobered the mood quickly. Shane shifted in his seat, fingers tightening slightly around his rifle.

"Best way to keep shit from getting out of hand is respect," Laughlin continued. "That means don't go barking orders at people like you own the place. These folks been through hell, lost homes, lost family—last thing they need is some twenty-year-old from Texas treating 'em like second-class citizens in their own country."

Loran nudged Shane. "Hear that, buddy? Be polite when you're intimidating the locals." He smirked and leaned back.

Shane barely reacted, just let out a quiet breath. Was it the cold? Was it the dizzying sight of what lay beyond the vehicle? He wasn't sure. But whatever it was, it had his eyes on the miles behind them and his mind further away.

Amid the ruins, there were signs of life clawing its way back. A man was out chopping wood beside a half-rebuilt home, his breath misting in the cold morning air. A woman in a headscarf swept the steps of a war-torn building that might have once been a shop. Clotheslines were strung between blackened buildings, colorful garments fluttering like defiant banners.

They passed through a small village where children played near a bombed-out husk of a bus, kicking around a half-deflated ball. Their laughter was thin, given the thick glass, but those expressions were real. An old man stood at the roadside, watching the convoy roll past with wary eyes, his hands tucked deep into the folds of his coat.

Laughlin kept going. "Biggest thing to watch for? The kids. They'll come up to you, beg for candy, cigarettes, whatever. Some of them are just kids. Some are working for someone who's got bad intentions. If a kid runs up and drops something at your feet, you don't pick it up, you don't kick it—you move your ass. Fast."

That has caught Shane's attention. He blinked, slowly turning his head briefly towards the front. He pursed his lips, nodded, and turned back to the window. Rodriguez let out a low whistle. "Jesus. They really got kids doing that shit?"

Wilson, who had a couple years in the Army over most of them, nodded. "Happened in Somalia. Kid runs up, all innocent, drops a can, boom. And I don't mean the fun kind."

Loran scoffed. "The fun kind? What the hell kinda parties you go to, man?"

Wilson grinned. "The kind that end with MPs dragging me back to base."

A chuckle rippled through the vehicle, but it was short-lived. Shane wasn't the type to run his mouth like Loran, but he was absorbing everything. The part about the kids stuck with him. The thought of a kid running up to them with a bomb didn't feel real, but then again, neither did being here in the first place.

"Point is," Laughlin continued, "you don't let your guard down. Not for anyone. Not for the old guy selling apples, not for the kid with the big eyes, not for the pretty girl giving you the once-over."

"Wait, hold up," Loran interjected. "Are we talking regular pretty or 'I just walked through a war zone, and she still looks good' pretty?"

"Don't matter, 'cause you'll keep your dick in your damn pants, boy," Laughlin snapped.

Shane let his gaze drift, watching Bosnia's shifting face through the tinted window. The conversation became white noise once more.

Two women walking close to the ruins of what had once been a building—maybe a home, maybe a shop. One was pale, with dark hair pulled into a low knot beneath a wool scarf. The other had tan skin and dark eyes and carried a child wrapped in a heavy blanket. Maybe she was his age, maybe she was older, wrapped in a thick shawl that concealed almost every inch of her aside her face. Their clothes matched the same faded, oversized coats, likely given out by some relief organization.

As the Humvee trundled past, the women hesitated. Then, quietly, they shifted onto the same muddy shoulder where the convoy had already passed. They trusted the tracks left by military vehicles—if the soldiers had driven over it without an explosion, then it was safe enough to walk. It was a grim kind of logic, the kind you learned in a place where one wrong step could kill you.

Then, the dusky one looked at him. Well, probably, at the glass mostly, but perhaps she had caught a glimpse of him through the tinted glass. There was no fear in those dark eyes, no gratitude either. Curiosity? Maybe, but observation at most.

She tilted her head slightly, studying the vehicle as if trying to see through the glass, past the faceless figure seated the closest to it inside. But distance swallowed the moment, and soon, she and her companion faded into the scenery. Two ghosts navigating a landscape still haunted by war.

The Humvee hit a deep pothole, jolting everyone in their seats.

"Shit, Sarge," Rodriguez muttered, gripping the wheel tighter. "These roads are worse than the ones back home."

Laughlin snorted. "Yeah, but here, the potholes might kill you."

Loran made an exaggerated show of glancing around. "Hey, quick question—how the hell did we end up on the scenic route to hell? I thought Bosnia was supposed to be pretty."

"It is," Wilson said, peering out the window at the snow-covered hills in the distance. "If you ignore the part where half of it got blown to shit."

They drove in silence for a bit, the reality of their situation settling in. Outside, Bosnia rolled by—ruined villages, people bundled up against the cold, the occasional makeshift repair job that spoke of re-silience more than recovery.

Shane found himself thinking about the woman he'd seen earlier. The way she'd tilted her head, watching them go. Something about it stuck with him, though he wasn't sure why. Maybe it was because she hadn't looked scared. She'd just... watched.

"Alright," Laughlin said, breaking the quiet. "One last thing. You got a lot of ideas about what a bad guy looks like. Might think you can spot 'em easy. Well, I got news for you—no, the fuck you can't." He sighed, leaning back. "We've established kids being involved in this, ladies and old folks. But it doesn't stop there. If you meet another American soldier or even a NATO boy...but you can't remember see-ing him at camp or something, then don't be stupid and trust him. Ask for proof. Uh, Sarge's name, CO assigned to the mission's name. CO's rank. Anything that all of you dipshits would know."

"And if he doesn't?" One of them asked, furrowing his brows.

"Then he ain't one of you now, is he?"

Shane saw Wilson nod slowly. Rodriguez glanced at the side mirror but said nothing.

"You're gonna meet people who look like your neighbors back home," Laughlin went on. "People who sound like 'em too. But that don't mean shit. You stay sharp. You stay professional. And you don't assume a damn thing."

Silence settled in again, this time heavier. The convoy had been on the move for nearly forty minutes, weaving through a countryside that told its own war story. Shane's rifle now rested against his thigh; however, his eyes never stopped scanning the passing terrain through the reinforced window.

It had been the same in the beginning—gray sky, bare trees, and snow-covered fields broken up by the occasional farmhouse. But as they traveled deeper, closer to Kiseljak, the landscape shifted. The scars of war became more pronounced. Entire villages stood abandoned, their homes roofless and gutted, skeletal remains of what had once been lives. Some had been burned out completely, only charred beams and crumbling walls left to mark where families had once lived.

He could tell when they were moving through different areas—not by signs, but by the way things changed. In one stretch, Croatian flags hung from damaged homes, red-and-white checkers stark against the gray. Further on, the flags were blue and yellow, Bosnia's new national emblem, though many looked like they had been torn down and hastily put back up. The Serbian areas had their own markings—graffiti in Cyrillic, slogans on walls that he couldn't read but that someone like Laughlin probably could.

They passed a town where the minaret of a mosque still stood, though the building beneath it had been blown to hell. It had collapsed in on itself, a heap of stone and splintered wood, but the spire remained, stubborn against the sky. In another village, a church had been reduced to rubble, the cross that once sat atop it now lying twisted in the dirt.

This place wasn't Bosnia. Not really. It was pieces of Bosnia, hacked apart, still bleeding, still raw.

Shane glanced toward the front seat. Laughlin was talking to Wilson, his voice half-drowned by the roar of the Humvee's engine. Loran, beside him, was already getting restless. He kept shifting his legs, stretching them out, then pulling them back, his knee bouncing.

"Jesus, how much longer we got?" Loran muttered.

"Not long," Laughlin replied, not looking back. "Stop bitchin'."

Loran huffed. "I ain't bitchin'. I'm just sayin', if I wanted to spend my morning getting my nuts frozen off in the back of a goddamn Humvee, I'd have signed up for a different kind of deployment."

Rodriguez chuckled. "What, like Hawaii?"

Loran shot him a look. "I was thinkin' more like Germany, but yeah, Hawaii don't sound bad either."

Wilson shook his head. "You ain't built for Germany, Taylor. Too many rules. You'd end up arrested or married."

Loran grinned. "Shit, long as she's got a nice rack, I ain't opposed."

Laughlin snorted. "You think some German girl's gonna put up with your dumb ass?"

"I dunno, Sarge. They say opposites attract."

Shane shook his head slightly, but he wasn't really listening.

Up ahead, there were signs of life. A small market, or what passed for one out here. A handful of stalls were set up along the roadside, mostly selling whatever people could scrounge together. Firewood, sacks of grain, some canned goods with labels in languages Shane couldn't read. The people here were bundled up, moving carefully across the icy ground, but he could tell they weren't just locals. Some were displaced, faces thin, clothes mismatched and worn. Refugees, probably. People who had lost their homes in places too dangerous to return to.

"Y'all ever think about what happens after this?" Wilson asked suddenly.

Rodriguez raised an eyebrow. "After what?"

"This. The mission. Bosnia. What happens when we pull out?"

Laughlin grunted. "We don't worry about that. Ain't our job."

"Yeah, but..." Wilson hesitated. "I mean, we come in, we keep the peace, but what's stoppin' 'em from goin' right back to killin' each other when we're gone?"

"Nothing," Laughlin said bluntly. "Maybe a year, maybe five. Maybe they hold out longer. But mark my fuckin' words, the first time some politician back home decides this shit ain't worth the money, we're outta here, and this place burns all over again."

Then Loran clapped his hands together. "Well, this has been a damn uplifting chat, but can we please talk about something that doesn't involve landmines, kids with bombs, or me keeping my hands to myself?"

Rodriguez smirked. "Like what, Taylor? You wanna talk about your feelings?"

"Hell no. I wanna talk about your ol' lady."

Rodriguez groaned. "Jesus Christ, here we go. Why did I even tell you about her?"

"Nah, I'm serious," Loran said, smirking. "Boy's got himself a girl back home. Writes him letters and everything. Probably spritzes 'em with perfume, too. I bet he sniffs 'em before bed like some lovesick bitch."

Laughlin exhaled through his nose. "Taylor, I swear to God..."

"What? It's sweet," Loran said, grinning like an asshole. "Ain't it, Rodriguez? You still keepin' her picture in your helmet, or did you upgrade to jerkin' it to Sears catalogs like the rest of us?"

Rodriguez shot him a look. "Taylor, I hope you get shot in the ass."

"That ain't a no."

Wilson snorted. "Maybe she already dumped his ass, and he just ain't tellin' us."

Rodriguez flipped them both off. "Y'all are fuckin' children."

Loran leaned in toward Shane, stage-whispering, "He *still* didn't say no, though." Shane let out a breath through his nose. Not quite a laugh, but close. Loran caught it and nudged him.

"There it is!" Loran clapped his hands. "Look at that, boys. We got ourselves a goddamn miracle—Alexander cracked a smile."

The tension in the Humvee lightened, if only slightly. The convoy pressed on, the cold seeping in, the road stretching ahead. They were still at least an hour from Kiseljak. An hour from their first real mission.

***

He kept his eyes forward, watching as Kiseljak came into view.

The town sat in the valley, the river cutting through its center. There were buildings intact, shops, and makeshift stalls. People moving, trying to live like things were normal. But even from here, he could see the places where war had left its mark—bullet holes in walls, windows covered with plastic sheeting instead of glass, shops rebuilt on foundations that had once been rubble. Some turned to watch the Humvees pass, eyes unreadable. Others ignored them entirely, too used to foreign troops rolling through their streets to care anymore.

And Shane couldn't shake the feeling that someone was watching.

Maybe it was just his nerves. Or maybe it was something else.

He noted the checkpoint ahead—three NATO vehicles positioned across the road, a handful of soldiers standing guard, weapons at low ready but not relaxed. A few sandbags were stacked near a small concrete barrier, not nearly enough to stop anything serious, but a deterrent nonetheless.

Their Humvee slowed, then stopped as Laughlin leaned out the window, signaling to one of the NATO troops. The man, a British soldier by the look of his gear, stepped forward, rifle slung across his chest.

"Americans?" the Brit called out.

"Yeah," Laughlin replied. "First Platoon, Bravo Company, outta Tuzla. You, the welcoming committee?"

"Something like that," the Brit said, stepping aside to let them through. "Pull up past the barrier. Captain's expecting you."

The convoy rolled forward, stopping near a cluster of buildings that had been converted into a temporary operations center. As they dismounted, Shane took in his surroundings—the faded shop signs, the narrow streets, the burned-out husks of buildings further down the road. The air smelled like damp earth, burning wood, and exhaust.

A few other NATO troops stood nearby, a mix of Brits, Germans, and a couple of Canadians. Their gear was slightly different—some wore winter camo, others had different loadouts—but they all carried the same weight in their eyes.

A captain in a NATO-marked jacket approached, his hands shoved into his pockets.

"Staff Sergeant Laughlin?" he asked.

"That's me," Laughlin said, squaring his shoulders.

"Captain Davis, Royal Infantry. You'll be relieving us on the southern checkpoint and market patrols. Town's mostly quiet, but don't let that fool you. There's been some trouble near the eastern bridge—small arms fire last week, no casualties, but enough to keep us on edge. Locals aren't hostile, but they ain't exactly friendly either."

Laughlin nodded. "Copy that. What're we looking at for security measures?"

Davis gestured toward a rough map taped to the wall of the nearest building. "Three main checkpoints. One at the south end of town near the market, one at the bridge, and one up near the municipal building. We've got a small detachment stationed here at the ops center, but it's mostly just for logistics. Your guys will be handling foot patrols near the market—keep an eye on the stalls and watch for anything out of place. The checkpoint teams'll be checking vehicles coming in and out. You get a bad feeling about something; you stop it before it gets into town."

Laughlin turned to his men. "You hear that? No fuck-ups. No lazy eyes. You see somethin' off, you call it in. You stop a vehicle, you check it right."

"What's the protocol for vehicle checks?" one of the soldiers asked, already running through what he'd learned in training.

Davis glanced at Laughlin, who gave a nod.

"Alright, boys," Laughlin said, turning fully to one of his own. His eyes landed on Shane. "You. Walk me through it."

Shane straightened. "Driver keeps hands visible at all times. We approach from an angle, not straight on. No bunching up—one man watches the driver, one clears the back. If it's a truck, we have 'em step out while we check the cargo."

"Good," Laughlin said, then turned to Wilson. "What're your escalation steps if a driver refuses?"

"Start with verbal commands," Wilson replied. "If they don't comply, escalate to show-of-force—weapon at the low ready. Still noncompliant, we pull 'em out, detain, search the vehicle fully."

Laughlin nodded, satisfied. "You check under the damn thing too. Ain't just the trunk you gotta worry about. They'll strap explosives under the chassis if they're feeling creative. Rodriguez, how you gonna check for that?"

Rodriguez didn't hesitate. "Mirror on a pole, go slow, look for wires or anything outta place. If it smells like fuel or anything chemical, back the fuck off and call it in."

"Good," Laughlin said. "See, this is how you stay alive. You assume every car is carrying a bomb, but you don't go making a damn scene unless you got a reason."

Davis folded his arms. "One more thing—don't let 'em crowd you. Market gets busy; people'll try to get close. Could be nothing, could be someone looking for a chance to grab a weapon. Keep 'em at arm's length."

Laughlin turned to his men. "You heard him. Keep your heads up. We ain't playin' mall cops here. This ain't a goddamn joke."

Loran exhaled. "Christ, Sarge, we get it. You're killin' the vibe."

Laughlin shot him a look. "Good. You keep that 'vibe' killed, and maybe you won't get your dumb ass shot."

Shane adjusted his gear, scanning the street beyond the makeshift command post. The town looked quiet enough, but the quiet places were the ones that got you killed.

This wasn't home. It wasn't even close.

Eight

Market Day

The eastern checkpoint was nothing more than a reinforced road-block—two concrete barriers set just wide enough for a single vehicle to pass through, flanked by sandbags and an old, rusted metal drum someone had repurposed as a trash bin. Shane stood near the edge, rifle slung across his chest, scanning every face that moved past the checkpoint. The market was just getting started, vendors setting up their stalls with wooden crates of produce, sacks of grain, and tables covered with everything from handwoven scarves to old Soviet-era tools.

A man in his late 40s shuffled past, shoulders hunched against the cold, a cigarette barely hanging onto his lower lip. His hands were rough and stained; probably a laborer or a mechanic. No bulges under his coat, no stiffness in his posture that suggested he was hiding anything. Just a guy starting his day.

Next, a teenage boy—maybe sixteen—jogged past, cradling a loaf of bread under one arm. He moved too fast, too eager. Shane tensed slightly, watching the way the kid's eyes flicked toward the soldiers and how he kept his distance. Then, just as Shane was about to say something to Loran, the boy skidded to a stop near an older woman, breathless, and handed over the bread with a sheepish grin. His grandmother, maybe. Shane exhaled, shifting his stance.

A middle-aged woman in a faded headscarf walked through, her shoulders squared and her face hard as stone. Shane noticed the way she avoided looking at them, her eyes fixed straight ahead. But that wasn't necessarily a bad sign—half the locals still weren't used to foreign soldiers being here. He let her pass, though he made a mental note of her just in case.

Then there was the man with the limp. Early 30s, unshaven, and wearing a thick coat that looked a size too big for him. Shane's gut tightened as he tracked the man's uneven gait. Something about the way he moved set off an instinct—like he was favoring more than just a bad leg. His right hand never left the pocket of his coat. Shane took half a step forward, ready to call out—

Then the guy stopped at a stall, reached into his pocket, and pulled out a handful of dinar notes. He was just buying potatoes.

Shane swallowed, feeling Loran's eyes on him. He didn't say anything; he just rolled his shoulders and kept watching.

A trio of men came through next, walking close together, speaking low in Serbo-Croatian. They were younger, mid-20s, the kind of guys who might've been soldiers themselves just a few years ago. One of them had a scar that ran from his eyebrow to his cheekbone. They glanced at the checkpoint but didn't linger. The one with the scar muttered something, and they all laughed.

"Friendly bunch," Loran muttered beside him.

"Yeah," Shane said, not looking away.

The last one that caught his attention was a little girl—maybe five, maybe younger—clutching a woman's hand as they walked past. Her coat was too big, sleeves nearly swallowing her hands. But it was her eyes that got him. She looked right at Shane, wide-eyed, curious but wary. Her mother pulled her along, not stopping, not acknowledging them.

Shane exhaled through his nose and shifted his weight again.

"Jesus, man," Loran finally said, voice low enough that only Shane could hear. "Loosen up a little. Your face is probably making folks nervous anyway."

Shane sighed. "Fuck off."

Loran grinned but didn't push it. He just kept watching the crowd, the same as Shane.

By late morning, the routine at the checkpoint settled into a steady rhythm—watch, assess, check, clear. Nothing flashy, nothing dramatic. Just the kind of work that required patience, discipline, and an eye for detail.

The market was busier now, the quiet trickle of early risers giving way to a steady stream of vendors, shoppers, and the occasional donkey cart rattling over the uneven road. Shane and Loran stood their post at the eastern entry while Wilson and Rodriguez handled the initial contact, directing foot traffic into an orderly line with short, clipped instructions.

"Documents," Wilson said, holding out a gloved hand as an older man in a wool coat stepped forward. The man produced a folded, slightly worn identification paper. Wilson barely glanced at it before passing it over his shoulder. "Taylor."

Loran took it, his eyes scanning the details. Name, birth date, and place of residence. It all looked fine, but he held it a beat longer than necessary, watching the man's face. No nervous shifting, no darting glances. Just mild impatience.

"Where you headed?" Loran asked, handing the ID back.

The man jerked a thumb toward the market stalls. "Buying flour," he muttered in accented English.

"Alright, go ahead," Loran said, stepping aside. The man shuffled past without another word.

Rodriguez waved the next person forward—a woman in her 50s, head wrapped in a dark scarf, carrying a small basket. Wilson took her papers and handed them back without much fuss. But then came a younger guy, maybe mid-20s, moving with just a little too much purpose.

"Stop," Wilson said, stepping slightly into the guy's path. "ID."

The man handed it over, jaw tight, shoulders stiff.

Shane watched from the side, fingers resting against his rifle sling, his weight evenly balanced. He was watching everything—the way the guy's left hand twitched at his side, the way his eyes didn't settle on any one of them, how his breath was just a little too controlled, like he was making an effort to stay calm.

Wilson studied the ID before passing it to Loran, who gave it a once-over and then held it up. "Where you coming from?"

"Bus station," the man said. His accent was thicker than the others.

"You live here?"

"Visiting family."

Loran didn't respond right away. Instead, he handed the ID to Shane. Shane took it, eyes flicking to the name and the date of birth. He didn't recognize the town listed as the place of residence, but that wasn't unusual. What caught his attention was the faint smudge along the bottom of the document—like someone had handled it before the ink had fully dried.

Rodriguez shifted slightly, angling his body just enough to cover the side while Wilson stepped to the right, subtly boxing the man in.

"You got a bag?" Shane asked.

The man's lips pressed together. "No."

"Turn around."

For a second, it looked like the guy was going to argue. Then he exhaled sharply and did as he was told, spreading his arms slightly. Rodriguez stepped in and gave him a quick, professional pat-down—wrists, pockets, waistline, ankles. Nothing.

Shane glanced back at the ID again, then at the man. He didn't like it. Something about him felt off. But feeling off wasn't enough to detain someone.

"Alright," Shane said, handing back the papers. "Move along."

The man grabbed them, eyes flicking to each of them before he walked past a little too stiffly. Shane watched him go, cataloging every step, but the guy just melted into the crowd.

"Something was up with him," Wilson muttered.

"Yeah," Shane agreed, but that was the end of it.

The next person coming through was a kid. Couldn't have been more than sixteen, maybe seventeen. Too young to be on his own, too old to be just another tag-along with the market crowd. He had a lean build, sunken eyes, and a nervous energy that immediately caught Shane's attention. The boy's hands flexed on the strap of the satchel slung over his shoulder—tight grip, adjusting like he was making sure it stayed close.

Shane's gut told him something was off.

"ID," Wilson said, holding out a hand.

The kid hesitated just a second too long before reaching into his jacket. Shane caught the way his fingers trembled slightly, how his breathing picked up—shallow, controlled, but faster than it should be. He was afraid.

That was the first bad sign.

Wilson took the ID, flipping it over and scanning the details. Loran had already shifted slightly, angling himself for a better look at the bag.

"What's in the bag?" Loran asked, voice casual but firm.

"Just...just things," the kid said. Accent thick. Voice just shy of steady.

Loran gave Wilson a glance.

"Set it down," Wilson said, nodding toward the ground.

The kid hesitated again. That was the second bad sign.

Shane adjusted his grip on his rifle. The safety was still on, but his finger wasn't far from it.

"Now," Wilson said. The kid exhaled hard through his nose and crouched, placing the bag at his feet. He stepped back, hands out slightly to his sides in a gesture that was supposed to look harmless. But Shane still didn't like it.

"Open it," Wilson said.

The kid's lips pressed together. Another hesitation. Third bad sign.

Shane was already shifting his weight, ready for whatever came next. A glance at Loran showed he was thinking the same thing.

The kid finally crouched again, fingers fumbling with the bag's buckle. It popped open, and he pulled it wide.

Wilson leaned in first.

Clothes. A bundle of them. Some food—a hunk of bread, a wedge of cheese wrapped in wax paper. A rusted pocketknife. A few scattered coins.

It was mundane. But something was off.

Wilson frowned, reaching inside. He pulled at the bundle of clothes. Something shifted underneath.

And there it was.

A bag of sugar. Another of flour. A tin of what looked like cooking grease.

All tucked away under the clothes, hidden like contraband.

Wilson exhaled through his nose and gave the kid a look. "What's this?"

The kid swallowed, rubbing a hand over the back of his neck. "I…was going to pay later."

"Uh-huh," Wilson said, deadpan.

Shane didn't react. Didn't shift. Didn't lower his weapon. Neither did Loran.

Because here was the thing—no one in the market was looking for this kid. No one was shouting, pointing, demanding something back. No vendors were making a scene about stolen goods.

And that meant it wasn't their problem.

Wilson studied the kid for another second, then reached down, grabbed the strap, and pulled the bag closed. He handed it back.

"Go."

The kid took it fast, dipping his head. "Hvala," he muttered before stepping back and walking off at a pace just slow enough to look normal.

Shane watched him go.

"Well, that was fuckin' anticlimactic," Loran muttered.

Wilson snorted. "Yeah, well. Kid's lucky. If he'd looked any jumpier, I'd have had to take my time."

"Shit, he looked like he was about to piss himself," Loran said.

Shane just exhaled and went back to scanning the crowd.

That was the job.

They cycled through the same process for hours—ID, check, clear. Some people barely acknowledged them, others threw them wary glances, and a few even offered polite nods. Occasionally, there was a cart to inspect, a bag to rifle through, and a hesitant teenager who had to be coaxed into handing over his papers.

The radio crackled every so often, updates from the other checkpoints. Nothing out of the ordinary. No threats. Just another cold morning in a country that hadn't quite figured out how to piece itself back together.

"Three-One," Loran called over the comms during a quiet stretch. "This is Three-One-Bravo. How's the west side looking?"

A short burst of static before the Staff Sergeant's voice came through. "Same shit, different angle."

Loran smirked, but Shane stayed quiet, eyes still on the crowd. It wasn't exciting work. It wasn't even particularly rewarding. But it mattered.

And so they kept at it.

Midday rolled around. The market ebbed and flowed with life, merchants haggling, buyers sifting through produce, the scent of bread and cured meats carried by the cold air. Shane was starting to recognize patterns—who came early, who lingered too long, who looked like they had business, and who just looked like they were waiting for something. It wasn't instinct, not yet, but it was getting there.

Then, a pair of women approached the checkpoint. Shane barely reacted, but he recognized them.

The fair one in the scarf, the dusky-skinned one with the baby—he'd seen them yesterday. Walking along the rubble-strewn roadside, the pale one carrying a basket, the other cradling the child, their footsteps cautiously following the tire tracks left by their convoy.

It was a long way from where he'd seen them last. That alone made him uneasy.

Wilson took the fair woman's ID first, flipping it over in his hand. He exhaled sharply as if bracing himself, then held the card up. "Tell me your date of birth."

She answered immediately, her voice even, and her shoulders relaxed. Wilson checked the details, then nodded, handing it back.

Then, it was the dusky-skinned woman's turn. Loran took her papers, eyes skimming the information. He paused when he got to the child's ID. "Who's the father?"

She hesitated. Not long. But just long enough for it to be noticeable.

When she did speak, her words came out low, a little jumbled. Not rehearsed, not polished, and Loran caught it. His expression shifted just slightly. "Sorry, what was that?"

She repeated the name, clearer this time, eyes set to the ground as if she was going to start sobbing there and then.

Loran glanced at Wilson, who gestured to the second ID in Loran's hand—one belonging to the young woman herself. It sported the same man's name. Loran's brow furrowed as he read something on the card, and then he made a quiet noise somewhere between a scoff and mild amusement.

"First time I've seen 'wife of' instead of a parent's name on an ID," he muttered, handing it back.

Shane hadn't spoken, but he was watching. The woman with the baby wasn't fidgeting, but there was something in the way she held herself, the way her arms tightened around the child. Her walking was a little too careful, definitely scared out of her mind. It was a sudden reaction; she hadn't been this jittery moments ago. Things checked out, and Shane concluded that it was probably only a natural response. Many civvies tend to be scared of armed individuals that up close and personal. Nevertheless, as she passed through the checkpoint, her eyes met his. As if, for a second, she might have seen beyond the glass yesterday.

He blinked. She tilted her head.

Neither's expressions changed, nor were any reactions given.

Then the baby started crying, and she turned her focus to shushing him, walking deeper into the market.

Loran exhaled. "Man, young moms are kinda hot—"

"Shut the hell up," Wilson said flatly before Shane even had to respond.

It was afternoon when it happened. An odd sensation. A prickling at one's skin, if you may. It was subtle at first. The kind of thing you felt before you could name it. A group of men approached the checkpoint—five, maybe six. Broad-shouldered, coats worn heavy, faces set like stone. They moved with the kind of confidence that wasn't about arrogance but something older, something rooted deep. They weren't here to start trouble. Not openly. But they wanted to be seen.

Shane adjusted his grip on his M249. **Not a threat.** But *something*.

Wilson was already moving, stepping forward. "ID," he said, holding out his hand.

The man in front, maybe mid-forties, squared his shoulders and reached into his coat. Not fast, but deliberate. The kind of movement that made men with rifles pay close attention.

Shane's heartbeat slowed, his focus narrowing.

Loran took a step to the side, casual on the surface, but adjusting his angle just enough to cover their flank. The man produced his ID, handing it to Wilson without a word. Wilson took it and flipped it open. His jaw clenched just slightly before he handed it to Loran.

Loran read, then let out a low breath. "Shit."

They were Serbs.

Not just Serbs—**Serb men** in a predominantly Croat market.

That didn't mean trouble. Not automatically. But in a town where ethnic tensions still smoldered beneath the surface, five Serb men moving together, making their presence known—it wasn't nothing.

Staff Sergeant Laughlin must have been watching because his voice crackled over the radio. "Hold 'em there."

Shane's grip tightened.

The men noticed the shift. They weren't stupid. Their leader—if he was the leader—lifted his chin slightly, eyes flicking between them. Then he spoke, his voice thick with an accent but firm. "Problem?"

Loran didn't answer.

Laughlin arrived within seconds, boots hitting the frozen ground with steady, measured weight. He didn't ask for an update. He took the ID from Loran, scanned it, and then fixed his gaze on the man in front. "What's your business here?"

The man didn't flinch. "Market."

Laughlin's expression didn't shift. "That so?"

The air felt tighter. It was not a full-blown standoff, but it was close enough that Shane's pulse stayed slow and controlled.

"You got family here?" Laughlin asked, voice flat.

A beat. Then the man nodded. "My sister."

Laughlin studied him for a long moment. Then, instead of responding, he turned slightly, eyes landing on Rodriguez. "Rodriguez, how many Croats we got left in Bratunac?"

Rodriguez blinked at the sudden question, but his response was immediate. "Not a lot, Sergeant."

Laughlin nodded. Then he looked back at the man. "You know why that is?"

Another pause.

The man's jaw tensed.

He knew.

Laughlin didn't move. Didn't blink. Just let the silence stretch.

Then he handed the ID back. "You boys behave yourselves."

The man took it, nodding once. "Of course."

Laughlin didn't respond. Just stood there, watching as the men passed through the checkpoint. They didn't speak to each other, didn't look around. They just walked.

Only when they were well into the market did Laughlin exhale through his nose. "Keep your eyes open. I'll go check in with our local liaison just in case."

No one needed to be told twice.

By 1400 hours, the market had settled into a steady rhythm. Vendors called out prices, children wove through the crowd, and the scent of grilled meat and fresh bread drifted through the crisp air. Shane had eased into the flow of their duty—watching faces, checking IDs, keeping the rifle at his chest like an extension of himself. He didn't feel relaxed, exactly, but the tension had settled into something manageable.

Then, something caught his eye.

He was scanning the ridgeline beyond the market—habit at this point, keeping track of anything above them—when a flicker of movement stood out against the backdrop of skeletal trees and frost-covered brush. A figure, half-obscured by scrub, shifting just enough to make Shane pause.

His gut tightened.

Could've been a civilian. Plenty of people used the trails up there, moving between farmsteads and smaller villages. But something about the way this one moved—slow, deliberate, stopping just as Shane's gaze landed—was off.

Shane kept his rifle steady, adjusting his stance slightly for a clearer view.

Then he saw another movement, ten meters from the first. *Someone else.*

They weren't walking a trail. They were watching.

Shane didn't hesitate. He pressed the transmit button on his radio, keeping his voice low and tight. "Three-One, this is Three-One-Bravo. Got movement on the ridge, one-four-zero. Two figures, ten meters apart. Paused when I saw 'em."

A brief crackle, and then Laughlin's voice came through, calm but alert. "Copy, Bravo. Confirm type?"

"Can't. No weapons visible. Not moving like hikers."

A few seconds of radio silence. Then: "Eyes on them?"

"Affirm. They're holding position."

"How high?"

Shane did a quick mental estimate, keeping his gaze locked. "One-fifty meters up. Overlooking the main square."

Laughlin and Wilson had already shifted closer, Wilson angling his head toward the ridgeline. "I got nothing," Wilson muttered.

Laughlin exhaled. Then his radio crackled again. "Three-One-Bravo, listen up. That high ground's got foot traffic. Farmers use it. Could be nothing. Maintain normal vigilance."

Shane didn't move his eyes from the ridge. "Copy."

"Don't escalate. Just watch."

"Roger."

Shane stayed locked on the spot. Thirty seconds passed. A full minute. Then, as quietly as they had appeared, the figures shifted again—this time moving back, fading into the trees.

Gone.

Shane didn't let out a breath. Just kept watching.

Loran, standing just behind him, exhaled through his nose. "Spooky bastards."

Shane didn't answer. He kept his gaze on the ridgeline, waiting for another flicker of movement, another sign of something more.

Nothing.

Maybe it was nothing. Maybe it wasn't.

Either way, he kept his rifle close and his eyes open.

Nine

The Arms of a Friend

1445 Hours

The first shot cracked through the air like a whip, shattering the market's routine.

For half a second, everything hung in eerie stillness. Then, the world detonated into chaos.

Civilians screamed, vendors abandoned their stalls, and baskets of fruit and bread tumbled into the dirt as people dove for cover. The market had gone from bustling to panic in the space of a heartbeat.

Shane's training kicked in before his mind fully processed what was happening. His left hand shot out, gripping Loran's vest and yanking him down hard behind the sandbagged checkpoint barrier.

"Contact! Shots fired—ridgeline!" he barked into his radio, already bringing his M249 up. His eyes swept the high ground, searching for the shooters, but the terrain worked against him—rocky, uneven patches of bare trees still standing from winter. Too many places to hide.

More gunfire erupted—this time from another angle, closer to the western checkpoint. A short burst, automatic fire.

"All checkpoints, report!" came Laughlin's voice over the radio, sharp and steady despite the chaos.

"Checkpoint East—shots fired from the ridgeline, no visual on shooters!" Shane responded, keeping his rifle tight to his shoulder.

"Checkpoint West—taking fire! At least two shooters!" another voice cut in.

"Checkpoint North—negative contact, securing civilians!"

"Stay low and hold position!" Laughlin ordered. "Do not return fire unless you confirm targets. Secure the civilians—push them behind cover!"

Shane's pulse hammered in his ears as he scanned the ridgeline. Movement. A dark figure shifting between the rocks—just for a second. He narrowed his sights, but the figure was gone before he could make the call.

"See 'em?" Loran asked, crouched beside him, rifle raised but finger off the trigger.

"Not clear enough."

More rounds snapped overhead, smacking into wooden stalls and punching through fabric canopies. Civilians were still scrambling—an older man had tripped, struggling to get up near a toppled fruit stand. A mother pulled her screaming child toward cover behind a truck.

Wilson and Rodriguez had already moved—Wilson was waving people toward the heavier cover of a concrete wall, his M4 angled upward as he scanned the ridgeline.

Shane kept his eyes locked on the high ground, voice steady as he relayed. "Still no solid visual. At least one shooter, maybe more. Firing from concealment."

"Fuckin' cowards," Loran muttered, keeping his head low.

"Checkpoint West—shooter at two o'clock, moving!"

Shane turned toward the western side of the market. There—just a glimpse of a figure disappearing behind an outcrop. Another burst of gunfire kicked up dust near the checkpoint.

Laughlin's voice snapped over the radio. "If you got eyes, call it! If you don't, hold fire!"

"Contact, moving west!" the soldier at Checkpoint West called out.

Shane clenched his jaw. They were trying to bait a response—force NATO to shoot first, maybe even hit civilians in the process. Classic insurgent tactic.

Laughlin knew it, too. "Do not engage blind! Keep civilians covered—local police are on the way!"

A lull. A few seconds of near silence, just the distant shouts of civilians and the wind cutting through the stalls.

Shane's grip on his weapon tightened. His eyes scanned the ridge-line again, every nerve in his body on edge. They weren't gone. Not yet.

Loran had always moved fast. *Too fast for his own damn good.*

Shane barely registered him, shifting beside him, rising from their cover in one fluid motion. His brain barely had time to process what was happening before Loran was moving.

There was a mother and child caught in the open—that young woman from before. The one with the shawl wrapped tightly around her head, her cold-bitten, dusky skin drawn tight with fear. The baby in her arms was crying; its wails lost in the rising chaos around them. She stood frozen, gripping the infant tighter, her feet rooted to the dirt like she didn't know which way to run.

Gunfire cracked again in the distance, sharp and sudden.

Loran didn't think. He acted.

"Come on!" he barked, waving her forward.

She didn't move. Didn't even flinch. Just stood there, wide-eyed, her chest rising and falling in quick, shallow breaths. Her arms tightened around the baby, as if sheer force alone could make the child disappear, shield him from whatever hell was unfolding around them.

Shane saw it—the way her fingers trembled on the fabric of her shawl, the way her lips parted slightly, forming some half-thought word she never got the chance to say. A small, desperate attempt at control, at understanding.

It didn't matter.

Loran moved forward, half a step out of cover. Just enough to grab her arm, just enough to snap her out of whatever frozen instinct had taken hold. She sucked in a sharp breath, eyes darting to him, filled with something between fear and sheer, blind trust.

She resisted for only half a second. A step back. The kind of hesitation that came from a lifetime of knowing that not every helping hand was there to save you. But then—

"Get down!" Loran ordered, yanking her forward.

She stumbled, baby clutched tight against her chest, and for a brief second, they were all just kids in this. Loran, barely in his twenties, still wearing the ideals of a young soldier who hadn't yet learned that some people were just too far away to reach in time. Shane, watching, knowing, but moving too slowly. The woman, not much older than them, was trapped in a war she had never signed up for, her breath coming in harsh little bursts as she scrambled to follow.

Shane saw it in her eyes. The shift from fear to something rawer. A gut-deep panic as she tried to say something—her lips moved, forming words in a language neither of them spoke. Something pleading, desperate. Maybe trying to tell them she had another child somewhere, maybe trying to say *thank you,* maybe just trying to breathe through it. But she never got the chance to finish. Loran had just enough time to lower his rifle and help her into the cover when—

CRACK.

The bullet hit fast.

No warning. No scream. Just the brutal, wet impact of metal punching through flesh.

Shane felt it before he saw it—hot blood splattered across his cheek, warm and thick. It dripped down his skin, beading along his jawline, the sharp metallic scent flooding his senses. Loran jerked back, his knees buckling as his whole body recoiled. His eyes shot wide, unfocused, mouth parting in a silent gasp. His rifle slipped from his hands, clattering uselessly against the dirt.

For a split second, it didn't register.

Then Shane saw the wound.

A jagged hole was torn through the right side of Loran's neck, just below the jaw. Arterial red gushed instantly, spraying in pulsing spurts, painting his collar, his vest, and the air itself. His skin, already paling, looked worse against the deep, crimson flood seeping down his throat. His hands clawed upward, fingers trembling as they pressed against the open wound, trying—desperately, instinctively—to hold himself together.

But there was no stopping it.

Shane lunged forward, catching him before he hit the ground. Loran's weight sagged into him, deadweight already, his body shuddering violently against Shane's arms. The heat of him, the slickness of his blood—Shane barely noticed, his focus locked on the torn, pulsing ruin of his friend's throat.

"Fuck! Taylor—stay with me!" Shane's voice cracked, his hands pressing down hard, trying to stem the bleeding. But it just kept coming. Warm and slick, gushing between his fingers in thick, pulsing waves. It poured down his wrists, soaked into his sleeves, and pooled beneath them in the dirt, turning the dust into something dark and sticky.

Loran's breaths came sharp and ragged, choking. Gurgling. His lips moved, but no words came out—just wet, sucking noises, drowning in his own blood. His body convulsed in Shane's grip, spasms rolling through him in jerky, disjointed movements. His fingers flexed weakly, nails scraping against Shane's forearm, as if reaching for something—clinging to something.

"Medic! Medic now!" Shane roared, but the chaos around them swallowed his voice whole. Gunfire still cracked somewhere in the distance, shouting, screaming, the panicked rush of civilians trampling over broken stalls and discarded belongings. None of it mattered. None of it was louder than the sound of Loran drowning.

Shane tightened his grip, shoving his knee under Loran's shoulders to prop him up, but it didn't help. Blood. Too much blood. The wound was deep—too deep—and every desperate, gasping breath sent another rush spilling out over Shane's hands. It was slick and hot, coating his fingers, filling the creases of his knuckles, smearing across Loran's already paling skin.

Loran's eyes darted around wildly, unfocused, searching. Looking for something. Someone. Then they locked onto Shane's.

Panic. Confusion.

And something worse.

Recognition.

Like he understood. Like it had finally clicked, what was happening, what it meant. His lips parted again, and this time, there was sound—weak, garbled. Shane leaned in, desperate to catch it.

But all that came was more blood.

A fresh wave bubbled up, seeping from the corner of his mouth and dribbling down his chin. He tried again—his throat spasmed, his whole body seizing with effort. A rattling, choking noise clawed its way out of his throat, his eyes widening—too wide.

Shane pressed harder. "Don't you fucking die, man. They're coming, alright?" His voice was rough, shaking, his breath coming too fast. "Stay with me, Taylor—goddamn it, just hold on."

Loran's fingers twitched against Shane's arm, weak. Slipping.

His body bucked once—hard. Blood spurted violently, a final pulse, hot and strong, before it slowed. His mouth fell open. His limbs sagged, muscles going slack all at once, his weight heavier somehow.

Shane felt it.

The moment it happened.

A breath that never came. A pulse that never followed.

Loran's chest shuddered once—then stilled.

Shane's hands trembled where they pressed against the wound, now useless, blood seeping between his fingers like sand through a sieve. His own breath hitched. He squeezed his eyes shut for half a second, jaw clenched so tight his teeth ached.

Then something inside him shut off.

He inhaled sharply, forcing air into his lungs. His arms tensed, hands slipping from Loran's throat. Bloodied fingers wrapped around the grip of his M249, moving with cold, mechanical efficiency.

Shane turned. Sighted down the barrel. The first target was already moving, scrambling for cover.

Shane fired.

Shane clenched his jaw. "You're okay, man. You're gonna be okay." It was a lie, but it was the only thing he could say. He pressed harder against the wound. Loran's body twitched, fingers curling weakly against Shane's sleeve.

The medic was running toward them now, shouting something, but Shane barely heard him over the rushing in his ears.

Loran coughed—a terrible, choking sound. More blood bubbled up past his lips, spilling down his chin.

His eyes started to glaze over.

"Stay with me, goddamn it!" Shane snarled, shaking him. "Taylor!"

No response. His chest still rose, but it was shallow, slowing. His hands slackened.

The medic shoved Shane aside, working fast, clamping down on the wound, trying to stop what Shane already knew was unstoppable.

Loran's body gave one last shudder—then stilled.

His eyes, still open, stared past Shane at nothing at all.

Shane didn't move. Didn't breathe. His hands were still covered in warm blood, his heartbeat a roaring drum in his skull. The woman and her child had scrambled away, the infant wailing, but he barely noticed.

The gunfire had stopped. The world had gone eerily silent.

Loran was dead.

Shane didn't have time to think.

The world narrowed to blood, gunfire, and rage.

Loran's lifeless weight slumped against him, head tilted back, eyes still open—unseeing. Shane barely registered the medic shouting something, barely noticed the woman huddled with her child behind a toppled fruit cart, her arms wrapped tightly around the infant as she trembled in silence.

All he saw was movement on the ridgeline. The bastards were still there.

Shane snatched up his M249, where it had fallen. His hands were still slick with his best friend's blood, staining the grip and trigger, but his mind had already gone cold. Automatic.

He settled into a firing position, planting his knee into the dirt for stability, pressing the butt of the weapon firm into his shoulder. Eyes locked on the ridgeline. He spotted them through the trees—dark silhouettes shifting against the pale sky. Five targets.

Adrenaline roared through his veins, drowning out everything else.

He lined up the first one—center mass—finger tightening over the trigger.

The M249 rattled in his grip as the burst of 5.56mm tore through the target. The man jerked violently, staggered, and collapsed backward down the ridge.

Shane was already shifting.

The second bastard ducked behind a cluster of rocks, but not fast enough. Shane's next burst sent chips of stone flying before the rounds punched through him. He crumpled.

Shane didn't linger. Instinct drove him to shift his position slightly, keeping his profile minimized behind cover while his eyes locked onto the next target. The third man—running, breaking left toward cover. Shane adjusted.

Breathe. Track. Fire.

He squeezed the trigger in controlled bursts, his M249 kicking against his shoulder as he led the target, compensating for movement. The rounds found their mark, ripping into the man's side and dropping him hard. The body twitched, hands clenching briefly before going still.

Shane scanned. Two more.

The fourth was hesitating now, shifting his weight like he was trying to decide whether to fight or run. Shane watched the tell—the brief flex of muscles before the man bolted, retreating toward the trees. Shane's grip tightened.

He adjusted for the incline, compensating for the uneven terrain and the slight sway of his own rapid breathing. His sights tracked smoothly. Another burst. The first rounds caught fabric, and the next tore through flesh. The man staggered, his body twisting with the impact before he collapsed mid-stride, legs kicking out violently as he skidded to a stop.

One left.

The final shooter scrambled up the ridge, pushing through loose dirt and rocks in a blind panic. Shane shifted, planting his elbows for stability as he braced his bipod against the crate. His finger rested on the trigger guard for a half-second—quick assessment. Distance. Wind. Angle.

Exhale.

He squeezed the trigger.

A controlled burst spat from his barrel. The fleeing figure jerked, arms flailing as the rounds struck center mass. His body arched backward, momentum carrying him for half a second before gravity won, and he pitched forward, tumbling down the ridge in a lifeless heap, dust, and debris kicking up around him as he rolled.

Silence.

Not the tense, expectant kind. Not the heavy quiet of men waiting for the next shot.

Just... nothing.

Shane blinked against the sweat burning in his eyes, his grip iron-tight around the weapon. Slowly, he lowered the barrel, scanning the ridge with sharp, practiced precision. No movement. No more threats. The bodies were still. His ears rang, but beneath them, he could hear the distant shuffle of boots, the murmur of voices from the market below.

He pivoted, his training running on autopilot—situational awareness.

The market had gone deathly still. People crouched behind overturned carts, pressed against walls, wide-eyed and shaking. Some stared at him. Others at Loran. Shane turned, breath catching, his sharp eyes still scanning the area. The woman with the baby was still crouched behind the fruit cart, her child tucked under the shawl. Her gaze darted from Loran's body to Shane standing. Slowly, she reached out—small, trembling fingers brushing against Loran's cheekbone.

She gently closed his eyes.

Then she pulled back, pressing her forehead to the baby's, rocking him slightly as he whimpered against her chest.

Shane sat back on his heels, staring at the blood-soaked ground, ears still ringing. His hands were steady. His breath was even.

The job was done.

But Loran was gone.

Ten

All Left Behind

Shane didn't move.

The world around him blurred at the edges, sounds distorting into a dull, distant hum. His rifle sat heavy in his lap, the barrel still warm from the rounds he'd just fired. The metal pressed against his gloves was hot enough to be felt even through the fabric.

Loran's body lay beside him, still, lifeless, blood pooling into the dirt.

The market had been loud before. He knew that. He remembered the shouts, the panic, the stampede of feet before it'd become quiet. But now, the noise came back in jagged waves—somewhere in the distance, a woman was screaming. Closer, someone groaned in pain, a low, wet sound. Boots pounded against the ground. Radios crackled. Orders barked.

And Loran—Loran was just... there.

Shane exhaled, chest rising in slow, uneven movements. His body felt disconnected, like he was floating just outside of himself, watching someone else sit there, hands caked in blood. It was still warm. Loran's blood.

His grip tightened around his M249. His fingers ached.

"Alexander."

The voice cut through the fog, sharp and commanding.

"Alexander!"

A heavy hand gripped his shoulder. Squeezed. The pressure jolted something in his brain, snapping his focus back just enough to register the figure in front of him.

Staff Sergeant Laughlin.

Laughlin's face was tight, mouth set in a grim line. There was no softness in his eyes, no sympathy. Not yet. Right now, there wasn't time for that.

"Hey! Get your goddamn head on straight, now!" Laughlin snapped, giving him another rough shake.

Shane blinked. His throat felt thick and dry. The copper tang of blood filled his nose.

"Move, soldier. Now."

It wasn't a request.

Somewhere behind them, tires screeched as NATO's quick reaction forces pulled into the market. More soldiers poured in, weapons raised, scanning for threats. Medics followed close behind, their red crosses stark against dust-covered uniforms.

"Fuck's sake—Fitz!" Laughlin barked, turning over his shoulder.

Sergeant Fitzpatrick was already moving. A broad-shouldered, battle-worn man in his late thirties, Fitzpatrick had the kind of presence that demanded attention the second he stepped into a room—or, in this case, a battlefield.

He crouched beside them, his sharp gaze flicking between Shane and Loran. A beat of silence passed before Fitzpatrick let out a low sigh, pressing his lips into a firm line.

"Shit," he muttered under his breath, shaking his head. Then, louder, "Alright, get him up."

Shane barely had time to process before Fitzpatrick grabbed him under the arms, yanking him upright with the kind of firm, practiced efficiency that brooked no argument.

Shane stumbled. His legs felt weak, and unsteady, like they didn't quite belong to him.

"I got him," Fitzpatrick said to Laughlin, before his attention snapped back to Shane. "Alright, kid. Listen up."

Shane stared at him, breathing shallowly.

"You need to pull it the fuck together," Fitzpatrick said, his tone sharp but not unkind. "You hear me?"

Shane swallowed hard.

Fitzpatrick's grip tightened on his shoulder. "I *said*, do you hear me?"

A second passed.

Then another.

Finally, Shane forced himself to nod.

"Good. Then get your shit in gear." Fitzpatrick turned, jerking his chin toward the perimeter. "We need boots securing this fucking market. That means *you*."

Shane's stomach twisted. He glanced down, just once, at Loran's body. His best friend. His fucking *best friend*.

Fitzpatrick sighed through his nose.

"Listen, boy." His voice was quieter now. Lower. Just between them. "I know. Alright? I fucking *know*. But we've got a situation here. And you got two choices—you either sit there and let this fuck you up, or you get back in the fight and *do your job*."

Shane clenched his jaw so hard his teeth ached.

Fitzpatrick nodded, reading the shift in his expression. "That's it. You're a goddamn soldier. Act like it."

With that, Fitzpatrick let go of his arm and stood, already moving.

Shane inhaled sharply. Then, finally, he moved too.

The market was still in chaos.

Civilians huddled in corners, pressed against walls, eyes wide with shock. A woman held a child against her chest, murmuring something in hushed, panicked words. The baby still cried, sharp, stuttering wails. Blood stained the ground, thick and dark, mixing with dirt and dust. A man groaned, gripping his leg where a bullet had torn through the muscle. Medics rushed past, their voices clipped and efficient as they worked through the wounded.

Nearby, Laughlin shouted into his radio, relaying details to command. Shane forced himself to keep moving. Step by step. One foot in front of the other.

His hands still shook. His heart still pounded. But Fitzpatrick was right; he was a soldier. And right now, he had a job to do.

Everything was a mess. Stalls knocked over, carts splintered, bodies in the dirt—some moving, some not. The smell of gunpowder and blood hung heavy in the air. The only sounds now were the low groans of the wounded and the sharp, efficient voices of medics moving through the wreckage.

Staff Sergeant Laughlin stood in the center of it all, radio in one hand, rifle tight against his chest. His expression was flat, his voice sharp as he fired off orders.

"Casualty report."

Wilson answered first. "Three civilians dead. Seven wounded. All attackers neutralized." A beat. "Taylor's gone."

Laughlin pressed his lips together and exhaled hard through his nose.

"Fuck." It wasn't grief. Not yet. Just a fact. "Secure the perimeter. I want this place locked down until QRF gets a full sweep done. Nobody moves unless we know who they are and what they want."

Fitzpatrick was already moving. "Copy. Garcia, Rodriguez, on me. Sweep for secondaries, any strays we didn't see. Santiago, keep eyes on the road—if anyone even *thinks* about rolling up unannounced, you call it before they get too close."

"Roger."

Shane hadn't moved. He still had blood on his hands—Loran's, still fresh, drying against his gloves. He flexed his fingers, the sensation barely registering.

Laughlin turned, looking at him.

"You good, Alexander?"

Shane didn't answer right away. No. He wasn't. But his rifle was loaded, and he was still standing. That would have to be enough.

"Yeah." His voice came out rough.

Laughlin studied him for a second but didn't push. No time for it.

Instead, he gave a single nod. "Damn fine work up there, soldier. You kept this from turning into a slaughter." Then, into the radio, "Break, break, break—this is checkpoint one. Engagement complete, five enemy KIA, multiple civilian casualties. QRF on-site. Requesting further instructions from Camp Eagle, over."

The radio crackled. "Copy, checkpoint one. Hold position and continue civilian triage. Additional med teams en route."

NATO's quick reaction force was already in motion, securing the area and questioning witnesses. A few aid workers in blue vests were crouched by the wounded, pulling out bandages and emergency kits.

One of them, a woman with a French accent, was pressing gauze to an older man's leg, speaking to him in slow, careful Bosnian. Another medic passed Shane without looking at him, kneeling beside an old woman with blood on her headscarf. A teenager, probably her son, held her hand as he babbled something in...whatever language he was speaking at this point. Shane looked away.

Wilson and Rodriguez took up positions along the perimeter, rifles ready. Garcia and Fitz were near the far end of the street, scanning what was left of the crowd. Most of the civilians had run, but some still lingered, eyes wary, whispering to each other. Some were watching the soldiers. Some were watching the bodies.

"Any signs of a secondary threat?" Laughlin asked.

"Negative," Fitzpatrick replied. "No movement, no runners. Just a lot of people trying to figure out what happens next."

"Copy." Laughlin glanced back at Shane, eyes steady. "Then let's make sure they don't have a reason to panic anymore than they already have."

Shane moved like a man on autopilot. Every order followed, every motion precise, but his mind wasn't there. It was trapped somewhere between the blood drying on his sleeves and the echoes of gunfire that still rattled inside his skull.

The perimeter was set—Wilson and Rodriguez had the southern road locked down while Fitz and Garcia patrolled the east side of the market, clearing stragglers and ensuring no one wandered into the wreckage. NATO's quick reaction force had taken over, questioning the civilians, their blue helmets standing out against the dust and debris. Aid workers moved in clusters, triaging the wounded, their hands stained dark with blood.

Shane didn't talk. He worked.

He lifted an overturned cart that had pinned a man's leg and let one of the medics stabilize it before they hauled him onto a stretcher. He helped an older woman, still dazed, to her feet, guiding her away from the carnage and toward one of the aid stations set up near the edge of the market. When he passed by a stall that had been torn apart in the chaos, he stopped long enough to pick up a scattered bundle of dried goods and handed them back to the stunned merchant, who accepted them in silence.

His hands shook. Not enough to be obvious. But enough that he felt it.

He could still see the ridgeline. Could still picture that shadowed figure moving between the rocks, the same one he had reported to Laughlin an hour before the shooting started.

Should have pushed harder. Should have insisted.

But it was too late for that now.

Low murmurs of medics and the occasional sharp cry of pain cut through the dim light cast by battery-powered lanterns. He had been moving supplies, holding IV bags, and doing anything they asked without question. It was easier to focus on the work, on the tangible weight of a box in his hands or the feel of gauze pressed against torn skin, than to let his mind drift back to the ridge.

He stepped into the next tent, and the first thing he saw was a young boy, maybe ten, sitting cross-legged on a cot. His face was smeared with dirt and dried blood, though the wound itself had already been bandaged—a long gash running from his scalp to his left cheekbone. It wasn't the worst injury here, but the boy wasn't crying, wasn't making a sound at all.

His eyes, hollow and glassy, flicked up to Shane and stayed there.

A medic crouched in front of him, checking his pupils with a small flashlight. "Concussion, likely mild," she muttered, mostly to herself. "Laceration's closed, nothing deep. Kid's still in shock, though."

Shane knew that look. He'd seen it before.

"Where are his parents?" he asked.

The medic exhaled sharply, tossing the flashlight back into her kit. "Gone."

The boy's stare didn't waver, like he'd heard them but didn't care. Or maybe he didn't understand.

Shane didn't know what to say. Instead, he just crouched and held out the canteen hooked to his belt. The kid took it after a second, moving slowly, like the weight of it...or perhaps of the moment itself was unfamiliar in his hands. He took a sip but didn't let go of the container.

Shane left it with him.

The second tent was worse.

A woman lay on her side on a bloodstained cot, her arm stretched out, shaking as a medic stitched a ragged wound just above her elbow. The flesh was torn wide—shrapnel, probably. Fragments of something had ripped through her, and it had already been a miracle they'd stopped the bleeding before she lost the limb.

She was sweating, her blonde hair sticking to her forehead, but her teeth were clenched hard enough to make the muscles in her jaw tremble. No pain meds. Either they didn't have enough to waste on non-critical injuries, or she'd refused. Some people did that. Some people wanted to feel every second of it, like it was a kind of penance.

Shane knelt, helping to hold her arm steady as the medic continued working.

She barely looked at him.

But as the needle pulled through her skin, her fingers curled involuntarily, gripping his wrist like a vice. It wasn't intentional. He could tell by the way her breath shuddered, by the way her gaze stayed locked on the canvas ceiling above them.

Shane didn't pull away. He let her hold on as long as she needed.

Another was a man—old, maybe mid-sixties, face lined with deep wrinkles that spoke of a life hard-lived long before this war. Or perhaps through it as well. He was propped up against a crate, his leg wrapped in thick bandages. From the way he held himself, the wound was high on his thigh, likely a bullet that had passed clean through. Lucky, in a way.

Shane had just finished handing off another box of supplies when the old man caught his arm.

His grip was strong despite the blood loss, fingers curling over Shane's forearm in a grasp that was almost... grateful.

He said something, his voice low and urgent.

Shane blinked. "I—uh—"

More words, faster this time.

Shane shook his head slightly, lifting his other hand in a helpless gesture. "I don't—I don't understand, man."

The old man huffed, then just patted Shane's arm, nodding once before releasing him.

Shane exhaled slowly, standing. He had no idea what had been said, but he didn't think he needed to. The man's expression—somber, tired, but thankful—said enough.

In the next tent, a teenager sat slumped against a cot, pressing a wad of gauze against the side of his abdomen. The makeshift dressing was soaked through, dark red creeping past his fingers. He winced as a medic peeled the fabric back, revealing a deep graze along his ribs.

"Could've been worse," the medic muttered.

The kid let out a sharp, humorless laugh, though it cut off immediately when the pain flared. He hissed through his teeth, muttering something in his own language.

Shane didn't ask. He didn't need to.

Instead, he helped the medic pull his jacket off the rest of the way, exposing the extent of the injury. Not deep enough to need stitches, but enough to hurt like hell.

The kid caught Shane's eye then, his expression shifting for just a second—something unguarded, something bitter. He said something, quieter this time.

Shane didn't know the words, but he knew that look.

It was the same one he'd seen in the mirror more times than he could count.

He just nodded.

The last one made his stomach twist.

Bloodied rags piled in the corner, hands worked fast and efficiently—tying bandages, checking vitals. Shane was helping hold down a man's arm as a medic cleaned out a deep graze when another voice called out.

"Need an extra set of hands over here."

He turned.

A medic was hunched over a man's hand, carefully working to re-align his fingers. Two of them were split open, jagged wounds tracing up toward his knuckles. It looked like he'd caught the edge of an explosion—maybe shrapnel, maybe debris. He was young, mid-twenties at most, his clothes torn and blood-spattered. He sat stiffly, eyes blank, as if the pain hadn't fully registered yet.

"Hold his hand steady," the medic instructed. "Gotta close these up."

Shane crouched, wrapping his fingers around his wrist, firm but careful. The man's pulse was rapid beneath his grip. The medic worked quickly, applying medical glue to the wounds and pressing the skin back together before reinforcing it with stitches where needed.

Shane watched, but his focus drifted.

To the far side of the tent.

A young woman sat with her back to the entrance, shoulders hunched forward. Her shawl was still in place, though loosened as it was pulled forward and stained with dust. He didn't need to see her face to know who she was.

She was feeding her child. Tucked against her chest, wrapped in the same cloth he'd seen earlier, the infant suckled quietly, oblivious to everything happening around them.

The same pair Loran had saved.

His grip on the injured man's wrist tightened for just a second before he forced himself to let go.

Livid. That was the only word for it.

Livid because Loran was dead. Livid because this young woman—this *one* woman—was the reason he had stood up, the reason he had been in the open, the reason he had taken that bullet.

But it wasn't her fault. Shane knew that.

Didn't make it easier to swallow.

He exhaled sharply, stood, and left without another word. There was another tent nearby. They'd need his help there, too.

***

The sun was slipping below the hills, casting long shadows over what was left of the market. Fires had burned out. Blood had dried. The chaos had settled into something quieter, but not peaceful. Never peaceful.

Shane had been working non-stop, clearing debris, reinforcing the perimeter, checking in with the medics—anything to stay moving. Anything to keep his hands busy and his mind from looping back to that exact moment, over and over again.

The low murmur of voices at the edge of the market caught his attention. A column of Humvees rolled up, dust curling off their tires as they came to a stop near the main checkpoint. Captain Mitchell stepped out first—broad-shouldered, rigid posture, a face carved from granite. Behind him, four MPs followed, their expressions unreadable.

Fitzpatrick was already there, standing just outside the command post. His eyes flicked to Shane as the officers approached, but he said nothing.

Mitchell wasted no time. "Sergeant Laughlin." His voice cut through the evening air like a blade.

Laughlin stepped forward, straight-backed. "Sir."

The captain's gaze swept the area, taking in the remnants of the firefight—the dead still being loaded into NATO transport trucks, the wounded huddled beneath aid tents. His jaw tensed.

"Brief me."

"Five attackers, all neutralized by Specialist Alexander," Laughlin reported, voice clipped. "One KIA—Specialist Loran Taylor. Multiple civilian casualties. QRF secured the perimeter, and we've been assisting with medical aid and recovery efforts since. Situation under control."

Mitchell nodded once. "Good work."

For a second, it seemed like that was it. Then, the captain turned his attention to Shane.

"Specialist Alexander."

Shane straightened instinctively. "Sir."

Mitchell's expression didn't change. "You are to surrender your weapon and report to command for questioning regarding the engagement."

Silence.

Shane felt the weight of every single set of eyes on him—Laughlin, Fitz, Wilson, Rodriguez, the MPs standing just behind Mitchell, hands resting near their sidearms like they were waiting for him to make this difficult.

He swallowed once, forcing his voice to stay steady. "Questioning, sir?"

Mitchell didn't blink. "Orders from Battalion."

That was all he said. No explanation. No details. Just orders.

Shane's fingers tightened around the grip of his M249 before he finally let out a slow breath and unshouldered it. He ejected the belt, cleared the chamber, and then held the weapon out butt-first. One of the MPs stepped forward to take it.

No one spoke.

Fitzpatrick was watching him carefully, but there was nothing he could say. Not now.

Mitchell nodded toward the vehicles. "Let's go."

Shane squared his shoulders and followed, his boots heavy against the dirt.

Eleven

Speak no Evil

The ride to Camp Eagle was colder than it needed to be. Not just because the heater in the Humvee struggled against the Balkan winter clawing at the canvas flaps, but because of the weight of silence in the cabin. Shane sat in the rear, wrists resting on his knees, fingers laced loosely together to avoid any appearance of restraint.

The two Military Police escorts rode in the front. One was a Staff Sergeant with a square jaw and no name offered; the other, a Specialist with a clipboard balanced on his thigh, scribbling notes every so often, like Shane was a specimen in a jar. Neither of them spoke to him, not even a nod. No shared cigarette. No small joke to cut the edge.

They kept their conversation clipped and internal, mostly concerning comms checks and waypoints.

"Approaching Camp Eagle main gate," the driver reported over the radio.

"Roger, gate has been notified. Stand by for secondary screening," came the reply through the squawk of static.

Secondary screening. That was new.

Shane watched the frost crawl along the inside of the plastic window-like veins. He could see the faint outline of the main gate guard shack, a makeshift structure of sandbags, plywood, and a coil of rusting concertina wire drooping like tired ribbon. A soldier in full winter uniform waved them through the first checkpoint, rifle slung but not at rest. Eyes hard and unsmiling.

The Humvee rolled to a stop between two concrete barriers. Armed guards stepped up, checked the hood, and the undercarriage with mirrors, popped the tailgate, and peered inside. Standard protocol, but it felt personal. They glanced at Shane as if already briefed on who he was. What he allegedly was.

The clipboard Specialists handed over a sealed manila envelope marked "RESTRICTED" in block letters.

"Special delivery," he said dryly.

Clearance took six minutes, but it stretched like an hour.

When they finally drove past the last obstacle, Shane caught his first view of Camp Eagle since deployment—an ugly sprawl of prefab shelters, mud-churned motor pools, and razor wire corralling the whole miserable patch of earth. The American flag snapped taut in the wind above the command building, frayed at the edges.

They parked near the administration complex. Shane was ordered to dismount. No salutes exchanged, no words of welcome or recognition. He climbed out, boots crunching on frozen gravel, and followed the two MPs through a gauntlet of watchful eyes. Soldiers paused in their tasks to glance at him, then just as quickly looked away, busying themselves with clipboards or fuel lines.

They led him to the Military Police administrative office, a squat, windowless structure next to the communications bunker. Inside, the air reeked of diesel heaters and institutional coffee.

The Staff Sergeant escort motioned to a chair bolted to the floor near the duty desk. "Sit here," he ordered.

Shane did.

An MP Lieutenant appeared next, flipping through a packet of paperwork with a practiced flick of his gloved fingers. He looked young. Too young to carry the authority on his collar, but his voice held no hesitation.

"Specialist Shane Alexander, United States Army," he began, reading directly from the document. "You are hereby assigned to restricted quarters pending completion of an official 15-6 investigation concerning actions undertaken by you on 16 January 1997 at Grid 14-Romeo-Bravo."

The words were sharp. Mechanical. Not a flicker of empathy.

"This investigation is convened under Army Regulation 15-6," the Lieutenant continued, "initiated by order of Task Force Commander Colonel Michael Harrison."

He passed Shane a carbon-copied notification, the yellow page marked "ACKNOWLEDGEMENT COPY." Shane's eyes skimmed it:

"...investigation will determine whether actions were consistent with standing Rules of Engagement, force escalation protocols, and applicable provisions under international law applicable to NATO operations in Bosnia-Herzegovina..."

"Sign here," the Lieutenant instructed, tapping the acknowledgment line.

Shane took the pen. His hand felt stiff, almost wooden, but he signed. He noted how steady his handwriting looked. Somehow, it felt like that mattered.

The Lieutenant spoke again, clipped and procedural. "You are directed not to discuss the incident in question with anyone except designated investigating officers, appointed counsel, or approved personnel cleared for need-to-know by the investigating authority."

A gag order. Official. Binding.

Failure to comply could be construed as obstruction under UCMJ Article 134. Shane knew the implication without needing it spelled out.

"You are restricted to Quarters Delta, Building Two," the Lieutenant went on. "Meals will be delivered to you at designated times. You are not to enter motor pools, arms rooms, CP facilities, or engage in radio transmissions outside approved check-ins. Your mail is subject to inspection. Visitation is denied pending further notice."

He flipped to another page.

"You will surrender personal communication devices now."

Shane pulled the battered Motorola handset from his cargo pocket and set it on the table. The MP tagged it with a property sticker and logged it into evidence.

"Do you understand these conditions as read to you?"

"I understand," Shane replied, his voice tight.

The Lieutenant offered a mechanical nod. "Good. Your compliance is required and expected. You will be notified of interview appointments as they are scheduled. Questions?"

Shane thought about it. Just for a second. *Why Loran? Why not me?*

But that wasn't the kind of question they wanted. "No, sir," he answered.

"Escort will take you to quarters."

Two new MPs appeared, different from the first pair, which seemed deliberate. Fresh eyes, no familiarity. They flanked him at a respectful distance, not too close to imply custody, but never more than a step away either.

As they walked out, Shane caught sight of a poster tacked on the office wall:

OPERATION JOINT GUARD:

MAINTAIN PEACE. MAINTAIN DISCIPLINE. MAINTAIN HONOR.

The words felt hollow now.

Outside, the morning sun had clawed its way over the ridgeline, throwing long shadows across the camp. Shane's shadow stretched thin and brittle ahead of him, like it belonged to someone else.

The walk to the Quarters took less than two minutes, but the moment felt eternal. Other soldiers avoided his eyes, or worse, fixed him with blank stares full of quiet judgment.

At Building Two, an MP opened the door and motioned him inside.
The room was bare-bones. Cot, footlocker, wall-mounted heater humming like an old man's wheeze. A single barred window let in pale daylight over the snow-caked parade ground.

"Wait here for further instruction," one of the escorts said, shutting the door behind him.

A dull metal click sounded as the bolt slid into place. Not locked from the outside—but the message was clear.

Shane stood for a long moment, staring at the chipped paint on the walls. His gear bag sat in the corner, already delivered. Stripped of any sensitive items. Sanitized. Impersonal.

He finally sat on the edge of the cot.

No clock on the wall. No radio chatter piping through. Just the faint noise of Camp Eagle grinding along without him, engines coughing, boots stamping in the cold, orders being barked across the yard.

He laced his fingers, elbows resting on his knees, and let his gaze fall to the floor.

15-6.

Restricted quarters.

Gag order.

Suspect, not soldier.

The weight of it pressed down on his chest, heavier than any pack he'd ever carried.

And somewhere in the back of his mind, beyond the protocols and procedures, the drills and directives, a quiet, corrosive thought took hold:

What if they've already made up their minds?

***

Shane pinched a jigsaw piece between his thumb and forefinger, turning it absently as he studied the half-formed cartoon dinosaur on the table. His eyes narrowed at the bright green curve of its back, scales drawn in thick, cheerful lines — ridiculous, really, for a place like this. He pressed it into place but left his hand there, resting on the puzzle as if steadying it might somehow steady himself.

Across from him, Mike Chisholm sat cross-legged, elbows on his knees, watching with the patient stillness of a man used to long silences. Around them, the rec room at Fort Leavenworth buzzed in low hums of quiet activity — a card game over in the corner, someone thumbing through a paperback with the cover torn off, a TV flickering in mute black-and-white above the door.

"You were saying," Chisholm prompted, his voice low but edged with purpose. Not pushy, just a nudge back to the task at hand.

Shane's gaze lingered on the puzzle a moment longer, then he drew a breath, chest tightening as he crossed the fragile gap between here and there — back to that morning in January of 1997 when the ride to Camp Eagle felt longer than the war itself.

He got his first real shower that night. The water ran rust-brown at first, then pink, then clear. He scrubbed until his skin burned, working Loran's blood from the creases of his hands, his arms, under his nails. His hands trembled so hard he nearly dropped the soap twice.

He couldn't say what hurt more — the physical rawness or the hollow ache that gnawed at him beneath his ribs. The numbness came in waves, like he was watching himself from the outside, a man pretending to be a man. And then the tide would turn, and he would double over in the stall, chest tight, mouth dry, grief rising like bile in his throat.

How the hell could they think he did wrong? How could *anyone* think that?

Rumors, like bad weather, had a way of creeping into every corner of camp. Even in isolation, he could feel it — soldiers who once nodded to him with casual familiarity now kept their distance. Some walked past his door without so much as a glance. Others, brave or perhaps stubbornly loyal, managed a quiet nod when they thought the MPs weren't looking. A couple tried to slip him notes — small gestures of support, folded slips of paper slid under his door before the guards caught on and cracked down.

Technically, they weren't supposed to. Orders were clear: no communication about the incident, no exceptions. But tension, like water, found its way through cracks. He could see it in their eyes when he caught glimpses of them across the compound — suspicion in some, pity in others. Worse were the looks from those who once laughed with him over cold MREs and bad coffee. Now they watched him like they didn't recognize the man at all.

The silence from leadership was deafening. No one briefed him beyond the formalities of the investigation. No one explained what would happen next. He knew only what he'd been trained to know: under the UCMJ, a 15-6 could lead to anything from full exoneration to court-martial, depending on the findings of fact.

And facts — brutal, undeniable facts — had a way of turning cold in the wrong hands.

****

The knock came just before 1800 hours.

Shane had been staring out the narrow barracks window, watching a gray curtain of sleet drag across the motor pool. He hadn't bothered to switch on the overhead light; the daylight — what little there was — had started to fade. His eyes were dry from staring too long, but he couldn't make himself look away.

"Alexander," a clipped voice called through the door. MP guard. "You got someone here."

Shane pushed off the bunk and opened the door halfway, blinking against the harsh corridor fluorescents. A tall figure stood there in Class B dress uniform — Staff Sergeant Kern, the company clerk. He held a manila folder tight against his ribs, posture stiff. Behind him, the MP kept his gaze neutral, the way they all did around Shane these days.

"Evening, Specialist," Kern said. His voice was formal, but there was a flicker of discomfort in his eyes. He was a paperwork guy, not a man built for these kinds of conversations.

Shane nodded once. "Sergeant."

Kern cleared his throat and opened the folder, reading from a typed memo.

"Notification to next of kin has been completed stateside," he began. "Specialist Loran Taylor will be prepared for transport to Dover Air Force Base within the next forty-eight hours."

Shane's jaw worked, throat dry. He swallowed and kept his voice steady. "He's going home."

Kern hesitated. "Yes, Specialist. He's being flown out with full honors."

Shane's fists clenched at his sides, nails pressing into his palms.

Kern continued, eyes fixed on the page like it might shield him from what came next. "Per command decision, you are restricted from attending the memorial ceremony scheduled at Camp Eagle prior to transport. Orders cite ongoing investigative proceedings and your status under review."

For a beat, the air in the room felt thin, like all the oxygen had been sucked out at once.

"Say that again," Shane said, low and tight.

Kern shifted his weight. "You're not permitted to attend the service."

"That's bullshit," Shane snapped, sharper than he intended. His voice bounced off the bare walls, too loud in the confined space. He forced himself to breathe, forced the heat under his ribs back down before it boiled over. "I fought alongside him. I—" His chest heaved. He ground his teeth until his jaw ached. "He was my friend."

Kern's expression flickered — a crack in the bureaucratic armor. But all he said was, "Orders are orders."

Shane took a step forward, and the MP behind Kern stiffened automatically, hand drifting to the butt of his sidearm. A silent reminder.

"I've done everything by the book," Shane said, keeping his voice firm and controlled, but it was shaking at the edges. "You know I have. I signed the papers. I took the restriction. I haven't said a damn word out of line."

"I know," Kern admitted quietly. He closed the folder against his chest. "But it's not my call."

Shane's chest burned — a hot, coiling thing that no amount of breathing could cool. Grief and anger wrestled just under his skin, twisting into something sharp and hollow.

"They're treating me like I did something wrong," Shane said, voice rough. "Like I meant for it to happen."

Kern's gaze flicked away toward the corridor floor. His silence was answer enough.

After a moment, Kern squared his shoulders, as if retreating behind regulations once more. "I'll leave the notification copy for your records," he said, placing the folder on the desk by the door. "MP will remain posted. You'll receive further instructions once your Article 32 hearing date is set."

He didn't wait for a response. He turned sharply on his heel and walked away down the corridor, boots echoing against the concrete floor.

The MP hesitated at the threshold. He wasn't required to say anything, but still, he gave Shane a brief, almost apologetic glance. Then he pulled the door shut.

The lock clicked into place.

Shane stood there, staring at the closed door, his breath tight in his chest.

Outside, the storm picked up, ice pellets ticking against the window like small bones. The dim room felt colder by degrees.

He looked down at the folder, at the sterile words printed in neat black ink. *RESTRICTED FROM ATTENDANCE.*

For the first time since the firefight, since the hollow explanations and the silent accusations, Shane felt the numbness crack. Beneath it, something hot and furious burned steady and bright.

"They already made up their minds," he said under his breath.

And this time, there was no one left to argue otherwise.

Twelve

Back Against the Wall

The Humvee's engine idled briefly before shutting down, leaving a heavy silence that pressed against Specialist Shane Alexander's ears. He sat motionless in the back seat, his uniform stiff with dried blood—Loran's blood. The metallic scent clung to him, a grim reminder of the firefight that had erupted less than two hours prior.

The door swung open, revealing the stern face of Sergeant Fitzpatrick. His eyes, usually sharp and assessing, held a flicker of something softer—concern, perhaps. But this was neither the time nor the place for sentiment.

"Alexander," Fitzpatrick's voice was gruff, all business. "Let's move."

Shane nodded mechanically, his body responding before his mind caught up. He stepped out onto the gravel, the crunch beneath his boots grounding him momentarily. The makeshift command post loomed ahead—a hastily erected tent reinforced with sandbags, its canvas walls stained with mud and soot. The NATO base at Kiseljak was a far cry from the fortified installations he'd trained in; here, improvisation was the norm.

Two Military Police officers flanked the entrance, their expressions unreadable beneath their helmets. One of them, a corporal with a square jaw and piercing blue eyes, gave a curt nod.

"Captain Reeves is expecting him," Fitzpatrick informed them.

The corporal stepped aside, unzipping the tent's entrance. "Go on in, Specialist."

Inside, the air was thick with the mingling odors of sweat, stale coffee, and damp canvas. A single overhead lamp cast a harsh, white light, illuminating the sparse furnishings: a folding table cluttered with papers, a map of the region tacked to one wall, and a few mismatched chairs. Behind the table sat Captain Reeves, his uniform crisp despite the day's events. His dark eyes locked onto Shane the moment he entered, assessing, probing.

"Specialist Alexander," Reeves began, his tone devoid of warmth. "Take a seat."

Shane complied, lowering himself onto the cold metal chair opposite the captain. Fitzpatrick remained by the entrance, arms crossed over his chest, a silent sentinel.

Reeves leaned forward, resting his forearms on the table. "I understand you've been through a lot today, Specialist. But we need to go over the events of the firefight while they're still fresh. Do you understand?"

Shane nodded, his throat too tight to form words.

The captain's gaze didn't waver. "Before we begin, I must inform you of your rights under Article 31 of the Uniform Code of Military Justice. You have the right to remain silent, the right to consult with counsel, and the right to have counsel present during this interview. Do you understand these rights?"

Another nod.

"Do you wish to have counsel present?"

Shane hesitated, the weight of exhaustion pressing down on him. The thought of prolonging this ordeal was unbearable.

"No, sir," he rasped. "I can proceed."

Reeves studied him for a moment longer before nodding. "Very well. Let's start from the beginning. At approximately 1430 hours, you and Specialist Taylor were providing security near the market square. Is that correct?"

"Yes, sir."

"Describe the initial contact."

Shane took a slow breath, forcing himself to recall the sequence of events with precision.

"Loran—Specialist Taylor—noticed a woman and child exposed in the open. He moved to assist them, breaking cover. That's when the first shots were fired from the ridgeline to the east."

Reeves made a note on the pad before him. "How many shooters did you observe?"

"Five, sir."

"Armed with?"

"AK-47s, from what I could tell."

The captain's pen scratched against the paper. "You returned fire immediately?"

"Affirmative."

"Approximately how many rounds did you expend?"

Shane's brow furrowed as he calculated. The M249's cyclic rate was high, and in the heat of battle, he'd fired in controlled bursts.

"Between 200 and 250 rounds, sir."

Reeves' eyes narrowed slightly. "Did you continue firing after the enemy ceased their attack?"

Shane's stomach twisted. He knew the implications of that question.

"No, sir. Once the threat was neutralized, I ceased fire."

The captain's gaze bore into him, searching for any sign of deceit. Finding none, he continued.

"Were you aware of the Rules of Engagement in place for this mission?"

"Yes, sir."

"Can you recite them?"

Shane swallowed, his mouth dry.

"Positive identification of hostile intent before engaging. Use of force proportional to the threat. Minimize collateral damage and avoid civilian casualties whenever possible."

Reeves nodded approvingly. "sDid you adhere to these rules during the engagement?"

"To the best of my ability, sir."

The captain's pen paused. "Explain."

Shane's jaw tightened.

"I identified the shooters' positions and returned fire to eliminate the threat. I aimed to suppress and neutralize, not to inflict unnecessary harm. Civilians were in the vicinity, and I was mindful of their safety."

Reeves leaned back slightly, considering his next question.

"Were there any indications prior to the attack that hostilities were imminent?"

Shane hesitated.

"Earlier, I noticed movement. I had informed Staff Sergeant Steven Laughlin immediately upon observation."

Reeves didn't move at first. He just studied Shane like he was trying to make out the parts that were still functioning. Then he tapped a knuckle twice on the folder and flipped the page again.

"You fired three distinct bursts at the final target," he said flatly. "Distance estimated at a hundred and sixty meters. Last engagement was at approximately 1448 hours. How did you determine that target was still a threat?"

Shane blinked slowly. His mouth was dry, lips beginning to crack from dehydration and cold air.

"He was moving uphill," he muttered. "Weapon still in hand. Didn't drop it. Didn't surrender. Didn't stop."

"Did he fire?"

"Not that I saw."

"So what made you engage?"

"He was breaking contact," Shane said. "Retreating to high ground. Could've regrouped, flanked, relayed intel. I wasn't gonna wait."

"Rules of Engagement state that if an enemy combatant is actively disengaging—"

"He wasn't just running," Shane cut in. His voice didn't rise, but there was a slight edge. "He was still armed. Still in the fight. That's not disengagement. That's repositioning."

Reeves let that hang in the air for a second. Then nodded slightly and jotted a note.

"How many rounds left in your loadout?"

Shane's eyes darted upward in thought. "About twenty in the belt when I stopped. Maybe less. I burned through over two hundred. Three boxes—one partial. Didn't reload the fourth."

"Standard issue is six hundred rounds per patrol. You expended over a third in under four minutes. Was there ever a point you ceased fire to reassess the threat?"

"I only fired when targets were visible," Shane said. "Didn't spray. Didn't fire blind. I identified five hostiles and neutralized five. No civilians were hit by my fire."

Reeves glanced at the folder. "We're confirming that. Ballistics are pending."

Shane nodded once. He didn't need confirmation. He remembered every squeeze of that trigger. Every figure through that sight. They were clear. They were armed. They were aiming at civilians.

They shot Loran.

"Why didn't you wait for confirmation from higher?" Reeves asked next, flipping a page. "You were ordered to maintain position. Laughlin didn't order direct engagement."

"He didn't have eyes," Shane said simply. "He was down at checkpoint two. I had line of sight. I had direct contact. I made the call."

"You bypassed the chain of command."

"I responded to an active threat. And I followed our escalation protocol—radioed it in, didn't fire until I confirmed muzzle flashes. I held position until the first shot dropped Loran. After that—"

He stopped.

Reeves waited. When Shane didn't speak again, he leaned forward slightly.

"After that, what?"

"After that, I did what I was trained to do," Shane said quietly. "Suppress. Neutralize. Protect civilians. Cover the perimeter."

The silence in the room stretched again. The only sound was the faint hum of a generator kicking on outside the prefab building and the steady tick of Reeves' pen tapping against the folder.

Reeves finally broke it. "Explain your position again. Orientation, visibility, and movement."

Shane took a breath. "We were positioned at the east checkpoint—concrete barriers stacked in a half-U facing the road. I had line of sight up the access path that runs toward the ridge, about 180 meters east-northeast. Visibility was clear. Cold, but no fog. Elevation about ten meters higher than our position."

Reeves nodded, making a rough sketch on the page.

"I had visual contact with five shooters," Shane continued. "Three initiated fire from the tree line, one from behind the ridge rocks, fifth emerged after about ten seconds from the eastern slope, moved uphill too. Standard-pattern AKs, from what I could see."

"You're sure of the weapons?"

"Distinct silhouette. No attachments. I could see muzzle flash. Heard the report." Shane's voice had gone cold now. Analytical. Like he was walking himself back into the moment. "Tactically, it was a deliberate harassment attack—short burst engagement. Hit and fade."

"Any indication they were part of a larger cell?"

Shane shook his head. "If they were, they didn't get involved. No follow-on. No reinforcements. No shadow movement."

Captain Reeves leaned back slightly in his chair, the folder open in front of him, but his attention fixed squarely on Shane.

"You said earlier that the fifth shooter was moving uphill when you engaged."

"Yes, sir."

"Running?"

"Yes."

"Was he firing as he moved?"

Shane hesitated. His jaw flexed, a tendon twitching under the stubble along his cheek.

"I didn't see a muzzle flash. But he was still armed."

Reeves nodded slowly, tapping the side of the folder with his pen.

"So, to clarify... after the fourth hostile dropped, there was a window of—how long would you say—ten seconds? Fifteen? Before you engaged the final target?"

Shane frowned. "I don't know. It was fast."

"Estimate."

"...Maybe ten seconds."

"Ten seconds," Reeves repeated, writing that down.

Shane shifted slightly in his seat. The blood in his sleeves had dried, turned stiff and scratchy. It itched, but he didn't move to scratch it.

Reeves went on. "During that time, was there incoming fire from any direction?"

"Not that I saw."

"So, no active fire. And the final individual was moving away from your position. Correct?"

"He was armed," Shane said again, firmer now. "He was headed toward the treeline. That slope leads behind the village. He wasn't retreating to surrender."

"I didn't say he was," Reeves said easily. "Just confirming facts. You made a call. I'm trying to understand the framework you used."

"I didn't have time for a framework," Shane muttered. "We were in the middle of it. There were civilians still out. A baby. A woman crawling on her knees behind a fruit stand. Loran—" His voice caught. He stopped himself.

Reeves didn't flinch. "You believed he posed a continued threat."

"I *know* he did."

A pause. Reeves clicked the end of his pen twice. Then, smoothly, he shifted gears. "Let's talk about the third shooter. The one who broke left."

Shane nodded once. "He tried to peel off and move between cover. I tracked him."

"How far did he get before you opened fire?"

"Fifteen meters. Maybe twenty."

"And?"

"Engaged before he cleared the stalls. Hit him twice. He dropped."

Reeves flipped to a different sheet in the folder—likely ballistic summaries. "Autopsy found three entry wounds. One in the back. Between the scapulae."

Shane didn't blink. "He was moving when I fired."

"Right." Reeves clicked the pen once more. "So… in both of these cases—the final two targets—your shots were taken after the immediate threat of fire had ceased."

Shane looked at him now. Long and hard. "If I'd waited, there'd be more bodies in that market. That's not conjecture. That's experience."

"I understand," Reeves said calmly. "But understand my job, too, Specialist Alexander. We have very clear parameters. Rule 5: *Engage only when hostile force is present, active, and posing a direct threat.* I need to determine if that line was crossed. Not by malice, but in the heat of the moment."

"I didn't cross it."

Reeves didn't nod. Didn't disagree. Just circled something in red on his page.

The door opened quietly, and Staff Sergeant Laughlin stepped in. His uniform was dust-caked and streaked at the knees. His eyes jumped from Reeves to Shane, jaw already tight.

"I asked to sit in," he said. Not a request. A flat statement.

Reeves didn't look up. "You're not part of CID, Sergeant."

"I was the senior NCO on site. That gives me oversight."

"You've already submitted your report."

"I'm not here to rewrite it," Laughlin said, stepping forward, boots crunching softly on the floor's grit. "I'm here because you're asking a soldier—who just lost a fellow boot—to give you a second-by-second breakdown of a live contact engagement where he saved over a dozen civilians. Maybe two dozen."

Reeves closed the folder.

"I'm following protocol, Sergeant."

Laughlin's eyes flicked to Shane. "He doesn't need a protocol right now. He needs someone who understands the difference between a damn firefight and a courtroom."

Shane stayed quiet, but something in his shoulders eased—just slightly.

Reeves didn't rise, didn't bristle. He just reached for the intercom phone.

"I'm asking you, as a courtesy, to step outside," he said mildly. "I'll notify you when we're done."

Laughlin's mouth twitched. Then he looked at Shane again—something sharp behind the expression. Regret. Frustration. "You did your job, Alexander," he said. "Don't let the desk jockeys convince you otherwise."

Then he turned and walked out, door closing a bit too hard behind him. Reeves sighed quietly. Reopened the folder. "Let's continue."

Shane rubbed a hand down his face.

"During your final burst," Reeves resumed, "were any civilians within your direct line of fire?"

"No. The fifth shooter was moving *up the hill*," he inhaled sharply, slightly ticked that he had to explain this over and over again. "There were *no* people behind him. The slope curves away into the woods. There was no crossfire risk."

"You're certain."

"Yes."

Reeves paused. "How about your backdrop? Anything flammable? Vehicles? Unexploded ordnance?"

Shane frowned. "No. Just trees and snow."

Reeves wrote that down. Then: "Was your elevation stable when firing the final burst?"

Shane blinked. "What?"

"Were you braced? Prone? Kneeling?"

"Kneeling. Braced the bipod on the low wall."

"Wind speed?"

Shane exhaled through his nose. "Low. Maybe three knots. Gusts under five."

"You're certain?"

"Yes."

Reeves stopped writing. Looked up.

"That's an extremely precise answer."

Shane stared back at him. "Because I remember everything."

There was a beat.

Then Reeves sat back. "It's a thorough account."

"That's what you wanted?" Shane asked. "Thorough?"

"I wanted accurate."

Shane didn't respond.

Reeves tapped the folder again. Then he leaned forward, elbows on the table.

"You're not being accused of misconduct, Specialist. Not yet. But your report will go before battalion review. Possibly brigade. And if someone believes you engaged after the threat had ceased, that becomes a legal matter."

"You weren't there."

"I know. Which is why I'm asking questions like these."

Shane's voice came quiet, hoarse. "I didn't shoot out of anger. I shot because if I didn't, people were gonna die."

Reeves studied him for a long time. Then gave a single nod.

"Staff Sergeant Laughlin's report says you requested to escalate to yellow alert status twenty-five minutes before the attack, citing movement on the ridge. Command denied it. Is that accurate?"

Shane nodded. "Correct."

"Did that affect your judgment during the firefight?"

"I saw shooters. I returned fire," Shane replied, wary of how they were going around in circles. "What happened before didn't change what I did during. I didn't act emotionally. I acted tactically."

There was a pause. Then, quietly: "Your friend was killed. Thirty seconds into contact."

Shane didn't respond.

"Are you saying that didn't affect you?"

He swallowed hard. His jaw clenched once. "Of course, it affected me. But it didn't compromise me."

Reeves didn't push the point. Instead, he stood and walked over to the map pinned to the whiteboard on the wall. He marked Shane's checkpoint and the ridge beyond it with a red X.

"Perimeter secured. Five KIA confirmed. Three civilian fatalities, seven wounded," Reeves muttered, more to himself than anyone else.

Shane sat still. The blood on his pants had dried in patches. The streak down his cheek had flaked into a crust. His right wrist throbbed from recoil, but he hadn't registered it until now.

Shane nodded, slowly.

"You'll be scheduled for a psychological evaluation tomorrow morning at 0600. That's standard. Don't read into it."

He didn't respond.

"Dismissed, Specialist."

Shane stood stiffly. Saluted. Reeves returned it, then motioned for the MP near the door.

"Make sure he checks in with medical before lights out."

The MP nodded, opening the door. Cold air hit Shane's face like a slap. The stink of burnt rubber and mud was stronger out here. As he stepped out of the makeshift command post, the world looked hazy—like someone had smeared grease across his vision. Trucks rumbled in the distance. He could hear boots crunching gravel, a medic shouting for morphine, the rustle of tent flaps, the hiss of radios.

***

The sky had gone steel-gray by the time Staff Sergeant Fitzpatrick caught up to Shane.

He found him out behind the maintenance hangar, squatting low beside a space heater someone had rigged to a rusted-out drum. Shane hadn't lit a cigarette, just turned one between his fingers like he didn't trust himself with the lighter.

"You're being summoned again," Fitzpatrick said, voice clipped. "Command tent. Bring your ID."

Shane stood. No questions. No reaction.

They walked in silence through the gravel paths, past pallets of supplies and rolled concertina wire. Everything was quieter now. The market was a smoking shell in the next valley, and the aftermath had turned into paperwork, radio traffic, and reports filed in quadruplicate. The real war had been pushed back into manila folders and official channels.

Inside the command tent, Captain Reeves was waiting with two Military Police. A different air hung in the room now—less inquiry, more formality. A sealed manila envelope sat on the table, along with a DA Form 268 and a typed memo bearing Colonel Brackett's signature block.

"Specialist Alexander," Reeves said, standing. "Reassessing the situation, this is formal notice that you are temporarily relieved of duty, effective immediately, pending the completion of a 15-6 investigation into your actions during the engagement at Grid 14-Romeo-Bravo."

Shane blinked. The words landed dull, as if through a wall of cotton.

Reeves continued. "You are to surrender your assigned weapon, magazines, and any sensitive items currently in your possession. You'll be transferred to Camp Eagle tomorrow at 0600 under escort."

He paused.

"This is administrative, not punitive. No charges have been filed. But until the investigation concludes, you're not to participate in patrols, live-fire drills, or field operations. You are confined to quarters unless otherwise directed."

The younger MP stepped forward with a canvas rifle bag. Shane didn't hesitate. He unclipped his sling, handed over the M249 like it weighed nothing at all. They took it silently. No ceremony.

Reeves handed him a copy of the notice. "You'll be billeted in barracks B-5 until transport arrives. Staff Sergeant Fitzpatrick will see to it."

Shane stared at the paper in his hand. His own name looked unfamiliar now, typed in bold across the header like it belonged to someone else.

"Am I under suspicion, sir?" His voice was hoarse.

"You're under investigation," Reeves answered. "That's not the same thing."

Shane didn't nod. Didn't move. The back of his neck prickled cold, even in the warmth of the tent.

"The ROE review is standard procedure," Reeves added, as if to soften the blow. "But there's language in your report and the CID summary that needs clarification. Namely, the duration between final incoming fire and your last engagement."

Fitzpatrick cleared his throat quietly.

"That'll be all, Captain?"

Reeves nodded. "That's all."

They stepped outside. The wind had picked up, carrying the bitter sting of coming snow.

Shane followed Fitzpatrick in silence toward the temporary billets. Somewhere nearby, a diesel generator coughed to life. The night around them was still—a different kind of quiet from the silence that had fallen after Loran bled out on his lap, but heavy all the same.

Halfway there, Fitzpatrick finally spoke. "This is bullshit."

Shane didn't answer.

"You did your job. That pain-in-the-ass Laughlin knows it, too."

Still nothing.

"Doesn't feel like it now, but this crap passes. It always does. Until then, head down. Don't give them a reason to tack anything on."

They reached the barracks. Fitzpatrick opened the door and gestured inside. Shane walked in, dropped his ruck onto the bunk without looking at it. A brown blanket, a folded towel, and a bottle of disinfectant sat waiting on the footlocker. Someone had prepped it, assuming he'd be dirty. Bloody. Worn out.

They weren't wrong.

"Transport's at oh-five-forty-five," Fitzpatrick said from the doorway. "They'll call you out by name."

Shane nodded faintly.

The door shut behind him. He was alone.

He didn't sit. Didn't undress. He stood by the footlocker and stared at his hands—still crusted with someone else's blood in the cracks of his knuckles, around the nails. Loran's blood. The boy had bled out quicker than Shane could curse. And now he was being sent back. With nothing but a duffel bag and suspicion at his heels.

He picked up the towel. Turned it in his hands like it might hold some other purpose. Then, wordlessly, he sat on the edge of the bed and began scrubbing the dried blood from under his fingernails, one finger at a time.

Thirteen

Frozen Hell

The sky over Camp Eagle had that flat, iron-gray look that didn't give away the hour. Might've been early morning, might've been midafternoon — didn't matter. The Balkan winter wasn't in the business of giving comforts.

Colonel Harrison stepped down from the Humvee, the door creaking too loudly in the frozen air. He was a tall man, not lanky, but all bone and command, wearing the lines of too many deployments like etchings across his brow. He didn't bother with the gloves, even in this bitter cold. He wanted to feel the papers in his hands. He wanted to feel the weight of this mess.

"Captain, give me that roster."

"Yes, sir," came the prompt reply from Captain Ellison, who handed over the manifest with the tight efficiency of a man who hadn't slept much.

The administrative building wasn't much warmer inside. The radiators clanged and knocked like they were choking on old iron. A single space heater buzzed in the corner, useless against the draft seeping in through the loose window frames. Harrison didn't sit. He stood at the head of the makeshift table, eyes skimming the list of names like a hawk circling roadkill.

"Let's get moving. I want every man with line of sight to that ridge in this office before dusk."

His team — three investigators, including a CID warrant officer and a legal advisor — snapped to work without fuss.

Outside, boots crunched across frozen mud. The daily grind of Camp Eagle went on, but there was an undercurrent now. A thickness in the air, like everybody knew this wasn't just some routine QRF deployment. This was about blood on the snow, and men being called to account.

****

The door clicked shut behind Specialist Wilson as he stood stiff before the table. His uniform was neat, but there was no mistaking the nervous energy running under his skin. He gave a sharp salute.

"Observation Post One, Sector Bravo, Specialist Jeremiah Wilson, reporting as ordered, sir."

"Take a seat, Wilson," Colonel Harrison gestured, voice flat but not unkind. He flipped open a binder, pages clipped with incident logs and radio transcripts.

Major Beckett sat off to the side, expression unreadable, pen already poised over a yellow legal pad. The recorder on the table clicked on, the red light steady.

"You understand this is an official inquiry under Army Regulation 15-6," Harrison began, by the book. "Your statements are recorded and can be used in any subsequent proceedings."

"Yes, sir."

Harrison's eyes settled on him, heavy. "Walk me through the morning of January 15th. From the moment you arrived at Kiseljak market."

Wilson's throat bobbed as he swallowed. He started from the beginning — early morning convoy out, cold enough that his fingers had gone numb inside his gloves. Set up perimeter security, mark sectors, and check comms. Rodriguez was on his left, Alexander further ahead, closest to the market's southern end.

"No disturbances at first?" Harrison asked, flipping a page in the binder.

"Negative, sir. Routine foot traffic. We checked IDs. Civilians moving between stalls." Wilson's jaw tightened. "Then a group of Serbs approached. Loud, but no weapons visible."

Harrison scribbled a note. "Staff Sergeant Laughlin?"

"Arrived on-site shortly after, sir. Checked our positions, spoke with Sergeant Kovačević—local liaison."

"Any change in posture?"

"None, sir."

"What about radio chatter?"

Wilson's face went tight, eyes darkening a shade. "Clear, sir. Until the first shots. We had no warning."

Harrison's tone didn't waver. "No indication of enemy movement on the ridge?"

"Negative." Wilson's lips pressed thin. "If there was, sir... *I* missed it."

There was a pause — not long, but heavy.

"Permission to speak freely, sir?"

"Granted, Specialist."

"Sir," Wilson inhaled deeply. "I was checking an ID and experiencing a language issue with a civilian short of hearing when the radio signal was being made between Staff Sergeant Laughlin and Specialist Alexander. I speak only to the best of my knowledge on what was observed at the ridgeline."

Shane sat at the edge of the room, silent observer, spine straight as rebar. He'd been told to sit in, as a witness to the full proceedings. But inside, his gut felt like it was coiled in barbed wire. He caught Wilson's glance, but it slid away fast, like both of them were afraid of what they might see in the other man's face.

Harrison nodded, unhurried. "Describe the opening of fire."

Wilson exhaled slowly. "Crack of the first shot. Echoed off the ridge, sir. Automatic fire followed. Incoming rounds struck the market entrance and checkpoint barriers."

"Response?"

"Staff Sergeant Laughlin wasn't present by then, sir." Wilson's voice was tight, professional, but Shane could hear it—the guilt packed behind every clipped word. "Specialist Alexander returned fire immediately. Private Rodriguez and I followed."

Harrison didn't lift his eyes from the page. "Enemy numbers?"

"Estimated squad-sized element, sir. Possibly reinforced by irregulars."

There was no pause this time.

"Was Specialist Taylor near you at the time of initial contact?"

Wilson swallowed hard. His fingers flexed in his lap.

"Affirmative, sir," he said quietly.

"Describe his actions."

Wilson's eyes flicked once again to Shane. Regret was carved sharply in his face.

"Specialist Taylor shifted to cover the eastern approach. Provided suppressive fire." A beat. "He was operating from behind cover for a while...before coming back out where he was shot."

Silence.

Shane's throat worked, but no sound came. His hands were fists in his lap, white-knuckled under the table. He stared straight ahead, like if he met anyone's gaze, the whole thing would come crashing down around him.

Colonel Harrison continued, steady as stone. "Was there any communication with Specialist Taylor after initial contact?"

Wilson's voice dropped low. "Negative, sir. He... he was hit early."

The recorder's red light kept burning.

The last member of the squad was called in. Rodriguez cleared his throat, back straight as the senior investigator fixed him with a stare that had peeled harder men down to their bones.

"Private Rodriguez," Colonel Harrison began, flipping to the next page in his folder, "state for the record your full name, rank, and unit."

"Private First Class Miguel Rodriguez, sir. Bravo Company, Second Battalion, part of Specialist Shane Alexander's fireteam."

"Good. Now," Harrison kept his tone even, "walk us through what you saw. From the moment your team arrived at the checkpoint, up to the incident at the Kiseljak market."

Rodriguez drew a slow breath, eyes fixed on the tabletop.

"Checkpoint was routine at first, sir. We had civvies moving through, couple of local merchants, couple refugees. Nothing stood out."

"You saw no enemy forces?"

"Negative, sir. But—" Rodriguez's brow furrowed. "Specialist Alexander did mention, over comms, that he had eyes on possible observation from the ridgeline. Couldn't get a clear PID—"

"PID?"

"Positive Identification, sir."

"Understood. Go on."

Rodriguez's hands rested on his knees, thumbs pressing tight. "Sergeant Laughlin was informed, as per my knowledge. Laughlin said to keep sharp."

"And Taylor?"

"Specialist Taylor was on overwatch, sir. Left flank, good view of the crowd and the market edge."

Colonel Harrison's pen tapped twice. "When did you first notice Specialist Taylor leave his position?"

Rodriguez's mouth flattened. His gaze didn't lift. "Right before the first shots, sir. He—uh—he moved outta cover."

"Why?"

Rodriguez exhaled through his nose, tight. "He saw two civvies, sir. A young woman, appeared Bosniak, maybe a migrant, to me. Dark eyes, olive skin. Cradling an infant, male. Er, skintone did not match, but it was hers as per documents. They had gone through the checkpoint earlier that day. Locals maybe. Refugees. I can't say for certain."

Harrison's eyes narrowed just a fraction. "You believe Taylor was attempting to assist these civilians?"

"Yes, sir." Rodriguez's voice firmed. "No hesitation. He went straight for them."

"And was he under fire at that time?"

"Negative, sir. Fire started just seconds after. Like they waited for him to step out."

"Ambush pattern," the JAG officer at Harrison's side muttered, making a note.

Harrison didn't flinch. "What did you do next, Private?"

"Took cover, returned fire, sir. Just like we were trained."

Harrison's gaze lingered on Rodriguez for a beat. "Anything else?"

Rodriguez hesitated — just long enough for the pause to speak for him.

"Sir... Taylor didn't have time to get 'em clear. He tried, but—" Rodriguez swallowed dry. "—he took the first rounds. Saw him drop. The civvies were able to get behind cover. He... was standing when they shot. Bullet through the neck, sir."

Silence crushed the room for a breath too long. Harrison's pen hovered, then scratched the line down.

Rodriguez's jaw worked once, twice, but he bit back anything more.

Harrison's tone never broke pace. "Dismissed, Private."

Rodriguez rose, saluted, and left the room with his shoulders tight, like he carried the weight of it all on his back.

Once he was out, Colonel Harrison cleared his throat, tapping the pen against his notes. "Specialist Alexander, we're going to go over this one more time. From the top. Describe your position at checkpoint Bravo, timestamp zero."

Shane answered flat, professional, his voice rasped from hours of this.
"Checkpoint Bravo, southeast corner of the market. Myself and Specialist Taylor were set on the eastern approach, overlooking the vendor lanes."

"Was there any verbal exchange between you and Taylor prior to the first shots fired?"

"Affirmative, sir," Shane said. "Taylor had eyes on civilians—I was keeping track of movement on ridges and above slope."

"And what about when he got out of cover?" Harrison didn't react, didn't so much as blink. Just scratched a note. "You didn't call him back?"

Shane's jaw tightened, a slight pulse at his temple. "Didn't have time, sir."

"Explain."

"Fire started the moment he moved."

There was a pause — not for effect, but as if Harrison was trying to find a crack in the wall Shane had built. He flipped the page on his clipboard.

"Was there a pause in the incoming fire before you returned fire?"

Shane's eyes hardened. "No, sir."

Harrison's brow lifted just a fraction. "None at all?"

"Negative, sir. They opened up, we reacted."

"You're certain."

"Damn certain."

Rodriguez and Wilson were in the next room, waiting for their turn in the gauntlet. Wilson had been tight-lipped from the start, no good answers because, truth be told, he barely had time to think before the market turned into hell. He didn't know much aside from the people he was checking. Rodriguez, though — Rodriguez had been up-front in his interview.

They played that back for Shane, too, as if they were testing his reaction.

Harrison scribbled again. "Specialist Aleanxder, when you returned fire, did you continue firing after the initial volley from the attackers ceased?"

"Sir," Shane said, cold but steady, "there was no cease. It was all within seconds. Close contacts. No lull."

"But you understand the concern."

"Sir," Shane's knuckles whitened under the table, "with respect, you weren't there."

Another pause. Harrison's face stayed stone flat. He leaned forward just an inch. "Humor me. After the first three attackers went down, did you fire upon anyone else?"

Shane's eyes met his square. "Final combatant was still armed, still moving, still a threat."

Harrison clicked his pen, slow and deliberate. "Final combatant was already wounded, Specialist."

"Wounded don't mean harmless, sir."

But as he turned to leave, Colonel Harrison's voice followed him, clipped and cool as winter steel.

"Before you go, Specialist — be advised, we'll be conducting on-site witness interviews in Kiseljak starting tomorrow. Civilian testimonies, forensic review."

Shane froze mid-step.

His fingers curled at his sides, tight enough to drive the blood from his knuckles. He didn't turn around.

"Understood, *sir.*"

There it was. That thin thread of irritation slipping into his tone. And they all caught it — the recorders, the scribes, the shadowy legal advisor in the corner. Harrison didn't flinch, just kept tightening the screws.

"Good. Dismissed."

Outside the admin building, the cold Bosnian winter hadn't let up. The wind tore down from the ridgelines like it carried a personal grudge. Rodriguez pulled his collar tighter and worked his jaw, chewing on the inside of his cheek like it was the only way to keep from saying too much too loud.

"You saw the way they were leadin' him in there," Rodriguez muttered, half under his breath, but loud enough that Wilson, standing beside him, caught it clean. "Line by line, they're buildin' a case."

Wilson glanced toward the door Shane had gone through minutes earlier, then back to Rodriguez. His eyes were dark, unreadable. "Yeah," he said after a pause. "They're pickin' at it like vultures."

Rodriguez's eyes narrowed. "They're railroading him."

Wilson's jaw clenched. He didn't want to believe it, but it was already too clear. "They want him hung out to dry."

Neither of them said more. They didn't have to.

Truth hung between them, bitter as gunpowder smoke.

Inside the interrogation room, Colonel Harrison was winding his finger in slow circles over a blank sheet of paper, like it irritated him just by being empty. Shane was almost out the door. The old reel-to-reel recorder ticked steadily, capturing every breath, every scrape of a chair leg, every tightened jaw.

"Specialist," Harrison said finally, his tone flat as pressed steel, causing Shane to face him, "would you say you felt... aggressive intent during the engagement? Perhaps bordering on excessive force?"

Shane's throat worked. He felt the muscles in his neck tighten, the burn in his chest rising, but he swallowed it. Hard.

"I felt the intent to survive, sir," Shane said, his voice even.

The pause that followed was sharp enough to cut a man clean through. Harrison let it linger long enough to feel like a deliberate tactic.

"Your close friend had just gotten shot in front of you," Harrison continued, eyes fixed on Shane like he could read the soul beneath the uniform. "That's all you felt?"

Shane kept his expression flat, deadpan, almost mechanical. But it was in his eyes — those pale, storm-worn eyes — that the truth lay buried. Beneath the discipline, beneath the training, there was a grief too raw for words, and a fury that hadn't yet found its place.

"Aside from the intent to protect the unarmed, like we're meant to?" Shane replied, meeting Harrison's gaze without a flicker of retreat. "Affirmative, sir."

Harrison's mouth ticked, not quite a frown, not quite anything human. He jotted a note without looking down, pen scratching the paper like a blade.

"We will recess," Harrison announced. "Stay available for further questioning."

Shane, already halfway to the door, scowled and nodded. His salute was sharp and practiced, but the rigid line of his spine betrayed the weight he carried.

"Yes, sir."

As he finally stepped out into the corridor, the fluorescent lights overhead buzzed with cold energy. Rodriguez was already moving toward him, falling into step like they were back on patrol, just two boots walking the wire.

"Stay sharp, man," Rodriguez said low, his eyes scanning the corridor as if it hid snipers. "They're tryin' to break you."

"They'll have to try harder," Shane replied, but it tasted like ash in his mouth.

Further down, Wilson was talking in hushed tones to Staff Sergeant Laughlin. Their faces were tight, unreadable, the kind of look men wore when they saw trouble coming and knew they couldn't steer clear of it.

As Shane approached, they cut the conversation short. Laughlin, for once, didn't lace his words with the usual rough sedge. He just clapped a heavy hand on Shane's shoulder, the weight of it more anchor than comfort. He held it there a moment longer than regulation called for, his eyes saying what his mouth couldn't in the open.

"Keep your head in the game, Specialist," Laughlin said, his voice a low growl. "We'll get through this."

Shane gave a tight nod. "Yes, Sergeant."

The hallway felt colder as they moved away, steps echoing like distant artillery.

Rodriguez walked beside Shane, silent for a moment, then spoke under his breath. "It's all a damn game to them. They weren't there. They didn't see what we saw."

Shane didn't answer right away. His jaw worked, tension running down the muscles of his neck and shoulders like live wire.

"They weren't there," he agreed finally, voice rough. "But they're gonna pretend they know better."

Wilson joined them at the corridor's end, falling into step without a word. His face was carved from stone, eyes shadowed beneath his helmet.

"They asked me if Taylor left cover for a good reason," Rodriguez said quietly. He used Taylor, not Loran. Protocol. Keep it clean, keep it professional. But Shane felt the sting of it anyway.

"What'd you tell them?" Wilson asked.

Rodriguez's mouth pressed into a thin line. "Told them what happened. He moved for those civilians. He saw them standing in the middle of that hell shower, and he went for 'em."

Wilson nodded grimly.

"They wanted me to say he hesitated," Rodriguez added, something bitter behind his words. "That he second-guessed himself."

Shane's hands balled into fists at his sides. He forced them to relax.

"He never hesitated," Shane said, voice like gravel sliding down steel. "Loran never second-guessed a damn thing." He paused, glaring at the floor. "That was always his fuckin' problem. The fuckin' bastard never hesitated!" Both Wilson and Rodriguez, who had walked a few steps ahead, turned around to blink at how Shane was just standing there. Hands still in fists and a face turning red with perhaps anger..or sadness, or maybe both.

"Not when Caleb Wade brought his pa's fuckin' bull to school and told him to go for a ride and not when Jenny Cooper dared him to jump off the fuckin' rooftop for a date," Shane wasn't stopping. His eyes were welling with tears, and his voice had started to slur with how rapidly he was speaking. "Fuckin' hell, he don't got no brain between those ears! Just a big stupid fuckin' heart he wore on his sleeve and that dick he used to think with." He sniffled, rubbing a hand over his eyes.

Wilson placed a bony arm around his shoulders as the two steered him outside with them. They stepped into the brittle cold. Snow crunched underfoot, the overcast sky casting a dull gray over the camp. Military vehicles lined the perimeter, frost clinging to windshields.

"Lord," Shane muttered, trying to keep himself together. "If that bastard was alive, I'd kill him myself." His voice was all gentle...adoring even.

Rodriguez exhaled slowly, his breath clouding the air. "They're gunnin' for you, man."

"I know," Shane replied.

"They're gonna spin it," Wilson said, watching Shane from beneath the brim of his cap. "Make it sound like you fired when the threat was gone."

"I know," Shane said again, tighter this time.

Rodriguez hesitated, then muttered, "They ain't askin' about what we did right. Only what we mighta done wrong."

Shane's jaw worked. He stared past them, to the distant ridgeline. He could still see the shadows there, just out of sight, like ghosts perched among the rocks.

"They want me to say there was a pause," Shane said, almost to himself. "That I waited, that I saw a lull before I fired."

Wilson's expression hardened. "There was no damn pause."

Shane looked at him, and for a beat, his eyes betrayed something deep and ragged.

"No," Shane agreed, voice rough. "There wasn't."

The door behind them opened. One of the investigation officers stepped out, clipboard in hand. He didn't say a word, but his eyes landed on Shane like Shane was already guilty.

Shane met his gaze, unblinking.

The officer moved on without a word, footsteps crunching away in the snow.

Rodriguez spat onto the frozen ground. "Asshole."

They stood there in a grim triangle of silence until Laughlin came out, too, shaking his head.

"They're headin' to Kiseljak," Laughlin informed them flatly. "They wanna dig through the scene. Talk to the locals. Bet *you* already knew that, huh?" his eyes landed on Shane squarely.

"Yeah, he told me." Shane's chest felt like it was caving in. His voice came rough. "What kinda witnesses?"

Laughlin gave a curt nod. "Civilian testimonies. Gonna try and piece it all together."

Rodriguez's face twisted. "Like the civilians saw a damn thing in that chaos."

"Some do...maybe even most, but they're gonna say what they think keeps their families safe," Wilson said, darkly. "And if that means throwin' us under the wheels, so be it."

Laughlin's eyes pinned Shane square. "You ready for that, Specialist?"

Shane squared his shoulders, swallowing the lump in his throat. "Yes, Sergeant."

Laughlin's gaze searched his face, then he gave a sharp nod and stepped back. Shane walked past, out into the brittle cold of the January air.

Snow clung in muddy drifts along the edges of the walkways, crusted hard by boots and vehicle tracks. He stopped just short of the motor pool, dragged a gloved hand down his face, and stared out toward the horizon.

Somewhere past those hills, Kiseljak waited. So did the ghosts of that day.

They were going to dig through the ashes, the shell casings, and the blood-soaked snow. And he knew it — he *felt* it, deep in his gut — they weren't looking for the truth. They were looking for blame.

He set his jaw tight against the cold, the fear, the bone-deep weariness that no amount of sleep would ever fix. His best friend was in a coffin halfway home, buried without so much as a damn goodbye. Now they wanted to bury him too — just not in a box.

In a report. In a charge sheet.

And if they found what they thought they wanted in that frozen bowel of hell, that'd be the end of him.

Fourteen

Half a Truth

The metal door creaked open on stiff hinges. Shane stepped into the dim barracks room and shut it behind him without flicking the light. He didn't need it. The shape of the bunk, the scuffed floor tiles, the clatter of boots left near the footlocker — all familiar like muscle memory.

He unzipped his jacket slowly. The fabric whispered as it peeled off, damp from sweat and cold. Tossed it toward the bunk. It missed and slumped halfway to the floor.

He stared at it for a beat.

Didn't pick it up.

He sat down on the lower rack and let his elbows drop to his knees. Head in his hands, fingers laced tight. Not praying. Just... holding something together that felt like it might come apart if he gave it a second too long to breathe.

The silence in the room buzzed louder than the firefight ever had. That kind of silence where you can still hear everything — boots slipping in slush, Loran's voice over the radio, the sharp bark of incoming rounds. The market. The blood.

His boots hit the floor heavy as bricks. He unlaced them like they were wired with trip lines. Every movement, deliberate, slow, like sudden action might trip something inside him.

The cot creaked as he lay back, staring at the ceiling. He didn't blink. Didn't move. Just lay there listening to the storm behind his ribs.

He closed his eyes and didn't sleep.

Outside, someone laughed faintly near the motor pool. The wind had let up a little, but it was still cold enough to keep most off-duty soldiers indoors. Staff Sergeant Laughlin stood near the side of the HQ, flicking ash off a cigarette with the kind of precision that came from habit, not enjoyment.

Sergeant Fitzpatrick stepped up beside him. No words at first. Just a lighter click and the soft draw of two NCOs settling into an unspoken rhythm.

"They done with the kid for today?" Fitzpatrick finally asked.

Laughlin nodded once. "For now."

Fitzpatrick shifted his weight, squinting toward the fence line. "He's holdin' up?"

"As much as a man can when the walls are closin' in." Laughlin didn't look over. "You know how this goes."

Fitzpatrick exhaled slowly. "Yeah."

"They ain't diggin' for truth," Laughlin added after a beat. "They're diggin' for *something*. Doesn't even have to be useful. Just enough to stick."

Fitzpatrick tapped the ash off his smoke. "You think he went over?"

"No." Laughlin's voice was low, firm. "But that ain't the question they're askin'. They're askin' if they *can* make it look like he did."

Fitzpatrick grunted. "Command's nervous."

"Someone wants a headline with a clean ending," Laughlin said, voice bitter. "Hero snaps, civilians caught in the crossfire. Tie it up in a bow."

"Even if it's bullshit."

Laughlin didn't answer. Just flicked the last of his cigarette into the snow and ground it underfoot.

"Not much we can do, is there?" Fitzpatrick asked.

"Not unless we wanna join him in the meat grinder."

Another long pause.

"Still," Fitzpatrick muttered, "he's one of ours."

Laughlin nodded, slow and heavy.

"Yeah," he said. "And that's why I'm stayin' close. Just in case."

They stood there a moment longer, not talking, letting the cold burn through the silence.

Then, without a word, they went back inside.

***

Camp Eagle 27 January 1997

The convoy rolled through the gates just after 0800. HMMWVs coated in grime from the winding roads between Tuzla and Kiseljak slowed to a halt near the admin building. The lead vehicle bore the stiff posture of Colonel Harrison in the passenger seat, his boots hitting gravel before the engine even cooled. The rest of the investigation team dismounted in practiced silence, hauling waterproof cases marked with evidence tags and manila folders secured with elastic bands.

Word spread before they even stepped through the doors.

By 0830, the photographs were already laid out across a long folding table inside the converted office they'd commandeered. Civilian witness statements—translated from Bosnian, Serbian, and even Croatian to English by contractors from Tuzla—were filed alongside them, bound, and initialed. Some statements, read aloud by a junior officer with a legal background, immediately turned heads.

"Witness claims the shooting started suddenly. No warning. Saw two American soldiers behind a market stall. One of them returned fire. The other was hit and fell."

Captain Raleigh, one of Harrison's legal advisors, frowned and leaned in. "Any detail about who fired first?"

"That's the thing, sir. It's murky. Some claim they heard shots from the hill. Others say they saw muzzle flashes from the American side."

Harrison grunted. "Convenient how it all becomes unclear when it matters."

Down the hallway, Shane Alexander stood in the shadows outside the glass panel near the old chow line, arms crossed, staring through the reflection at the room where the civilian witnesses were being processed. One by one, locals had been escorted into that sterile, re-purposed briefing room. Each of them sat across from the uniformed investigators and translators in folding chairs under fluorescent lights.

The translator, a wiry man in a windbreaker who looked more like a soccer coach than an interpreter, kept his tone level and soft, but the tone of the interviews didn't need volume to signal their weight.

Shane couldn't hear the words. But he could watch.

One older man with thick gray stubble gestured repeatedly toward a crude sketch map of the market drawn by someone on Harrison's team. He tapped furiously at a small cluster of stalls that Shane as-sumed was near where he had taken position, then mimed a gun recoil back and forth, like counting shots.

"He keeps repeating the same words" a young PFC seated in the room muttered to the translator. "What's he saying?"

The translator didn't immediately answer. Then finally: "'Too many.' He keeps saying, 'Too many bullets from that direction.'"

Harrison leaned in. "Ask him if he saw who the shooter was."

The question passed back and forth. The man shook his head firmly, then nodded at the hill drawn at the edge of the market. More mimed shots. Two fingers held up. One hand dropped as he slapped his palm—like someone falling.

Outside the glass, Shane's knuckles whitened against his elbow.

Another witness, a middle-aged woman with a headscarf and furrowed brow, dabbed her eyes as she answered questions. Her voice was measured, almost embarrassed, but her body trembled. At one point, she pointed toward the ridgeline on the map and drew a curved line through the air, then to the back of the market where the U.S. troops had been positioned. Again, more hesitation from the translator.

Harrison frowned. "Don't sugarcoat. What is she saying?"

The translator inhaled. "She says... she thinks the American soldier kept firing after it went quiet. Says she remembers him standing up, exposed, shooting upward. She thought it was strange."

"Strange how?"

"That it was so many rounds when the hill had already gone silent."

Raleigh scribbled notes furiously. Shane didn't need to hear it. He saw it in the reactions—the twitch of Harrison's jaw, the slow scribbling, the way the colonel leaned back like a man justifying his own suspicions. The evidence was being sorted, weighed for how well it fit the outcome they were already chasing.

Down the corridor, Rodriguez leaned against a concrete pillar, watching Shane.

"You all right, man?" he muttered.

Shane didn't look away from the window. "They're stackin' the deck."

Rodriguez nodded, lips a hard line. "That old guy—they made it sound like you went full Rambo."

Shane turned to face him. "I don't even remember how many rounds I fired. I saw movement on the hill. Loran was down. It wasn't math, it was muscle memory."

"You think they care about that?"

Shane's jaw clenched. No.

Inside the room, another civilian—a teen boy, maybe fifteen or sixteen—sat down nervously, glancing everywhere but straight ahead. His coat was too big, and his sleeves were nearly past his knuckles. The translator spoke gently, trying to put him at ease. The kid answered quickly, nervously. Shane could have sworn he'd seen him before. Perhaps he had. But honestly, every face before it went downhill was a blur to him. All except one, of course.

"He says he was in a stall near the fruit carts. Heard three loud cracks. Looked up and saw a soldier firing toward the mountain."

"Did he see who the soldier was?"

"He says no. But he says after that, he didn't hear anything else. No more shooting. Just the American firing."

Silence hung like smoke in the room.

Back outside, Staff Sergeant Laughlin appeared from the stairwell, crossing over with an unreadable face. He stopped beside Shane.

"They ain't showin' you the stuff that helps, are they?"

"Doesn't look like it."

Laughlin grunted. "I was up there. I saw the terrain. You don't get pretty engagements in valleys like that. It's fast, and it's dirty."

Shane gave him a glance. "You saw the hill? You saw where they fired from?"

"Yeah. Slopes were scattered with broken brush. Easy for muzzle flashes to disappear if you're not lookin' right. But the casings don't lie. We found plenty on that ridge. Problem is, those photos won't speak loud as a crying local."

"They'll believe the crying."

Laughlin gave a grim nod. "Yeah. And no one's gonna cry for Taylor."

Neither man said anything for a long moment.

Eventually, Rodriguez stepped over. "They done with the civvies yet?"

"Not even close," Laughlin said. "They got a few more scheduled tomorrow. Same drill. Maybe this time they'll get one who actually saw the trigger pulled."

Shane exhaled, slow and heavy. Through the window, the next witness walked in. Elderly. Limping. Holding a cane that looked like it had been repurposed from a broom handle.

Rodriguez shook his head. "Swear to God, it's like they're auditioning people for a court drama."

Shane muttered, "Hope they give me a script then. I'm tired of being the villain improv."

Behind them, inside the interrogation room, Harrison sat back in his chair and nodded to the translator to begin again. Another testimony. Another tally mark against Shane.

And outside, Shane stood silent, arms folded, bearing witness to a war being rewritten in real-time — one testimony at a time.

✳✳✳

It was getting late. He didn't- hell, who are we lying to? Shane Alexander definitely meant to listen long after the others had left for their duties of the day.

He wasn't sure how long he'd have to stay. He'd sat on the floor for a while, but he just...couldn't find it in himself to leave. He had to know. As if hearing it firsthand might make their bullshit more believable.

Heard *"the old man"* and *"ridge,"* his spine locked up like a jammed bolt.

"...claims he saw the whole thing from across the road," a voice was saying — calm, clipped, American. Probably Lieutenant Wallace, one of Harrison's aides. "He gestured toward the treeline. Said the Serbs were firing first, but made a motion like they went quiet just before our guy lit up the last ones."

A shuffle of paper. Then, a second voice — Harrison's, measured and irritatingly patient. "How long of a pause did he indicate?"

"Didn't give a time, sir. Just a hand raise. Kind of a 'stop, then go' motion."

"Seconds?"

"Maybe. Hard to say. Translator thought he meant a lull."

"Did he see our soldier—Specialist Alexander—*observe* the lull and then continue firing?"

A pause.

"No, sir. He said he saw muzzle flashes *from the ridge* again, just before the final burst. But he looked unsure. Kept glancing at the translator for confirmation."

"Sketchy," Harrison murmured. "Still, it supports a version of over-reaction."

Shane's jaw locked. He stayed silent.

It wasn't *entirely* a lie. That part made it worse.

The elderly man — the one they were talking about — had come in earlier that morning, hunched and slow, escorted by MPs and a young translator with a blue folder. Shane had seen him from across the gravel motor pool, limping up the steps in a battered coat. He remembered thinking the man looked like he had lived through *too many* wars to speak clearly about one more.

He'd been crouched near a fruit cart that day, Shane remembered. Around the ten o'clock mark. Maybe twenty meters from where Taylor had been hit. The old man would've had a partial view of the ridge-line *if* he'd looked up past the buildings and the crowd — and *if* he hadn't flinched like every other civilian once rounds cracked off.

And now here he was, giving hand gestures and "maybes."

"I want that statement translated fully," Harrison continued, shifting in his chair. "And I want a sketch from him — what direction he thinks the fire came from, and where he claims Alexander was when he returned fire. Let's see if he gets creative."

Wallace murmured something in assent.

Shane stepped back from the wall, his heart an engine in his chest. This wasn't about finding the truth anymore. It was about stacking assumptions until someone could sign off on a report and call it done.

Back in the hallway, one of the JAG officers brushed past him without a glance. Shane didn't move. He stared at the ground, running the man's hand gesture through his mind. A "pause," they said.

Maybe there *was* a pause. Maybe it was three seconds. Maybe it was half of one. But muzzle flashes were muzzle flashes, and no shooter alive waited politely for a ceasefire.

They think I had time to think.

They didn't understand that in a firefight, thought didn't work like that. You didn't *wait* for someone to reload. You didn't *calculate* odds. You saw movement, and you followed your training. Shane had aimed where the threat was and pulled the trigger because anything else meant going home in a bag beside Taylor.

And now some shaky old witness — probably more startled by the echo than the reality — was giving the kind of vague statement bureaucrats loved.

It wasn't a lie. But it wasn't the truth either.

And it was going in the report.

***

It was just past 2200 hours when Laughlin caught Shane alone behind the maintenance bay. Snow crunched under his boots as he stepped into the glow of the single overhead light, face hard-set and unreadable.

"Alexander," he said low, eyes flicking once toward the building behind them. "You got a minute."

Shane turned, cigarette halfway to his lips. "You ain't supposed to be out here either."

Laughlin ignored that. "I'm hearing things. Not rumors — whispers from inside that admin wing. Word's getting bent."

Shane just watched him, jaw tight.

Laughlin stepped closer, voice even lower. "You told me over the radio there was movement in the treeline. Someone watching. That radio log's still there. You did your job. Hell, you followed ROE. But they're cherry-picking witness statements. Interpreting things loose."

He paused a beat. The cold bit hard across the back of his neck, the kind that reminded him of Kansas winters growing up—no frills, no forgiveness.

As Shane took a drag off the cigarette, Laughlin looked at the kid. Really looked. Tall, quiet, square-shouldered, all that Oklahoma stillness sitting heavy in him. Country boy. Just like Laughlin had been once. Before the stripes, before the gray started edging his temples. Before the years started carving lines into his hands and face from too many cold FOBs and too many dead friends.

Same eyes, too—low-lit and tired. Eyes that didn't need to brag or beg. Eyes that watched the world like it might come apart any second.

Shane's voice came out rough. "How loose we talkin'?"

"They got a Bosniak farmer sayin' the firing paused before you finished the last guy. They're treating it like gospel, even though he couldn't ID who fired first or where anyone was standing." Laughlin shook his head. "Hell, the guy thought we were Russian when they brought him in. Translator had to walk him through what NATO even was."

And damn if that didn't make Laughlin's stomach turn. He'd told Fitzpatrick just yesterday—*They're settin' him up. They need a body for this drama, and the MPs already picked the understudy.* Fitz hadn't said much. Probably knew he was right, too.

Shane exhaled slowly, the cigarette smoke curling in the cold air. "You think they're fixin' to hang this on me."

"I *know* they are." Laughlin didn't blink. "And I've seen this game before. They want this wrapped up clean for the brass. Bad headlines don't play well. You? You're expendable."

He didn't say *like I was once.* He didn't need to.

His mind wandered for just a second—couldn't help it. He saw his daddy again, sittin' on that peeling porch in their busted lawn chair, half his face gone from a mine in the Cu Chi tunnels. Never did talk much after he came home. Ma did all the heavy lifting—kept the stove hot, patched clothes till her knuckles bled, and raised the rest of them up straight. She passed with her boots on, still hanging laundry the week before the stroke. That was just how things were.

Now, most of his siblings had families of their own. Christmas cards with babies on hay bales, husbands in ball caps, and wives holding toddlers by the arm. Hell, even his little sister had a husband and a second kid now.

And back home? His own wife had the woodstove going. Their girl—seven years old and fierce like her mama—probably curled up with her picture books, waiting for a call that always came late and never lasted long enough. He'd done his damnedest to stay whole, to be better than what war took from his daddy. That's what he promised his wife back in the church parking lot the day he shipped out.

He looked at Shane again. Kid had *just* started living. Twenty-one. Still had fire in his bones and maybe something good waiting when he got back stateside. A life not yet ruined.

And if this shit kept sliding the way it was? That life was about to get buried under the UCMJ code and a press release with sanitized language.

Shane looked away, the muscle in his cheek ticking. "Doesn't matter. I told the truth."

Laughlin stepped in close, voice hard. "Yeah, well, that and a buck'll get you a cup of coffee in Leavenworth if you don't lawyer up. Stop talking to them without representation, Alexander. You hear me? You got the right to counsel under Article 31. Use it."

Shane nodded once, slowly. "Roger that."

The sergeant hesitated, then added in a quieter tone, "This isn't justice, kid. It's theater. Get smart before they start writing your script."

He walked off without waiting for a response, leaving Shane alone under the flickering light.

And for one split second, as he stepped past the edge of the building, Laughlin felt like he was watching his own past twist itself into someone else's nightmare. Only this time, he wasn't the kid on the edge—he was the old hand watching the noose get tied. And he didn't like how tight it was getting.

***

The notification came three days later.

February 1st, 1997. The envelope was sealed, standard form letter with the weight of a sledgehammer behind it. He opened it at the edge of his bunk while Rodriguez sat on the next cot, eyes flicking up once, then away.

"Preliminary findings indicate violations under Article 118 and Article 92," Shane read aloud, voice flat. "Improper use of force, dereliction of duty, failure to adhere to ROE."

A pause. His fingers tightened around the paper.

"Effective immediately, Specialist Alexander will be assigned defense counsel under UCMJ protocol."

Rodriguez muttered, "Motherfuckers."

Shane folded the letter once, twice, tucked it into his footlocker. No words, no outburst. Just that same gnawing silence that had haunted him since Kiseljak.

Only now it had a shape.

And a date.

Fifteen

The Defense

The rec room at Leavenworth was quiet, the kind of quiet that made every shift of a chair or clink of a coffee cup feel louder than it ought to. Everything was the same: the linoleum floor, the metal tables, the men scattered about pretending they weren't where they were.

Shane sat at one of those tables, his arms folded, forehead resting on them like he might've dozed off mid-sentence. But he wasn't asleep. His fingers twitched now and then, like his body still hadn't learned to relax, even when there was nowhere left to run.

Chisholm sat across from him, one leg folded over the other, sipping the burnt coffee the guards called fresh. He leaned back in his seat, casual, like this was just some backwater diner and not a federal military prison. A man a few tables down flipped a page in a paperback; another guy muttered under his breath while jotting in a crossword. Nobody paid them any mind. Nobody cared.

"You know," Chisholm said, tapping the side of his cup, "I once represented a guy who swore up and down that powdered eggs were what started his PTSD. Said the smell took him straight back to a crash site in Kandahar." He shrugged. "Can't smell scrambled eggs to this day without breaking into a cold sweat."

Shane didn't laugh, didn't even snort. But there was the faintest twitch at the corner of his mouth. Not joy. Just recognition. The joke was stupid, and he appreciated that it was.

"Smells like powdered eggs in the mess sometimes," Shane muttered, voice muffled into his sleeve. "Makes sense."

He sat up just enough to draw in a breath, then leaned forward again, elbows on the table, heads low. His hands folded, knuckles pressed white.

"You ever have a dream that don't let go?" he asked. He didn't wait for an answer. "I left Bosnia months ago... but I still end up back there every night. Like some part of me stayed behind."

Chisholm said nothing. Just nodded once and waited.

Shane's voice stayed flat, like a man narrating something he'd watched happen to someone else. "Every time I'm supposed to sleep, I end up murdering some kid in Bosnia instead."

That word—*kid*—landed sharp.

Shane shifted his jaw, eyes on the table now. There was a faint groove scratched into the metal, maybe from a fork or a pen tip. He ran his thumbnail along it absently.

"I hear Laughlin's voice sometimes. Real clear. He's telling me to stop. Same way he did over the radio. Only difference is, I never do."

Still, Chisholm didn't interrupt.

"I know I'm dreaming," Shane said, softer now. "But my trigger finger doesn't care. It just keeps pulling."

The silence stretched. Shane didn't fill it.

Across the room, the crossword guy muttered, "Four-letter word for burden," and scribbled something in.

Chisholm set his coffee down. "Who's the kid?" he asked.

Shane's eyes flicked up, slow.

He opened his mouth, then closed it again. Something worked in his throat like he was swallowing down dry gravel.

"Loran," he said at last. Just that.

Then, after a beat—"Only it's not Loran as he was. Not that day at the market. It's him, the way I remember from high school. Fourteen. Skinny as hell. Always chewing on sunflower seeds."

He huffed a breath, not quite a laugh. "He's still got braces in the dream."

Chisholm watched him carefully, but didn't move. He let Shane sit with it.

Shane blinked hard and looked back down at the groove in the table. His fingers curled into a fist beside it, slow and tight.

No more words came after that. Just the soft hum of the overhead lights, the scuff of a boot against tile somewhere behind them, and Shane—still, finally, for the first time in that hour—quiet.

***

The meeting room wasn't more than a cheap table with hard plastic chairs and dull institutional paint on the walls that felt like it hadn't been fresh since the Nixon years. But this one had a folder already waiting on the table when Shane stepped in, and a man already seated on the other side, in service dress blues. Major's rank. Legal pad out, pen in hand.

"Specialist Alexander," the officer said, rising. "Major William Davis. Your assigned defense counsel. Go ahead and take a seat."

Shane gave a quiet nod and sat across from him.

Davis looked about ten years older, but twice as anxious. His short brown hair was regulation neat, his collar stiff. The look in his eyes said he'd read too much, too fast, and wasn't sure which part to tackle first.

"I, uh... I just received your packet this morning," Davis said, tapping the folder. "The charges are—serious. Potential violations of Articles 118, 92, and 135 of the Uniform Code of Military Justice."

He paused to let that settle. Shane didn't move.

Davis cleared his throat. "Let me walk you through what that means, in plain terms."

He flipped the folder open, as if the words might be more palatable written down.

"Article 118 is murder," he said bluntly. "If the prosecution can convince the court-martial panel that your use of force exceeded what was necessary, especially after the threat ceased—then they can argue premeditation, or at minimum, unpremeditated murder."

Shane's jaw didn't twitch, but his eyes darkened just a touch.

"Article 92 covers failure to obey orders or regulations. In this case, they're citing a possible breach of the Rules of Engagement—specifically, Rule 5."

He looked up at Shane, gauging comprehension.

"You remember Rule 5?"

Shane nodded. "Do not fire unless fired upon. And cease fire when the hostile act or intent is no longer present."

"Exactly," Davis said. "They're alleging that after a confirmed lull in enemy fire, you continued your barrage. That would—on paper—violate Rule 5."

Shane leaned forward, elbows on his knees. "They get that from the Bosniak witness?"

Davis hesitated, flipping a page in the file. "That... and from ballistic forensics. The investigative report suggests your last volley had a tighter shot grouping, indicating you'd already taken time to reacquire targets. Which they're interpreting as—"

"Deliberate," Shane muttered.

Davis nodded once.

"Article 135," he went on, "is a catch-all they're throwing in for good measure. Involuntary manslaughter under military law. It gives them a fallback if 118 doesn't stick."

He let that hang.

Shane stared at the floor. "So what's that mean? Realistically."

"If convicted on all counts?" Davis took a breath. "You're looking at decades. Twenty, thirty years. Maybe life, if they push for it under 118. Dishonorable discharge, loss of all pay and benefits, and a federal conviction on your record."

There was no dramatics in his voice—just hard fact. And maybe that made it hit worse.

Shane didn't move for a long stretch. Then, finally: "You ever tried a case like this before?"

Davis hesitated. "Not one with potential life sentence implications, no. Mostly administrative hearings. Article 15 appeals. A couple of low-level UCMJ violations."

Shane just nodded slowly, as if he already knew that before he asked. He leaned back in the chair, arms crossed now, like he was bracing for the next hit.

Davis looked down at the file again, then back at Shane. "Look... I'm not gonna lie to you. This is complicated. You're not being accused of pulling the trigger in a firefight—that's expected. You're being accused of pulling it *after*."

Shane's voice came quiet. "They weren't there."

"No, they weren't. But they have pictures. Witnesses. And paperwork that fits their version better than it fits yours."

He shut the folder.

"But the truth still matters. It has to."

Shane looked at him. For a split second, there was something hollow in his expression—like the kind of man who used to believe that, once.

"Alright, sir," Shane said. "Then let's see if it does."

***

The next time they met, Shane walked into the room with a fresh bandage on his knuckle from punching the edge of his bunk the night before. Davis didn't ask about it. Didn't even seem to notice. He was already seated, flipping through a binder filled with more redacted statements and grainy photos than anything that resembled the truth.

"Alright," Davis started, not looking up. "I've finally gotten a partial copy of the witness list from the prosecution. Still waiting on some of the translations."

Shane sat across from him, stiff and silent.

Davis tapped a page and turned it toward Shane. "This one's from a civilian male. Serb. Claims he was in the market when the gunfire started. Says there was a pause, maybe ten seconds, before the last rounds were fired."

Shane leaned forward and studied the paper. The name next to the statement meant nothing to him—*David Bogdan*—but the blocky handwriting under the translated section had one line circled in pen: *'I thought the shooting had stopped.'*

"That's not how it happened," Shane muttered.

"I'm just telling you what they've submitted," Davis replied. "The prosecutors are building their timeline on this guy and a couple others like him."

He turned another page. "Here—this woman, *Lilliya Karisimarova*. She told investigators she was shielding her children behind a bread cart. She claims she heard a second round of firing 'after the silence.'"

Shane's eyes followed her name to a smudged black-and-white photo attached to the bottom corner. She looked like somebody's aunt. Worn sweater. Real light hair. Sharp cheekbones. Terrified eyes frozen in place.

Davis flipped the page again, unconcerned with Shane's pause.

"This one's still untranslated. Statement's marked 'pending.'" He slid it past like it didn't matter.

Shane's hand landed on the sheet before it disappeared.

"What's his name?" he asked.

Davis squinted. "*Mustafa Savić.* Why?"

Shane didn't answer. Just stared at the unfamiliar name, trying to match it to a face in the market. He...almost could. Kid was young. Looked like he'd just stolen some food and greese and got away without causing a riot.

He glanced up. "And the U.S. statements?"

Davis shook his head. "Still incomplete. I've requested copies from CID. They're dragging their feet, claiming they're still validating chain-of-custody on evidence logs and processing digital files. Most of it's just... not here yet."

He sounded annoyed—but not angry. Like a man stuck in line at the DMV, not one defending a soldier's life.

"So we're supposed to build a case," Shane said slowly, "off statements I can't read and pictures taken after half the market bled out."

Davis finally looked up from the binder. "That's what we have, Specialist."

Shane leaned back in the chair, arms crossed, mouth tight.

"They're framing it like I was calculating," he said. "Like I had a goddamn stopwatch and a vendetta."

"Doesn't matter what you meant to do. What matters is what they can prove you did," Davis said evenly.

Shane stared at him. "And you believe them?"

"I didn't say that."

"You didn't say you don't, either."

Davis was quiet for a moment, then gave a little shrug. "Let me put it this way—intent is hard to prove, but easier to imply. You fired after the first wave of gunmen was down. That's what they're leaning on. Witnesses heard a pause. They're turning that into motive. You understand how this looks, don't you?"

"It looked like a goddamn warzone," Shane said sharply. "My best friend was bleeding out four feet from me. There were civilians crying, screaming, running in all directions. I was clearing sectors. I was looking for muzzle flashes, any movement—"

"But that's not in the record," Davis interrupted. "That chaos? That instinct? That's not what's in these statements. These people say the firing stopped. Then you kept going. The prosecution's not going to be interested in your heart rate or adrenaline spikes. They're going to hammer the timeline."

He slid another sheet forward. "*Milan Lukić.* Claims he was near the woodpile. Saw a soldier 'firing uphill when no one else was moving.' That's your position, Alexander."

Shane looked at the name. Lukić. Pale man, dark hair, slumped shoulders in the photo. A blur of fear and accusation.

He tried to remember the woodpile. Couldn't. There was so much dust. So much screaming. The roof had collapsed on the left side of the market—wasn't that near where—

He rubbed his eyes.

Davis, still flipping through pages, didn't stop. "There's a few more pending. And we haven't gotten any of the drone footage yet. It exists—they mentioned it in the initial summary—but apparently, it's 'classified for review' right now."

"Convenient."

Davis nodded, without looking up. "Very."

There was a long silence between them then. Shane watched his lawyer's hands moving over the papers, methodical, distant.

"Tell me something," Shane said after a minute.

Davis glanced up.

"You actually think I did it? Murdered someone?"

Davis didn't answer right away. Just sighed and sat back, closing the binder gently like a pastor shutting a hymnal.

"I think," he said finally, "that the people in charge want this case over. Neatly. Quickly. And if that means pinning it on a single soldier, especially one without rank or pedigree—then yeah, I think you're a convenient solution."

His voice was calm. Almost detached.

Shane nodded slowly.

"Just wanted to hear you say it."

He stood, flexing his sore knuckles behind his back.

"I remember every face in that market," he said quietly, eyes on the table. "Every goddamn one. But not like this." He motioned toward the photos. "Not in black-and-white. Not as statements on a page. I remember the kid missing half his leg. I remember the woman clutching someone else's baby. I remember Loran not breathing."

He turned toward the door but didn't move to open it.

"They think this ends in a courtroom," he said. "They're wrong. It never ends."

Davis didn't reply. Just opened the binder again and started reading.

Like the war was already over.

***

It was late, somewhere past 2300 hours, when Shane finally got access to the line. A tired sergeant at the admin desk handed him the receiver like it weighed a hundred pounds. Shane dialed slow, like dragging his fingers through mud. He hadn't called since the investigation started. Didn't see the point. Didn't want to hear the worry in their voices. But now, with the charges officially handed down, he knew he had to.

The phone rang four times before a familiar voice picked up.

"Hello?" Mary Alexander sounded like she'd been asleep.

Shane tried to speak, but nothing came out. He had to clear his throat and start again.

"It's me, Mama."

There was a sharp inhale. "Shane? Oh my God, baby—where've you been? I've been callin' every line they gave us. They told me you couldn't talk to nobody, and I—are you okay? Are you safe?"

"I'm fine," he lied. "Just... they had me under hold. Nothing personal, just part of the investigation."

Silence. Then softer, "Is it true then? What they're sayin'? Some kind of shootin'?"

Shane leaned against the cinderblock wall, his head thudding gently as he rested it back. "Yeah, Mama. There was a firefight. In Bosnia. In the market."

He paused, exhaled. Then, "Loran's gone."

The line went still.

"Gone?" Mary's voice cracked, and in the background, he could hear the creak of the old kitchen chair. She was sitting down now.

"He died a hero," Shane said, quieter. "Saved a little lady and a baby. Like somethin' outta a movie. Ran right into the open. Got 'em out. Took the hit instead."

"Oh, Jesus," she whispered. "Loran... that sweet boy. I remember when y'all used to tear up our backyard with those dirt bikes..."

Shane's throat tightened. He didn't respond. His jaw worked quietly while the silence filled the space.

Then another voice came on. Gruff, dry. "Shane. It's your daddy."

"Hey, Dad."

Tim Alexander didn't speak at first. Then he asked in that low, matter-of-fact way of his, "You in trouble?"

There it was.

Shane nodded slowly to himself. "Yeah. Got charged."

"What with?" Tim asked.

Shane's mouth felt like it was full of gravel. "They say I fired after the shooting stopped. Article 118—murder. Article 92—failure to obey ROE. Article 135—conduct unbecoming. Couple others. Doesn't really matter."

Mary let out a small noise, like her breath had caught sideways.

"You killed somebody?" Tim asked. Not accusatory. Just straight.

"I killed the ones who shot at us. The ones who murdered Loran," Shane snapped, then caught himself. His voice cracked. "I made sure no one else died that day. That's what I did."

He stood there, the cord wrapped tight around his knuckles.

"But it don't matter," he added. "None of it matters. They don't care what I did. They don't care what we saw. All they care about is how it looks in print. What the papers say. What the politicians say. I ain't a soldier to them. I'm a fuckin' headline."

He blinked hard. "They got what they wanted. A neat little villain."

Tim grunted. "Yeah," he said after a long moment. "Sounds about right. That's what they did to the boys in 'Nam. Didn't matter if they were pullin' babies outta rice paddies or fightin' ghosts in the fuckin' treetops. Still got spit on the minute they touched down at home."

He paused, then added, "Ain't no justice in war, son. Just survival and fallout."

Shane gripped the phone tighter. "You still believe in this system, Dad?"

Tim didn't answer right away. Then, with a gravelly sigh, he said, "I believe in my boy."

Mary's voice came back on, watery and strained. "Shane, we'll come out there. We'll—"

"No," he interrupted. "Please. Just... not yet. I gotta figure out what comes next. Just promise me ya'll be okay there."

He heard her breath hitch again. "Always."

The call ended quiet. No goodbyes. Just a soft click and a long silence.

Shane stood with the phone still pressed to his ear for a full minute before the sergeant gave him a look. He set it back in the cradle and walked out into the dark, the cold biting his skin like it had something to prove.

Sixteen

To Failure

Fort Bragg, North Carolina

Early March 1998

The C-130 touched down just after dawn, wheels screaming against the tarmac. Shane barely looked out the porthole window. The base looked smaller than he remembered—flatter, too. Maybe it was the fatigue. Maybe it was the weight of what was waiting.

Two MPs stood waiting on the tarmac. They didn't cuff him, but the message was clear enough. He wasn't home. He was back under restriction.

His orders were precise: placed in administrative holding within his original unit's rear detachment compound, stripped of his weapon and field gear, and confined to the barracks during off-duty hours. Technically, he wasn't under arrest—just "flagged." But the armed guards at the company HQ said otherwise.

They'd let him shave. Let him wear his uniform. But everyone who looked at him saw the charges hanging over his chest like a busted ribbon rack.

***

Major Davis was already knee-deep in pre-trial motions when Shane met with him that week.

"I've submitted three separate Article 46 requests under the UCMJ," Davis said, leafing through a manila folder in the cramped office space they'd been assigned. "One for access to all physical evidence collected at Kiseljak. One for the full transcripts of the 15-6 interviews. And another for the complete list of civilian and military witnesses—Bosniak and U.S. alike."

He leaned back in the chair and rubbed his temple.

"The prosecution's answer?" He held up a printed memo stamped in red: **DECLINED – NATIONAL SECURITY INTEREST.**

Shane stared. "What does that even mean?"

Davis glanced over the edge of the paper. "It means we're being stonewalled."

He dropped it onto the table. "Captain Reynolds claims the Department of the Army has classified certain witness identities under a joint State-DoD directive. Says some of the civilian witnesses are under protective status due to ongoing instability in the region. Claims releasing names or transcripts could jeopardize their safety or reveal methods of intelligence collection."

Shane scoffed. "So... what, they can use their testimony against me, but I can't even know who said it?"

"Welcome to selective transparency," Davis muttered. "Reynolds argues the witnesses are technically foreign nationals interviewed under SOFA constraints. So, their testimony's admissible under Rule 802, but we don't get access to it until the prosecution enters it as evidence at trial."

"And by then," Shane said, jaw clenched, "we're already playing catch-up."

Davis nodded. "Exactly."

He flipped to another sheet. "I also requested access to all radio logs and firewatch records from the FOB on the day of the incident. Anything that could corroborate your call about seeing movement on the ridgeline."

Shane's eyes narrowed. "And?"

"Partial release. They gave us the outgoing call from your checkpoint—your transmission to Sergeant Laughlin is there—but nothing about what came after. No recordings. No response. Nothing confirming your warning was ever acknowledged."

Shane leaned forward, voice tight. "So they're cutting out half the comms traffic, and calling it fair?"

"They're calling it operational necessity," Davis said grimly. "Reynolds claims the rest of the transmissions contain classified tactical data that can't be redacted without compromising signal intelligence protocols."

Shane was silent for a beat, then spoke low. "They're building this to bury me."

Davis didn't answer at first. He just tapped the edge of the folder. "I've filed motions to compel under RCM 701. We'll see what the judge says."

"And if the judge sides with them?"

"Then we go in blind."

Shane stared at the blank wall across the room, jaw tight. "Feels like I already am."

***

The next day, another motion was filed—this time demanding a deposition from one of the Bosnian translators who'd handled civilian interviews. Reynolds responded within 48 hours.
"

Witness unavailable. Location unknown. Believed to have relocated under witness relocation agreement through NATO forces."

Shane read the line twice, then looked up. "They lost the translator?"

Davis shrugged. "They say she was a temporary hire through IFOR's civilian contractor pool. Used a false name, minimal records. Nothing we can trace."

Davis opened the next folder on the table—one thicker than the others, its corners bent from overhandling. Inside were pages stapled to black-and-white photocopied photographs, names typed in bold above paragraphs written in Bosnian, Serbo-Croatian, and fragments of rough English. A sticky note marked *Pending Translation - March 1997* clung to the top page.

He laid it out flat and jabbed a finger at the pile.

"Well, what about *these*?" His voice sharpened, but not loud. Just tight, tired, and done with the dance. "Statements taken almost thirteen months ago. Some of these folks were interviewed within forty-eight hours of the shooting. There's timestamps. Initialed receipts."

He flipped a few pages forward, holding one up between two fingers for Reynolds to see.

"Here's a woman—*Amira Begović*. Thirty-seven. Market vendor. Witnessed gunfire from 'multiple directions'—her words, not mine. No official translation submitted. No chain of custody follow-up. Not even a redacted version."

He let the page drop and flipped to another. "Here's *Nedim Sokolović*. Older male. Retired military, based on the markings on his coat." He turned the photocopy toward Shane briefly.

The man in the image had pale skin, thin lips, and hard eyes beneath a furrowed brow. His hair was cut short and graying at the sides, his build thick through the chest and shoulders, but the deep creases across his face and neck told a story of too many winters and too much loss.

"Looks like someone whose words might carry weight," Davis added dryly. "Statement marked: *'heard return fire from upper treeline af-*

ter seeing soldier assist civilians.' Again, untranslated. No reference number."

Shane remembered the papers with incomplete work from last year, too. That teen. His statement wasn't in the pile either.

He flipped again. "These." A sigh escaped his lips as he pointed to three of the witnesses where nothing had been translated. One was even missing the photograph. "*Emir Begović*, farmer and this," he pointed to the statement, then to the single question mark beneath it in place of translation. "Is also incomplete." It was the same case with *Lubov Maarijen*, the statement below Emir's. The last might as well have been a ghost. No image, no translation. Just a name; *Nad'a Hussein*...and a long ass Slavic paragraph under it.

"This girl," he said, tapping another page, "*Zehra Halilović*, nine. There with her aunt. Saw someone pull a child out from under a table near the meat vendor's stall. No one followed up with her. She was cleared to leave with an IFOR escort. End of note."

He didn't stop.

"Here. *Danail Dukov*. Vegetable stand worker. Middle-aged. Statement flagged with a question mark—interrupted mid-interview, possibly due to shelling near the checkpoint."

Another: *Sabina Ramić*, early thirties, bruised face in the photo, one hand bandaged. A loose paragraph beneath the image ended with: *'young boy in uniform shouted when shots came twice.'*

Davis looked up, the paper still in his hand. His tone didn't rise, didn't accuse—but it pressed hard enough to draw blood.

"You telling me none of these are relevant, Captain?"

Reynolds didn't answer. He adjusted his collar, looked briefly at the manila stack.

"Intelligence is still reviewing language consistency," Reynolds said coolly. "Priority assigned to direct-line witnesses. These are considered peripheral unless they're subpoenaed."

Davis gave a faint scoff. "Peripheral?" He tapped the girl's photo again. "You think a nine-year-old watching her market get lit up is peripheral?"

He leaned back, arms folding.

"Sir, with all due respect—either these folks saw something that matters, or you collected this paper trail just to keep the optics clean."

Reynolds looked unmoved. "The government will fulfill all obligations under discovery. When it becomes relevant, you'll be notified."

Shane watched the exchange in silence. Davis didn't slam anything, didn't curse, didn't grandstand. But the air in the room had gone stiff, like the moment before thunder.

He quietly gathered the stack back together, straightened the pages, and closed the folder. Once the two stepped out, Davis hummed, nodding at Shane, who was staring at the floor with his head miles away. Davis's voice, when it came, was flat and firm. "Then I'll make damn sure the judge sees this pile and decides for himself what relevance looks like."

Shane snorted. "Convenient."

"Extremely."

Davis shook his head. "This is how they do it. Build a case with partial visibility. If we can't refute what we can't see, they win by default." He buttoned his jacket. "I'll keep pushing. Just don't expect anything resembling a level playing field."

"Given what you said last year," Shane looked at him for a long time, then said quietly, "You don't think I got a shot, do you?"

Davis hesitated. His professionalism warred with honesty for half a second.

Then: "I think you're walking into a courtroom where half the evidence has already been pre-stamped."

He didn't smile. Didn't soften it.

"I'll do my job, Specialist," he said. "But you'd better get ready to do yours too."

Shane nodded slowly.

"Roger that, sir."

***

Early March 1998 – Fort Bragg, North Carolina

The rental car barely came to a stop before Mary Alexander stepped out, clutching her purse like it might float away. She wasn't crying. Not yet. But her face told the story—creased and lined deeper than a year ago, lips drawn tight, eyes scanning the transport lot like she'd misplaced something precious.

Tim followed a half-step behind her, his stride slower, deliberate. He'd worn his old 82nd Airborne windbreaker and a ball cap pulled low. There wasn't much hair left beneath it these days, just that hard-set jaw and squint that didn't soften even when he spotted his boy.

Shane came down the steps with a Staff Sergeant escort trailing behind. His uniform hung looser on him than it used to. Shoulders not slumped, not exactly, but less sure. His gait, once full of that twenty-something spring, was now heavier. Not from weight, but from the kind of wear a man doesn't shake.

Mary stopped in front of him. She didn't speak right away. Just reached out, one hand barely touching the side of his face, thumb brushing his cheekbone.

"Jesus, baby," she whispered. "You look hollow."

Shane offered a faint, crooked smile. "Hey, Mama."

Tim didn't speak. He just reached out, gave Shane a firm handshake that turned into a brief, two-second hug with a hard clap to the back. Then he stepped aside, standing near but not too close.

Mary finally broke, grabbing her boy tight, her fingers curling into the back of his jacket.

"I'm okay," Shane said quietly. "I'm okay, I promise."

She didn't believe it, and no one corrected her silence.

***

Two days had passed.

You ever wonder how civvies and even the military expect too much out of these kids? It's not trying to get all yellow bellied, it's a fact. Humans can only do and hold so much pressure. It's like sometimes everyone just chooses to forget that these are, in fact, just boys.

That they'd freshly gotten a kiss from some prom date. That the touchdown they'd scored during high school football was one of their biggest achievements. That they had only just begun to spin their hopes and dreams into something tangible.

Yes. They were just boys trying their hardest to fill in the boots assigned to them. And if you ask us, they try with such determination.

Nevertheless—

The courtroom was standard Army issue bare walls, government-grade linoleum, single U.S. flag in the corner. Brigadier General Louis Nolan sat at the raised platform, his uniform crisp, his expression unreadable behind thick glasses, and the neat press of silver in his hair.

Major Davis stood before the bench, his briefing folder open. Captain Reynolds was positioned opposite, flanked by two junior officers from the prosecution team.

"Your honor," Davis began, "the defense renews its request for complete transcripts and translations of all Bosnian civilian witness statements collected between January and March 1997. These materials are directly relevant to our response to the government's theory of unlawful use of force."

Nolan didn't blink. "Captain Reynolds?"

Reynolds stood with his usual careful economy of movement. "Sir, the government's position remains unchanged. Several of those statements fall under NATO security protocols. Witnesses were either cooperating with IFOR intelligence assets or have since been placed under protective status due to the volatile nature of the region."

He slid a document across the table to the judge's clerk. "Referencing enclosure B-6, these individuals were part of ongoing intelligence operations at the time. Releasing unredacted material could endanger cooperative arrangements still in play."

Davis raised a brow. "With respect, sir, the defense is not asking for operational details—just the direct statements made about the events at Kiseljak. Most of these individuals were vendors and civilians. Their words were collected as part of the 15-6, not a classified HUMINT brief."

Nolan glanced down at the packet. "Captain, can the government provide redacted versions that preserve the core witness observations?"

"Some, sir," Reynolds said. "But others cannot be validated due to name changes or displacement during post-war reconstruction. Translation services were subcontracted, and some original notes are incomplete or illegible."

Davis stiffened. "That's convenient."

Nolan's gaze snapped up. "Major Davis—careful."

"Yes, sir." He nodded, stepped back slightly.

Brigadier General Nolan tapped his pen once, then again. "Motion to compel full disclosure is denied. The court will allow the redacted excerpts previously approved. Additional disclosures will be reviewed in-camera for national security clearance."

Davis didn't show much reaction—just closed the file, slid it to the side, and stepped back to his table.

The next motion dealt with defense plans to call retired Major Emil Kovac as an expert on regional insurgent tactics—Kovac had served as a NATO liaison in Sarajevo and was familiar with the area's irregular fighters. The prosecution objected, claiming his testimony strayed too far into classified assessments.

After a brief recess, Nolan ruled to limit Kovac's input to "general observations not derived from operational briefings."

By the end of the hearing, it was clear where the weight leaned.

Shane sat at the defense table through it all. Said nothing. Hands folded in front of him. The muscle in his jaw twitched once during Reynolds' remarks about "the fog of war" being "insufficient justification for deviation from ROE."

Outside, as the defense team packed up, Davis glanced at Shane.

"You holding up?"

"They've already written the ending, haven't they?"Shane shrugged. "I really thought...you know? A year's gone and I thought hell, maybe God's on my side, but I guess not."

Davis didn't argue.

***

It was later that same evening. A pot of burnt coffee sat untouched at the end of the long metal table. Shane sat at one end, arms folded, his sleeves rolled halfway up, boots untied, eyes locked on the wall but seeing right through it.

Major Davis took his time organizing the files—slow, deliberate. Not for effect, but because every inch of this case felt like dragging dead weight uphill with a rope that frayed more by the day.

He finally sat across from Shane and opened a slim folder marked with a pink cover sheet.

CONFIDENTIAL:

PRELIMINARY DISCUSSION MATERIALS – **NOT AN OFFER.**

"Look, Specialist," Davis started, tone low, even. "We need to talk about what this is shaping up to be. The court's rulings are mostly going in favor of the prosecution. I can argue until I'm blue in the face, but without full access to those civilian statements, without the photographs admitted, and with half our tactical context limited to redacted summaries—it's going to be an uphill fight, blindfolded, with both hands tied."

Shane didn't speak. Didn't blink.

Davis pressed on. "They've built a narrative around escalation and excessive force. They're not saying the firefight wasn't chaotic. They're saying that after the chaos, *you kept going*. That the threat was neutralized and you continued engaging."

He tapped the folder gently. "Now, there's been some informal feelers. Nothing official. But Captain Reynolds and his team are entertaining the idea of a plea deal. Something along the lines of reduced charges—reckless endangerment, maybe negligent discharge of weapon under ROE breach. Non-punitive separation. No brig time, no dishonorable."

He paused, gauging Shane's face. Still blank.

"I'm not saying you're guilty. I'm saying the government doesn't have to prove guilt beyond doubt, the way you might think. This isn't a civilian court. This is a military tribunal. The rules of evidence are narrower. The discretion of the presiding officer—General Nolan—is broad. He controls the admissibility. He controls sentencing. There's no jury. Just him. Just command influence."

Another pause. Davis leaned forward slightly, voice quiet. "You take a deal, you control the outcome. You get to write the ending, at least partially. You walk out with a general under honorable or maybe even an OTH if we push back hard enough on characterization. But you get *out*. You go home. You rebuild."

He gave it a beat.

"If this goes to verdict, and Nolan decides you used excessive force? That you violated ROE? You're looking at years, son. And not in a soft place either. Fort Leavenworth doesn't care if you had good intentions. They'll care about whether you followed orders. Whether your fire discipline held under pressure."

Davis let that settle in the air. It wasn't a threat. Just facts.

"I need you to *think* about it, Specialist Alexander. Not tonight. But soon. Before Reynolds turns formal and puts something worse on the table."

He closed the file with a soft *snap*. Then sat back, waiting.

Seventeen

The Devil Works for NATO

April 7, 1998 – Fort Bragg, North Carolina

The courtroom was a converted administrative hall tucked deep within the legal operations wing of the XVIII Airborne Corps headquarters building. It smelled faintly of waxed floors and coffee gone cold. The panel sat in silent formation, each one in full service uniform, hands folded on the polished wood in front of them, eyes neutral.

Specialist Shane Alexander sat at the defense table in Class A. He looked smaller in the uniform now than he had a year ago, the frame thinner beneath the wool, skin pale and drawn. Major Thomas Davis, crisp and expressionless, sat beside him, legal pad open, pen perfectly aligned atop it. Across the room, Captain James Reynolds, the trial counsel, stood behind the government's table, already prepared to speak.

Brigadier General Louis Nolan, the presiding judge, entered at 0900 sharp, his presence announced with the sharp bark of "All rise."

His face was unreadable, posture exact, the silver star glinting against his lapel.

"Court is now in session," he said. "United States versus Specialist Shane Alexander."

Reynolds rose for his opening, walking slowly toward the panel. He kept his tone respectful but firm, voice clear.

"Members of the court, this case is not about bravery. It's not about sacrifice. It is about discipline. It is about lawful conduct under stress. It is about accountability under the Uniform Code of Military Justice."

He turned briefly to glance at Shane before continuing.

"We will show that Specialist Alexander, in the aftermath of his friend's death, lost control of his fire discipline. That he continued to engage after the enemy threat had ceased. That he violated clearly established Rules of Engagement—specifically Rule Five: *Do not fire on personnel who are withdrawing or surrendering unless they continue to pose a threat.* We will show that Specialist Alexander ignored this rule. And in doing so, he crossed a line that every soldier in a peacekeeping role is trained never to cross."

Reynolds returned to the government's table and nodded to his co-counsel. The evidence presentation began immediately.

First came the ballistics reports: carefully collated, labeled, and color-coded. An Army CID forensics specialist walked the panel through photographs of the Kiseljak market square—before and after the engagement. Red pins on a large diagram marked impacts from

Shane's M249. Green ones marked impacts from hostile AK-pattern rifles.

"The final cluster of impacts," the specialist explained, "occurred in a tight pattern roughly four meters west of the attackers' last known position. Based on casing distribution and impact angles, this final burst was not returned fire. It was initiated after a 2.5-second lull in hostile gunfire."

Major Davis objected, citing the imprecision of battlefield ballistics timing and the impossibility of confirming firing sequences without audio. General Nolan allowed the evidence to stand, noting that the panel could weigh credibility.

Next, Reynolds called Colonel William Harrison, the officer who had led the initial 15-6 investigation in Bosnia. Harrison took the stand with a stack of paperwork and a digital timeline printed in binders for each panel member.

He walked them through it: timestamps, radio logs, witness summaries. He made no dramatic claims, just pointed facts delivered in that careful, emotionless tone of a man who'd learned long ago to keep sentiment out of reports.

"Based on the cumulative review," Harrison stated, "we estimate that hostile fire ceased at 1429:11 local time. Specialist Alexander's final burst of six to eight rounds occurred at 1429. The only movement observed from the attackers during that interval was a retreat northward toward tree cover. There is no evidence they continued to fire at that point."

Major Davis stood. "Colonel, were you on site during the engagement?"

"No, sir."

"So your timeline is reconstructed from statements, radio logs, and ballistics?"

"That is correct."

"No audiovisual evidence?"

"None that were recorded in real time, no."

"Thank you."

But Reynolds wasn't finished.

At 1125 hours, he requested the court's permission to play translated excerpts from Bosnian civilian testimony—video clips gathered from the Camp Eagle interviews months prior.

The first was a grainy video of an older woman, perhaps in her sixties, wrapped in a heavy scarf, hands trembling as she gestured in the air. Her voice was flat, the subtitled translation appearing in white lettering at the bottom of the screen.

"The soldier with the big weapon kept shooting. The men were already falling back. He didn't stop."

Davis was on his feet instantly. "Objection. This excerpt omits context. The defense has not received full translations of these testimonies."

"Overruled," General Nolan said without looking up from the screen. "The court will consider this material in conjunction with the full record, once completed."

Except the record wasn't complete. Davis knew it. So did Reynolds.

Another video played—this one a middle-aged man, clean-shaven, wearing a worn peacoat. He gave a similar account: raised voices, gunfire, chaos, then calm—and then the sound of automatic fire once more.

Shane sat motionless, fists clenched beneath the table. He didn't blink. Didn't flinch. But his jaw was locked so tight it hurt.

By 1400 hours, the prosecution introduced the ballistics expert from the Army's Weapons Effects Lab. He stepped forward with a laptop, external projector, and simulation software loaded with data from the 15-6 report.

"Using trajectory analysis, acoustic delay modeling, and reconstructed positions based on statements and terrain mapping," he said, "we've developed a visual simulation of the engagement."

The lights dimmed. The projection began. It showed simplified figures—green for NATO personnel, red for attackers, yellow for civilians. It rendered the movement, the firing arcs, the staggered pace of combat in neat little bursts of color-coded fire.

At the end of the simulation, there was a visible pause—then a green cone of fire erupting toward red figures, turning away.

"Final engagement began 2.5 seconds after last confirmed hostile fire," the expert repeated.

Davis rose again. "Sir, is this simulation an accurate reproduction of combat dynamics?"

"It's based on the best-available data."

"But does it account for fog of war, adrenaline response, threat ambiguity?"

"It's a forensic tool, not a psychological one."

"And it assumes attackers were retreating?"

"Yes, based on positional mapping."

"Thank you."

But the panel had seen it. The pause. The deliberate burst. Neat, simple, damning.

Shane didn't move. His heart was hammering behind his ribs, but his face gave nothing.

Major Davis leaned over slightly and whispered, "Stay with me."

The first day closed at 1530 hours with General Nolan dismissing the court for the day. "Government, continue with witness testimony tomorrow. Defense, be prepared to present after government rests."

The panel filed out, their faces unreadable.

Shane remained seated long after they'd gone, eyes still fixed on the last frame of the simulation. Green fire. Red silhouettes. And a silence that told no truth at all.

Shane wasn't sure if his brain had simply stopped working or the world had because the time between the next session flew by as if it were mere seconds.

On day two, Major Davis stood, his voice cool and exact as he adjusted his glasses and approached the government's star witness—the prosecution's ballistics expert. The courtroom was still, save for the steady scratch of pens and the soft rustle of uniforms shifting in wooden seats.

"You're confident in your simulation," Davis began, tone courteous but edged. "Down to the second. Down to the bullet."

"Yes, sir," the expert replied.

"Tell me—were you there in the Valley that day?"

"No, sir."

"So you determined exact timings—who fired first, who stopped firing, who turned and who advanced—based on audio, drone footage, and scattered rifle shells in an echoing valley during a firefight involving twelve separate weapons."

The expert hesitated. "We used synchronized audio and time-stamps."

"In a valley. Surrounded by cliffs. With echo. In the middle of an ambush." Davis let that settle. "You've never served in combat, have you, sir?"

"No, sir."

Davis gave a slight nod and returned to the defense table. The moment marked a shift.

They began their case.

Staff Sergeant Laughlin took the stand first. Stern, weathered, his voice steady.

"It hit hard and fast," he said. "I was down on a different checkpoint but our men are taught to handle and trust me; handle is what they did." He shook his head. "There wasn't time for a count. There wasn't a plan. We were walking civilians back, and they were everywhere. Specialist Shane Alexander, operating as Three-Three Bravo at Checkpoint One, didn't hesitate. He didn't wait to see who might be lining up a second shot. He returned fire, like we're trained."

He spoke of Shane's record—commendations, discipline, his quiet leadership. And of the Rules of Engagement.

"You want the perfect call? That's in a classroom. Not in a ditch with bullets tearing through your interpreter."

Then Sergeant First Class Fitzpatrick spoke.

"You don't pause and ask if hostilities have ceased when you're under fire," he told the jury. "You engage until you're sure it's done. I've trained this soldier, and I've seen him work to get his weapon locked and loaded right. I'd trust him in a heartbeat. What he did was by the book—as it applies in real life, not paper."

A tense moment followed when Davis tried to enter new evidence—a freeze-frame showing a dead insurgent with his weapon still raised. But the prosecution objected. It hadn't been disclosed during discovery.

The judge agreed. It was ruled inadmissible.

At the defense table, Shane's fingers clenched. His mouth twitched, but he stayed silent. Davis touched his arm—subtle, grounding.

Then came Shane's turn.

The courtroom quieted. The kind of quiet that meant something sacred or dangerous was happening.

Shane stood.

"I remember the sun was in my eyes," he began. His voice was raw, and softer than expected. "And then he dropped. Just dropped like someone'd cut the strings. And I didn't think. I just—I picked up his rifle and started covering the civilians. There was a girl with a baby. I remember that. I remember thinking she looked like someone I used to know."

He paused. His jaw clenched.

"And I kept firing. Because they weren't stopping. And because if I hesitated—" he trailed off.

The prosecutor stood.

"So you're saying you didn't know if they were retreating?"

"I'm saying it didn't matter. You don't pause to take attendance in a firefight."

"But according to the audio, fire had slowed—"

"Ya think I was countin' bullets?" Shane snapped, raw emotion in his voice. "Ya'll think I stood there, doin' math?" He was breathing harder now. "You wasn't there. You ain't seen what they was gonna do to them folk down there. You ain't seen what they did to Lor—"

"Let me clarify," the prosecutor cut in smoothly. "So, Specialist, you're stating that you *intentionally ignored* the shift in the sound of fire?"

"I didn't *ignore* anything. I was reacting. There were still flashes from the tree line, still rounds hittin' the dirt. You don't stop to con-firm every shot in real time."

"But your helmet cam didn't show active fire at that angle after ten seconds."

"My helmet cam didn't have a 360 view. And it didn't have my ears. Or the dirt hittin' my uniform. Or the cries behind me from people tryin' not to die."

"You had civilians to protect, yes. But you had responsibility, too. You *kept* firing."

"Yeah, I did."

"Were you aiming at specific targets, or simply shooting suppressive fire?"

Shane blinked. "I shot at what I could see. At movement, muzzle flashes. I wasn't shootin' for fun."

"But it's possible, isn't it, that some of those targets were retreating?"

"It's possible one of 'em was takin' a smoke break, too. That ain't what I saw."

"Then what *did* you see?"

Shane opened his mouth to speak, then closed it again.

"I saw a field of chaos," he said finally, quieter now. "Smoke, dust, movement, blood. Loran's blood. I saw him—"

"You mean Specialist Taylor?"

Shane flinched. "Yes. Specialist Taylor."

"You understand the importance of detachment in an engagement review, don't you?"

"You ever buried your best friend?" Shane asked instead of answering.

The judge leaned forward. "Specialist—"

"Yes. I have actually, Specialist."

"Well, I *didn't*," Shane answered. "I just watched him bleed out in my arms. I wasn't allowed to say goodbye when they flew him back home."

"So, you're saying there's lack of detatchment?"

"I'm saying you're fuckin' outta your—"

"Specialist—!" The judge called louder this time.

Shane held up a hand, apologetically. "Sorry, Your Honor." He stared ahead.

"Let's get back on track," the prosecutor said crisply. "Would you agree that your emotional state may have compromised your decision-making?"

"I'd agree that if I didn't act, a mother and her baby would've died. That's what I agree to."

"And yet, we have no confirmed casualties among the civilians."

"That's 'cause we stopped it. That's the whole point."

The prosecutor tilted his head. "You mean *you* stopped it?"

"Me and my team. The ones who bled for it. Who died for it."

"So you see yourself as the hero in this story?"

Shane's knuckles whitened on the witness rail. "I see myself as the one who was there."

"You shot unarmed men."

"You sat in a room and watched it a month later. That's what *you* did. They weren't unarmed and you know it." Shane looked toward the gallery. His mother sat beside his father, hands clenched in prayer. The prosecutor opened his mouth to press further—

—and that's when Shane snapped.

"I wanna say what I *really* think of this process. What I *really* think of you. But I won't. Because I know who's watching. And I know how this goes. You put a soldier on trial for doing his job—then act surprised when he doesn't fold into your story."

He paused.

"But I'm still here. And I stand by what I did."

He stepped down without being dismissed. No one corrected him.

The court recessed in silence.

***

Arthur Miller once wrote, "*You can be better! Once and for all you can know there's a universe of people outside and you're responsible to it.*" But in uniform, Shane had begun to wonder if that universe ever really looked back. You bled for the mission, broke your body for it. You brought results—they pinned ribbons on your chest. Then you came home, hollow and scared, and they fed you silence. Until one day, they didn't need you anymore. Or worse, you became *inconvenient*.

That was the part they didn't put in the pamphlets. Not the weight of what you carried. Not the way your own government could look past the blood on your boots just to chase the dirt under your nails.

And now, they were here to clean their hands of him too.

The next morning, the courtroom carried a different weight. The crackle of morning chatter had been replaced with a brittle silence. Major Davis rose immediately after roll call, requesting to briefly recall Specialist Shane Alexander to the stand.

He stood with a composed expression, the fatigue under his eyes belying a night of little sleep. Shane looked steadier than he had the day before, but no one missed the way his knuckles were white against the edge of the witness stand. The court allowed the brief recall.

"Specialist Alexander," Davis began gently, "yesterday, during cross-examination, your emotions understandably got the better of you. I'd like the panel to hear—briefly—how you see your responsibilities as a soldier."

Shane blinked slowly, his jaw tight. "My responsibility was to my team. To the civilians. To the mission. And to the truth."

"And you believe you upheld that responsibility?"

"Yes, sir."

"Thank you."

There were no further questions. Davis sat, knowing it wasn't enough to undo the damage. The panel members—a mix of officers and seasoned NCOs—had seen many soldiers under stress, but rarely one unravel so publicly. His outburst the previous day still hung in the air. It had been raw, human, and undeniably real. But it had also pierced the careful decorum of the courtroom, leaving behind a trace of doubt that Davis could feel growing like mold between the cracks.

Captain Reynolds stood.

He moved with the calm assurance of a man who knew procedure was his friend.

"Members of the panel," Reynolds began, pacing slowly in front of them, "I will now offer the closing argument for the prosecution."

Shane's jaw twitched.

"Let me be very clear: this case is not about whether Specialist Alexander was brave. He was. It is not about whether he served with honor. He did. It is about whether, on April 17th, 1998, he violated Rule 5 of the Rules of Engagement."

Shane flinched.

Rule 5. Again.

He'd heard it recited so many times he could almost mouth the words along with Reynolds. It had been quoted in the field, in training briefings, on laminated cards, in posters at the firing range, and now in every damn hour of this trial. It rang like a drumbeat in his skull, each word another hammer blow. He didn't even feel his breathing shift, not at first. Just the sound of Reynolds's voice droning on, and the faintest buzzing at the edges of his hearing.

"Rule 5: Once the hostile act or intent ceases, use of deadly force must also cease. This is the cornerstone of military discipline in combat."

There it was again.

He tried to focus on the floor tile near his boot. A little crack along the grout line. It split like a tree branch. His heartbeat fluttered. His vision sharpened strangely, then blurred at the edges.

"We are not judging Alexander's bravery," Reynolds continued, "We are evaluating his *judgment*. Audio forensics show a lull in enemy fire. Civilian interviews confirm a moment of quiet. And Specialist Alexander continued to engage. That is excessive force. That is a violation."

Shane was barely hearing him now. His palms had gone slick. He felt the cold sweat slide between his fingers, resting on the grain of the witness rail. His throat tightened, but he couldn't clear it. A faint ringing had started in his left ear. Or maybe both.

He tried to shift in his seat, but his limbs felt heavy. Too heavy. Like they were being pulled into the earth. His stomach clenched, nausea curling up his throat. He didn't move. He couldn't. He'd trained himself not to twitch, not to flinch, not to show weakness.

But his body was *screaming*.

"He did not stop. Not when the threat ended. Not when the mission was complete. He continued. And people died. That, members of the panel, is why we're here."

Reynolds' voice snapped into painful focus, louder than it had been seconds ago. Shane's ears throbbed. His breathing shallowed, chest rising but no air coming in. Sweat was trailing down his back. Every part of him screamed to run. Or to yell. Or to hide. He gripped the edge of the seat beneath the table. Counted four beats of his pulse. Then four more. Then another four.

No one noticed.

Or if they did, no one said a word.

Reynolds finished his argument with a rehearsed pause, then returned to his seat. The prosecutor sat like a man satisfied with his work. Like he had put the final nail in the lid.

Major Davis stood.

He didn't pace. He stepped forward slowly, letting the silence breathe before he began.

"Specialist Shane Alexander is not on trial because he made a mistake. He's on trial because he survived a moment no man should have to relive, and did what he was trained to do."

Shane forced himself to listen. He tried to pull his focus back in. Davis's voice was calm, but firm.

"The prosecution wants you to measure combat in seconds. In decibels. In forensic timing and digital noise. But war isn't neat. It doesn't pause to let you assess it like a physics problem."

The ringing in Shane's ears was fading now. Not gone. Just quiet enough that Davis's words could cut through.

"Specialist Alexander saw his best friend die. Not just a fellow soldier—his *brother*. He didn't have time to grieve. He didn't retreat. He did what every man and woman in uniform hopes they'd do in that moment: he protected the innocent. He held the line."

Davis turned toward the panel. "You are all soldiers. You know what a firefight is. You know the difference between a battlefield and a courtroom. Please don't let hindsight become a weapon."

Shane stared at the floor again, jaw clenched.

"The prosecution will have you believe this is about one rule. But this case is about *context*. About judgment in real time. About humanity in hell."

Davis let the silence stretch.

"You cannot punish someone for being human under inhuman pressure."

He stepped back.

The judge turned toward the jury box.

"Members of the panel, I will now read you your instructions. You must determine guilt beyond a reasonable doubt. If such doubt exists, you must acquit. You will consider all evidence presented, testimony given, and arguments made. You are to apply the law as instructed without prejudice or sympathy."

As Judge Nolan read on, Shane let his head fall slightly. His throat burned. He hadn't cried in two years. He wasn't about to now.

"The court is in recess until a verdict is reached," the judge concluded.

The seven members of the panel filed out.

No one spoke.

Shane was led quietly back to confinement.

Behind him, the courtroom emptied slowly.

And somewhere in the silence, Rule 5 echoed once more in Shane's mind, like a drumline that refused to stop beating.

Eighteen

Far Away

April 29, 1998 – Fort Bragg, North Carolina

The holding cell was a squat concrete square with peeling green paint, just wide enough for a bench and a stainless-steel toilet that glinted cold under the flickering ceiling light. No sound made it through the thick door, but the hum of the overhead vents and the occasional shuffle of a guard's boots passing by. It wasn't cold, not exactly, but the kind of stale, air-conditioned room that gave off the feeling of winter without the weather.

Shane sat on the bench with his elbows on his knees, hands loosely clasped, eyes unfocused. The overhead light buzzed, clicked once, then held. He'd stopped watching the clock hours ago. Or maybe minutes. Time didn't matter in here.

The jury was still deliberating. That's all he'd been told. He figured if the decision was easy, they'd have come back fast. That used to seem like a good thing. Now he wasn't so sure. It left room for hope, which was crueler in long doses than in short supply.

He scratched absently at the inside of his wrist. The skin there was dry, a faint white line from an old mosquito bite. He used to get eaten up every summer back home. Zena, Oklahoma. A dot on the edge of nowhere, where the grass grew in patches and the wind never stopped moving.

He thought of his father, probably sitting straight-backed in one of those hard courtroom pews just down the hall, probably hadn't said a word in over an hour. Tim Alexander had fought in Vietnam—sort of. The war ended five days after he landed in-country, just long enough to give him a regulation haircut, a rifle, and a return ticket. He never made it outside the wire. Shane used to tease him about that when he was younger, not understanding the weight his father carried for doing nothing *because* the fighting had stopped. Tim never laughed at those jokes. Just said, "I was ready to go. That's what mattered."

Shane never quite bought that. But sitting in this cell now, he wondered if maybe that *was* what mattered. Not what you got to do. Just being willing when it came.

He leaned back against the cool wall, let his head rest, eyes drifting closed. There wasn't sleep waiting on the other side—just pictures. Memories he hadn't invited, but didn't have the energy to push away anymore.

He was five again, sitting cross-legged in the yard with a Tonka truck and a paper towel tube for a cannon. His dad had come home from the feed store in his boots and dusty jeans, squatted down in the dirt with him. They made war sounds, dug trenches with a stick, fought an imaginary enemy that always lost by suppertime. Shane remembered the way Tim grinned—not wide, but enough that the lines at his eyes creased up. He remembered that exact grin. Hadn't seen it in years.

Another flash—he was maybe seven. Mary was standing over the stove, flour on her cheek, bowl in one hand and wooden spoon in the other. She was patient with everything but mashed potatoes. "No lumps," she'd said, over and over, pointing at the pot like it was sacred. He'd mashed with both hands, grunting with effort while she corrected his grip, her other hand resting lightly on his shoulder. They'd eaten the whole bowl before his dad even got home.

And books. God, he used to read. Back when the world felt bigger and slower.

The Adventures of Huckleberry Finn—he remembered reading it on the porch during a thunderstorm, rocking back and forth with a flashlight under a blanket because the power went out. He couldn't get enough of the river. That wide, muddy Mississippi, where anything could happen. Some part of him still wanted that—just to drift, no uniform, no orders, no lines in the dirt that made men enemies.

Treasure Island was next. He remembered pressing the pages flat to stare at the map. His finger had traced the "X" like it meant something real. Sometimes, as dumb as it sounded now, he used to imagine himself sailing with Jim Hawkins, wind at his back, nothing ahead but the horizon.

Then *The Jungle Book*, and the idea of a boy raised by wolves surviving on his wits. He'd thought that one was a little far-fetched, but he still read it twice. There was something about the wild that stuck with him. The idea of a world that didn't ask for permission. Just took what it needed to keep moving.

He opened his eyes. The light buzzed again. No footsteps yet.

Loran had always wanted to get *out*. Away from their little town, the dusty fields, the same faces at church every Sunday. Loran used to talk about Nashville like it was heaven and New York like it was Mars. He wanted the noise, the traffic, the music on every street corner. Shane didn't care about cities much. He didn't hate Zena. He just wanted to do something that mattered.

Not fame. Not even glory. Just something that, when he looked back at his life, he wouldn't feel like he'd slept through the whole thing.

He'd once told Loran that if he could do anything, *anything*, it'd be to float down the Mississippi with a satchel of books, some fishing line, and a flask of something warm. Just drift until he hit New Orleans, see if the music was really as good as folks said. No map, no plan. Just the river.

"Man," Loran had laughed, "you'd last two days before you got lost or sunburned."

"Yeah, well," Shane had grinned, "at least I'd get there slow."

In this cell, slow was all there was.

He rubbed his hands together, not for warmth but rhythm. The same motion he used to make while waiting for his mama to drain the potatoes.

He didn't pray. Not because he didn't believe in anything—he just didn't know what words to use anymore. He figured if God was listening, He already knew. And if He wasn't... well, then silence was just as good.

Outside, beyond these walls, his parents were waiting. Tim, with that stillness he'd carried since 1975. Mary probably clutching a tissue that had long since shredded. He hated knowing they were out there. Hated more that he couldn't tell them anything—couldn't reassure, couldn't promise, couldn't fix.

He leaned forward again, fingers laced. The metal door stayed shut. No word yet.

And so he sat with his memories. Quiet company. Better than none at all.

***

The heavy bolt slid back on the cell door with a metallic rasp, and a second later, Major Davis stepped inside. Uniform pressed sharp as ever, briefcase in hand, face drawn tight from lack of sleep. He glanced around like the place offended his sensibilities, then gave Shane a nod.

"You holding up?"

Shane shrugged. "Same as this morning."

Davis leaned his back against the far wall, adjusting his sleeves before speaking again. "They're still in deliberations. Four hours and counting. Not exactly textbook."

Shane didn't say anything.

Davis glanced at him, expression unreadable. "Could mean one of two things," he said. "They're hung up on something, or someone's not buying the full prosecution narrative. Either way, it's not a rubber stamp. That's... something."

He opened his case, pulled out a small notebook, flipped through a few dog-eared pages, then snapped it shut again. "I'll be honest with you, Specialist—I don't know which way this goes. But they're not asleep at the wheel in there. They're talking. That buys us more than I thought we'd have by now."

Shane gave a small nod, but his gaze had drifted away—past Davis, past the walls, the floor, the steel. He wasn't really hearing him anymore.

In his mind, he was back in Georgia. Fort Benning. The muggy pine air, the sand getting into his boots, the smell of sweat and scorched dirt from the firing range. Loran had been there too, always one row over, grinning through pushups and mouthing off under his breath to their drill sergeant in a way that never quite got him caught. He made every exercise a contest—who'd shoot tighter, run faster, pull off a cleaner gear check.

Then came the backyard, a patchy sprawl of crabgrass and red dirt. It was fenced in with old wood and rusted nails. A plastic wiffle bat lay discarded by the steps, and Shane, all lanky limbs and scraped knees, crouched beside an overturned bucket they were using as second base. Loran, grinning wide under a mop of dark hair, had braces that caught the sunlight like chrome. He wore his Air Jordans unlaced, his jeans rolled up just above his socks—cool in a way Shane never could quite pull off.

It was the summer of '89, late July, heat shimmering off the shingles, and both boys were fourteen and free.

Loran had just hit a lopsided home run over the fence—well, what counted as a home run in backyard rules—and was rounding the bases with theatrical flair when the sound cut through the air.

A roar, low and fast. The kind that made your chest buzz and your ears pop for a second. Both boys stopped and looked up.

An aircraft streaked across the sky—silver, fast, and no doubt military. It was gone as quickly as it came, banking east, leaving behind only a thin white scar across the blue.

Loran stood there in the middle of the yard, squinting against the sun, and raised his hand in a wave. Not wild, not showy—just a clean, steady salute.

Shane squinted up too and laughed. "They can't see you, dumbass."

Loran shrugged, hand still raised. "Doesn't matter. I see them." He dropped his hand and picked up the wiffle bat again, tapping it against his palm. "Bet they work hard. Probably deserve a wave."

Shane never forgot that. Not the way he said it—so simple, so sure.

In the present, seated stiff-backed in that sterile room with nothing but fluorescent hum for company, Shane blinked hard against the memory. His jaw tightened, and he almost spat.

Those same people. The uniforms, the salutes, the hard work. The ones he'd waved to. The ones he'd wanted to be like. The ones Loran had saluted with all the blind faith of a kid staring up at something bigger than himself.

They were the same ones now willing to ruin his life. To take his service and twist it into something disgraceful. Not a moment of hesitation.

Work hard, do they?

Yeah. Undoubtedly.

But they didn't deserve that damn wave. Not anymore.

He sucked his teeth, peering up and squinted at Davis who was saying...well, *something*.

Shane's brain had heard too much of all that. It wanted out. So, it went back to Bosnia.

That foreign gray light, always seeming like dawn or dusk, never full sun. He could still feel the cold in his knuckles from those endless patrols. Loran had always been a magnet for both trouble and charm. Probably would have been the reason for Laughlin to put chastity belts on them all at some point. "One pretty girl and I'm settin' down roots," he used to say, holding up his fingers like a scout's oath. "Swear it."

Shane had rolled his eyes. But truth was, he'd thought about it, too. About a life.

He'd imagined staying in. Finishing his second enlistment, maybe a third. Moving up the ranks slow and steady. Another deployment or two, then back stateside. A wedding—quiet, maybe a church back home, his mama in something powder blue, Tim in that old suit he wore to funerals and graduations. The woman didn't have to be flashy. Just kind. Just someone who didn't mind the silences. Someone who'd sit beside him on the porch during a thunderstorm and let the coffee go cold.

He'd thought maybe they'd have kids. Maybe not. Didn't matter much. Some Christmases with too many gifts under a crooked tree. A couch they both fell asleep on while some dumb movie played. The sort of life that didn't make headlines.

He was a romantic, though he'd never owned up to it. Not the flowers and poems kind—he was terrible with words—but the kind that believed a simple life could be the most beautiful thing in the world.

Major Davis was still talking, something about procedure and panel dynamics, but the words blurred into the hum of the light overhead.

And then, uninvited but welcome, came a different kind of thought.

He could almost see her—his maybe-wife—standing at the stove, her hair pulled back, smiling at something he'd said as he walked in the door. His parents would be there too, older, faces more lined, but proud, the way they were in that one photograph from graduation. There'd be kids—at least a couple. One with a missing front tooth, the other with braces and a gap-toothed grin. They'd run full-tilt, arms flung wide, hollering *Daddy's home* as they tackled him at the door.

That vision didn't stay long. It was too warm, too *far away*.

But what lingered—what held—was something simpler.

Just him and Loran again.

The two of them sitting at the edge of some river they couldn't name, boots kicked off, feet in the water, rifles set aside. No borders. No rules. Just sky and current. Letting the water steer them somewhere quiet. Somewhere that didn't ask for anything but breath and time.

He closed his eyes. Didn't sigh this time.

Didn't move.

Just sat there.

Letting himself believe.

***

The metallic clatter of boots echoed down the corridor just after 1900 hours.

A sergeant stepped into the holding cell. "Jury's back. Time to move."

Shane stood without a word, spine straight, jaw set. The cuffs were fastened without ceremony. He didn't flinch. Just followed orders like always.

Two MPs flanked him as they walked the narrow hallway toward the courtroom. Fluorescent lights buzzed overhead. Somewhere distant, a door slammed.

He didn't look at the floor. Didn't glance around.

By the time they reached the double doors, his face was stone—calm, unreadable. Military bearing etched in every line. But beneath the surface, his thoughts moved like water under ice.

The doors opened, and he stepped inside.

Nineteen

Closer to Home

The courtroom was packed wall-to-wall—officers in Class A uniforms, suits, and skirts, a few reporters cordoned off behind a row of folding chairs, pens poised, waiting to scribble down a name that would carry weight in headlines for a few days and fade the next.

Specialist Shane Alexander stood at attention beside the defense table. Boots polished, belt aligned, cover absent. Hands rigid at his sides, shoulders squared. His uniform fit looser than it had the year before, his face hollowed out by months of investigative seclusion, but his bearing was regulation-perfect. A soldier until the end.

Sergeant First Class Bassey, who'd been flown in from D.C. for the formality, stood at the center of the courtroom. Black folder in hand, voice smooth as ceremony required.

"The United States versus Specialist Shane Michael Alexander, United States Army…"

The stillness that followed felt unnatural. Even the air vents in the ceiling hummed low, like they knew to keep quiet. Shane's ears registered the words but didn't grasp them in real time. His focus was singular—don't flinch, don't blink, don't let them see a goddamn thing.

"...having been found guilty by this General Court-Martial of the following charges..."

A pause. The sound of a page turned slowly, deliberately.

"Charge I: Violation of Article 118, Uniform Code of Military Justice. Murder. Guilty."

His mother, somewhere behind him, stifled a sound. Shane didn't turn. He kept his eyes fixed straight ahead.

"Charge II: Violation of Article 92. Failure to obey a lawful order. Guilty."

His jaw tightened. Just barely. Major Davis didn't look at him—didn't need to. Both of them had known the odds coming in.

"Charge III: Violation of Article 134. Acts bringing discredit upon the armed forces. Guilty."

Each word struck with a clean, deliberate cadence. Not harsh, not vindictive. Just official.

Judge Nolan didn't shift. He sat like a stone at the bench. Unbothered. Perhaps, even relieved. Captain Reynolds folded his hands before him, barely suppressing the smirk at the corner of his mouth.

And then came the sentence.

"For the offenses of which you have been convicted, the court sentences you to the following: Reduction in grade to E-1. Forfeiture of all pay and allowances. Confinement for a term of forty-three years. Dishonorable discharge from the United States Army."

Forty-three years.

Not life. But long enough that life outside would be unrecognizable when—or if—he walked out.

The air didn't move for a moment.

Major Davis finally turned toward Shane. Just slightly. His mouth twitched—not in surprise. Not even dismay. It was more like a resignation. They'd tried. Fought tooth and nail. And the system, well... it did what it always did when the narrative had already been written.

Shane inhaled through his nose. One breath. Then another. Still at attention. Not a crack.

He remembered Loran at Fort Benning, day three of boot, their rucksacks weighing like anchors, both of them sweating bullets in Georgia heat, and Loran cracking a joke about how even prison chow might taste better than the MREs they were issued. "Bet the portions are warmer," he'd said.

That same Loran had died in Bosnia, in a market square, pulling a child and a young woman out of the line of fire. Shane had emptied half a belt of 5.56 into the treeline because there was no other choice. Because it was them or more civilians—more blood in the dirt. And now they called it murder.

The court recessed. Shane was ordered to remain standing as the jury filed out. One by one. Some glanced his way. Most didn't.

When they were gone, Judge Nolan issued the customary final instructions, voice devoid of warmth.

"This court is adjourned."

The gavel tapped once. Not a slam. Just protocol.

A pair of MPs moved in behind Shane, their hands lightly brushing his arms, not gripping yet. Not until they got him out the side door. A different exit than the jury, the press, or even his parents.

As the courtroom began to empty, he finally turned his head—just enough to see them.

His mother, Mary, looked stricken, one hand clutching her chest, the other clamped onto his father's forearm. Her lips moved like she was praying. Tim Alexander stood beside her, stone-faced. He didn't blink. Didn't falter. Just held her up. Shane gave them the smallest nod. Not a goodbye. Not a thank you. Just a silent acknowledgment. That he saw them. That he appreciated them being there.

Then he was led out.

Down a hallway that smelled of institutional wax and detergent. White walls, flickering lights. Turn after turn until the courtroom was far behind. Not once did he stumble or hang back. He marched like he always had—head high, steps sharp, a soldier to the core.

They brought him to a temporary holding cell until transport could be arranged. Fort Leavenworth. That was the next stop. But not yet.

He sat down heavily on the cot. Alone now. No ticking clock, no lawyers, no salutes. Just silence. He leaned forward, elbows on knees, and pressed his hands together.

Forty-three years.

Not for negligence. Not for desertion. Not for cowardice.

But for doing what he'd been trained to do. What they'd drilled into him since day one.

He thought of the patch on his sleeve. The oath he took. The metal in his hand when everything went to hell.

He thought of Loran waving at a military jet when they were teenagers, braces flashing in the sun, saying they probably deserved a wave.

He'd saluted too many times. He'd meant it. Every goddamn time.

And now?

Now they'd cut off that same arm and left him to bleed.

***

The chapel was quiet. Empty but for the dusty scent of wood polish, old hymnals, and tired prayers hanging in the air like forgotten smoke. No candles burned. No voices rose. The stained glass held the late morning sun like it didn't want to let it go, casting streaks of blue and blood-red across the pews.

Shane sat near the front, elbows on his knees, hands clasped—not in prayer, just in habit. His uniform was clean but faded, same as every other inmate in the block. His boots were scuffed. He hadn't shaved that morning. No one had said anything.

Chisholm slid in beside him with the quiet scrape of denim on wood. A couple of seconds passed before he spoke, not loud, just enough to echo in the hush.

"That kind of sentence hollows a man out," he said, like he was talking about a thunderstorm rolling in.

Shane didn't look at him.

"I ever tell you 'bout sweet Sister Maddy?" Chisholm grunted, scratched the back of his neck, then leaned forward with a smirk creeping onto his face. "Had a thing for a nun once," he said. "Real looker. Sister Maddison. Long neck. Big hands. Bigger, uh, well, everythin' else; I know—shoulda run the other way, but damn if temptation didn't come in rosary beads."

Shane let out a breath. Not quite a laugh, not even a scoff. More like the sound a man makes when something hurts, but he doesn't want to admit it.

"Knew her family 'cause well, everybody knows everybody in a small town, maybe a few years younger than me." Chisholm grinned. "Swear to God, back in Kentucky, the woman ran a church school. Couldn't stop 'visiting' every week. Told everyone I was volunteering for community leadership—what I was really doin' was blowin' my ammo reserves on fantasy confessions." He made a loose hand gesture. "Shoulda seen her with a ruler."

Shane finally turned to glance at him, then back at the front. "You're sick."

"Guilty as charged," Chisholm said, the grin fading into something older, something closer to bone. He let the silence settle again. Then, quieter: "You remember that thing I asked you first time we met? About your jury?"

Shane nodded slowly.

"I asked if you'd taken a proper look. You said no."

Another nod.

Chisholm leaned back, looked up toward the vaulted ceiling like he was trying to remember something exact. "I been thinking on it. Had time. Dug a bit, too—some records, the names. All of 'em had military ties. One was married to a battalion XO, now serving as a military medic. Another, an infantry admin desk jockey. One was a logistics officer. Rest were enlisted backgrounds. Not one who had served, but from what you've told me, Davis had already told you that."

Shane blinked, jaw visibly tightening.

Chisholm went on, soft and certain. "Now, they weren't all hardasses. Not saying they were crooked. But that ain't a jury of your peers, Shane. That's a firing squad in dress uniforms. Not one of 'em had a background in law. No one who could've weighed the rules of engagement against real battlefield psychology. No mental health experts. No blue-collar folks who'd maybe seen unfairness in the system. Just career uniforms and dependents who'd learned how to salute from birth."

He turned, letting that sit with weight.

"You were judged by people who've spent their whole lives inside the same machine that chewed you up. You think they were gonna see you? *Really* see you?"

Shane didn't answer. His hands curled tighter.

"I said it that day, and I'll say it now," Chisholm added, tapping the wooden pew. "That wasn't justice. That was theater. They just needed it wrapped neat. A tidy headline. And you, son, you were the ribbon."

Shane's eyes stayed forward, fixed on the simple brass cross bolted to the altar wall. His face gave nothing away. But his silence carried the weight of knowing—and not knowing—what to do with the truth.

Chisholm leaned back against the pew, the wood creaking like it was tired of holding broken men.

"I got a stack of papers on my desk back in New York," he said. "Keeps me busy. Bunch of notes, clippings, some doodles of Sister Maddison in fishnets—don't judge me. You find God your way, I'll find mine."

Shane didn't react, but Chisholm caught the faintest twitch at the corner of his mouth. That was enough. He reached into the front pocket of his worn correctional jacket and pulled out a folded sheet, creased from being opened too often. He ran a thumb over the edge.

"I wasn't supposed to give a damn," Chisholm said, gaze lowering to the page. "But I was in the library one day—God knows why—and I bumped into this guy. Name was Milo Jovanović. Said he used to be a translator with NATO. Volunteered after the war. Said he got stuck translating witness statements for some of the U.S. units trying to make sense of what the hell happened in all those towns nobody could pronounce."

Shane finally turned toward him. Quiet, but watching.

"Milo was a chatterbox. The kind who tells you his whole family tree before you know his last name. Said his wife left him, blamed his halitosis, but he thinks it was the war trauma." Chisholm paused. "Pretty sure it was the halitosis. Man smelled like a goat's lunch."

Shane let out a ghost of a breath. Might've been the closest thing to a laugh since the verdict.

"But," Chisholm went on, serious again, "Milo said something that snagged me. He mentioned Kiseljak. Said he was there after the shooting. Helped coordinate the local interviews for your battalion's legal guys. Then he squints and goes, *Funny thing, one of the clearest testimonies I ever translated never made it into the report.*'"

Shane's brow furrowed. "What do you mean?"

Chisholm unfolded the paper, tapping a line with one finger. "Old Bosnian shepherd. Name was Emir Begović. He was out early that morning tending his sheep on the eastern hill. The opposite hill from where the gunfire came from. Had a damn-near panoramic view. He saw the ambush unfold from above, start to finish."

The name rattled something loose in Shane's head. Not a sticky tab—he remembered it now, faintly, a ghost among the pile of untranslated witness statements Davis had shown him during trial prep. Just pages marked 'Pending Translation' or red-lined for language issues. Emir's had been one of them. Buried with the rest.

"His testimony wasn't in the trial evidence," Chisholm added. "Not even as an appendix. Milo swore he translated it himself and handed it to the CID liaison. Said the old man described the shooters, their position, the sequence. Said the guy didn't see Taylor directly—but his version lined up with two others."

Shane looked up again.

"One was a woman named Lubov. Said she was across from the last shooter—saw him retreating, confirmed he was still very much armed. Her words: '*I saw it. He was not surrendering.*' Described the mayhem, and saw someone pulling civilians down behind a fruit stand. Didn't get a name, but her timeline backed the shepherd's exactly."

Chisholm's eyes sharpened. "The other one, though—the last of the untranslated ones—was apparently real close. Said she ducked behind a burned-out vendor truck. She saw it all. Mentioned '*the other one*'—they'd expected Taylor, obviously. But Milo said when she was shown pictures of the soldiers on site, she pointed to both you and Taylor."

Shane blinked. "She pointed to me?"

"That's what Milo said. Clear as day. Said the woman didn't speak much. Might've been half in shock or just you know, typical Bosniak. But when he showed her the ID sheets, she jabbed at your photo and said, 'That one. He was good.'"

Shane stared at the wooden cross mounted above the altar. Memory flitted behind his eyes like static. That moment—too loud to be clear, too fast to freeze.

Chisholm leaned forward.

"You mentioned a girl too," he said quietly. "When you told me everything. You said Taylor grabbed a little lady and a child."

Shane blinked hard, then slowly nodded. "Yeah."

"You seen her face in any of the witness photos?"

Shane shook his head slowly. "No. I never did."

Chisholm sat back with a sigh and rubbed the back of his neck. "Seen anyone without a photo with the statements?"

"I...I guess. I don't remember a name."

"Ah, well, guess, now I get to tell you that I've located and visited Emir to hear it all myself." Chisholm hummed, stretching his arms over his head.

Shane looked like he'd just been electrocuted. Not in the cartoony sense—no eyes bulging, no sparks shooting out of his ears—but in the way a man goes still, like his body hasn't caught up to the idea that something buried deep just got unearthed.

Chisholm stopped mid-sentence, eyebrows rising. "What the hell's that look for?"

Shane blinked. A second passed before he muttered, "You should've started with that."

Chisholm gave a slow shrug, half sheepish, half stubborn. "Can't just lead with the ace, man. Procedure matters. I needed your whole story before I dropped anything. Otherwise, I don't know what connects, what doesn't. Plus, if I'd just told you about Emir right off the bat..." He gave a lopsided grin. "You'd have missed out on all my world-class jokes."

"Your jokes suck," Shane said, still staring straight ahead, the words automatic and dull.

"Thank you for your service," Chisholm replied, deadpan, then chuckled, giving Shane a moment to let his pulse settle. "Anyway, like I said, I tracked Emir Begović down about six weeks ago. Lives in a little village tucked behind a ridge southeast of Kiseljak. Place barely has power, and you'd miss it if you blinked. Took me two separate drivers, a bribe, and a guy with a truck that coughed every time we turned left."

He shook his head like he still couldn't believe the trouble.

"Emir's still sharp. Old but sharp. He remembered that day like it happened last week. Said he watched the whole firefight from up on the slope. He'd taken his flock up early and got stuck behind a boulder once the shooting started. From where he was, he could see the market, the shooters, the U.S. troops—everything."

Shane was quiet, but now leaning slightly forward, elbows on his knees.

"I recorded him. Subtitled everything," Chisholm said. "He said there was *no pause* in the gunfire. Not a lull. The last shooter was still trying to fire as your unit returned fire." He inhaled deeply. "Emir said he saw muzzle flashes from the attacker's position even as your friend was pulling the little lady out of the line of fire."

Shane nodded slowly. "Yeah. I just covered for him. He was the one who ran in."

"So, they've said." Chisholm glanced at him. "Emir said the woman dropped something. Slipped maybe, or tripped, he wasn't sure. But the soldier had to drag her and the kid both. Mentioned when Taylor got shot. Then went on to say you were still engaging the final shooter—last one wasn't dead yet."

Shane's jaw tensed. "I knew it."

"Well, Emir confirmed it. And here's the kicker—he said he *was* interviewed. NATO investigators, CID guys, whoever—they came up, talked to him, took notes. Milo said he translated Emir's statement himself. But that testimony never made it to your trial. Not even a mention in the footnotes."

Shane looked over at him, voice quiet. "They buried it."

"They buried *a lot*, apparently." Chisholm nodded grimly. "Lubov's statement? The woman who saw the last shooter running across the alley? She lined up with Emir's timeline perfectly. Described the soldier dragging civilians to cover. She didn't name anyone—but her statement reinforced everything Emir said."

"Then why wasn't she called?"

Chisholm let out a breath. "Because she got mysteriously ill a week after those interviews. Hospitalized. Diagnosed with something vague and neurological. Couldn't testify. CID closed her file when her husband said she'd been overworked."

Shane's brow furrowed. "Jesus..."

Chisholm nodded once, then leaned forward.

"And then there's the third one. The woman who was closest to the shooting—Na'ada Hussein. Milo had mentioned her name but didn't think much of it until I pressed. Claimed she was young. Had a baby," he paused only to peer at Shane, who looked like a lightbulb had just gone on in his head. "Said she *hid behind a cart when the bullets started flying. She saw everything.*"

Shane looked up at him, eyes narrowing. The name triggered something, but it was blurry, like a voice heard through thick glass. He stared down at the floor. "What she look like?"

"Took me damn near a month, but I found her. No photographs in the original file, no ID numbers. But Milo had mentioned something about her skin tone—light tan, he said. The natural kind. Not sunburned. Said it stood out in Bosnia, *'like a splash of warm sand on a snowy day.'*"

"Poetic."

"That sounds familiar, doesn't it?" Chisholm gave a small smile. "That helped. I asked around some medical volunteers who were in-country after the war. Found her in a small community farther inland, not far from Doboj. She'd relocated after the war—no phone, no internet. Apparently, she'd only been visiting Kiseljak for a market day. But she's alive; still real young, poor thing. And the kid? Saw him running like a foot tall menace."

Shane didn't speak for a long time.

When he finally did, his voice was rough. "So what now?"

Chisholm looked him square in the eye. "Now we file. Prosecutorial misconduct for withholding exculpatory evidence. That's the first brick. We start building a new petition—request a retrial, maybe even full dismissal. Emir's statement, Na'ada's testimony, the medical timeline for Lubov—all of it gets packaged. If I can get Milo to write a sworn declaration, that's even better."

Shane didn't move. His breath was steady, but his hands were clenched.

"I've heard that before," he said quietly.

"I know," Chisholm replied. "But this time, there's something they can't ignore. You didn't make this shit up. They did."

There was a long pause. The chapel was still. Dust swirled through a beam of light near the stained glass window. No prayers, no hymns. Just air and tension.

Shane finally looked up.

It wasn't relief on his face. Not joy. Just something heavier than resignation. Something that hadn't stirred in years.

Hope. Small, worn, but alive.

"I'm not saying it'll work," Chisholm said gently. "But I am saying it's real."

Shane didn't answer right away. He looked forward again, gaze landing on the wooden altar, his voice barely above a whisper.

"If it does work... it's not just for me."

"I know," Chisholm said. "It never was." With that, he got up, ready to leave. As he started down the aisle, he paused, glancing over his shoulder.

"Oh, and Shane?"

Shane turned slightly.

"That nun? She never did confess." He smirked. "But I did."

"Oh, *fuck off.*"

Twenty

Dust in the Wind

November 1998 came in colder than usual, the wind rolling off the Kansas hills, biting through even thick field jackets. Fort Leavenworth's chapel stood half-empty most days now, except for the usual handful of men who clung to whatever faith or habit had kept them human. Shane Alexander sat through those days with the patience of someone who'd learned time wasn't a thing you fought anymore—it was a thing you wore, like a set of handcuffs no one bothered to unlock.

That morning, Mike Chisholm had gone quiet after chow, head bent low over the battered table in the attorney conference room, finalizing the last few details of Shane's appeal packet. A cup of burnt coffee steamed next to his hand, untouched. Every few minutes, he'd grumble to himself, cross something out, then rewrite it in smaller, angrier letters.

Shane sat across from him, arms crossed over his prison-issued shirt, watching. He didn't ask questions. Chisholm had promised news, real news, not just court dates or lawyer-speak. So he waited.

At last, Chisholm slammed his pen down, shoved the papers into a manila envelope, and leaned back in his chair, stretching like a man sore from carrying a load too heavy for one back.

"That's it, brother," he said, voice rough. "It's filed. The bastards have it now."

Shane shifted, heart hammering harder than he wanted to admit. "You're sure you covered it all?"

"Affidavits from Begović. Sworn statement from our translator friend—Milo's been damn near heroic about backing it all up. Cited Brady violations, procedural suppression, even threw in a little due process cherry on top. They'll have to respond."

"They gonna?" Shane asked, voice tighter than he intended.

Chisholm gave him a look. "Oh, they'll respond, alright. Problem is, their first move's gonna be denial. Always is."

***

The military prosecutors fired back within two weeks, swearing up and down they'd never heard of Emir Begović during the investigation. Shane read the copy of their response Chisholm slid across the table, jaw clenching tighter with each line.

"They're lying," he muttered.

"No shit," Chisholm said. "But lying ain't illegal. Suppressing evidence that coulda helped your case? That's another story."

The next tactic was more creative. The prosecution argued that, even if Begović had been interviewed, his vantage point on the hillside was too far and too obscured to be reliable. Shane could practically hear the smirk in the way the words were typed—"poor visibility," "inconsistent memory," "lack of military expertise."

"They're calling him blind without saying it outright," Shane said.

"They're covering their asses," Chisholm corrected. "See, they can't admit they knew about him without admitting they picked through the witness statements like a man picking crabshells for meat. Only kept what fit their story."

He paused, running a hand through his buzzed hair, the gray showing clearer under the harsh fluorescent light. "And that's what's gonna make the appeal stick. Maybe not quick. Maybe not easy. But we've got 'em by the balls now."

Through November, December, and January, Shane fought not to hold on too tight to that thread of hope. Every time a guard banged on the cell bars for mail call, his stomach twisted.

Sometimes it was just a card from his mom—a picture of a farm dog tangled up in Christmas lights, with "thinking of you, sweetheart" scrawled inside. Sometimes it was a short note from his dad, written in that tight block handwriting that had once filled after-action reports in Vietnam: "Stay strong, son. We're proud of you."

Once, when no one was looking, Shane pressed the paper to his forehead, as if he could absorb it somehow, like heat from a stove.

Letters turned into occasional visits. After almost a year, he had finally let them back in. His mom would bring him thick, homemade cookies wrapped in plastic bags that the guards would tear open and inspect. His dad sat beside her, jaw locked, one hand always resting lightly on Mary's knee, like he was holding her together by touch alone.

Shane never cried. Not in front of them. Not when he was shackled at the ankles, led in like some murderer. His father's eyes stayed dry, too. Only Mary wept silently, a tissue twisting between her fingers, her lipstick worn clean away by the time visiting hours ended.

They talked about normal things—cousins getting married, repairs needed on the old house, whether the Panthers would ever figure out how to win a damn game. It was the only way any of them knew how to keep breathing.

By February, Chisholm had submitted more motions, more exhibits. Depositions, diagrams, photographs of the hillside where Begović had stood. He found a forensic photography expert who swore under oath that Begović's line of sight was "clear to 600 meters on a cloudless day," and it had been cloudless that morning at Kiseljak.

Prosecutors pushed back hard, trying to get the appeal dismissed. They argued technicalities—wrong format, wrong filing location, missed deadlines. Chisholm countered every point like a man swatting flies. Every time Shane thought they'd finally buried him for good, Chisholm came back swinging.

Even when hope cracked open the door a little, Shane wasn't stupid enough to walk right through. Not yet.

He carried that anger like a rucksack he couldn't set down. Not just at the people who'd railroaded him, but at the system itself—the uniforms he'd once saluted, the officers he'd once respected, the rules he'd believed meant something.

They didn't. Not when it mattered.

There were nights he lay on his narrow cot, staring at the low ceiling, feeling that betrayal like a splinter working deeper under the skin.

But there were better nights, too. Nights when he let himself picture home. His mom's fried chicken. His dad's gruff laugh after too much whiskey. A porch light left on just for him.

Those nights, he almost dared to believe he could still have something after all this. Not the same life. But a life worth living.

March brought a new letter.

Chisholm slid it across the table with a grin.

"They're rattled," he said.

The military courts had agreed to hold a preliminary hearing to decide whether Shane's case warranted reopening based on "newly discovered evidence." It wasn't a guarantee. But it was the first real crack in the dam.

"Get ready," Chisholm said. "We're about to see how deep this rabbit hole goes."

After a long minute, he said, voice rough, "Mike?"

"Yeah, bud?"

"You really think...this'll fix it?"

Chisholm leaned back, hands folded behind his head, studying him like a man weighing the truth.

"No," he said finally. "Nothing's ever gonna fix it. But it might set it right."

Shane nodded once, slow and heavy. He could live with that. Maybe that's all any man ever really got—a second chance to tell the truth and hope someone finally listened.

***

April 1999 brought storms—real ones that battered the Leavenworth walls with sideways rain, and quieter ones in Shane Alexander's life, the kind you felt more than you heard.

For weeks, the case file Chisholm had managed to pry loose from the original court-martial had been sitting like a weight between them. Thousands of pages, most of it boilerplate: witness lists, map diagrams, after-action reports, transcripts so dry you could feel your brain cracking just trying to get through them.

Every evening after meetings with Shane, Chisholm would sit at the battered table in the law library, reading by the dull yellow light, tapping a chewed pen against the folder in a steady rhythm like a metronome counting out someone else's life.

Then, one Thursday afternoon, something shifted.

Shane saw it before Chisholm said a word. His lawyer froze, finger resting on a page halfway down a typed list. His whole body stiffened, the casual slouch straightening like a man who'd just heard a twig snap in the dark.

"What is it?" Shane asked, voice low.

Chisholm didn't answer right away. He flipped back two pages, then forward three, scanning fast, mouth pulled into a grim, hard line. Finally, he looked up, eyes gleaming behind his glasses.

"They interviewed Begović," Chisholm said, voice flat.

Shane's heart kicked. "You're sure?"

"Positive. His name's right here—Emir Begović. Date, time, place. Signed witness intake form." Chisholm tapped the page with the back of his pen. "And here's the kicker: no corresponding witness statement filed. None."

He flipped through the next section—statements from other civilians, soldiers, the market vendors—and sure enough, Emir's testimony wasn't there.

"Son of a bitch," Chisholm muttered, almost reverently.

Shane leaned forward, staring. It was real. Proof. Not a maybe, not a hunch. Real, tangible proof they'd *had* the witness. Chisholm dropped the page flat on the table and leaned both hands on it like he might crush the whole system through sheer force of will.

"This is it," Chisholm said, almost to himself. "They can't weasel out of this one."

He stood so fast his chair scraped backward. Started pacing, raking one hand through his hair. Shane just sat there, feeling like he'd been punched—not in a bad way, but in that gut-emptying, staggering way that came when something you barely dared hope for actually happened.

"You gonna file it?" Shane asked after a minute.

"Damn right," Chisholm said. "Gonna drop it on 'em like a goddamn piano from the fifth floor."

Chisholm barely slept, hammering out the supplemental brief. Shane was half convinced he wasn't human. It didn't matter when Shane came. Afternoon allotted time, yard time, hell if he skipped lunch and was escorted to the tiny attorney's office on base where he'd insisted to have set up shop just until case was done; Chisholm was always awake and working.

Nevertheless, he attached scanned copies of the buried intake forms, witness interview logs with Emir's name crossed off, even a memo that referenced "culling unreliable testimony for clarity"—a memo no decent prosecutor would ever want to see daylight.

When Shane saw the final packet, thick enough to kill a man if you threw it hard enough, he felt something he hadn't in a long, long time.

Not just hope.

Momentum.

By late April, the appellate court issued a terse, barely-contained order: government counsel was to respond fully to the new evidence.

The prosecutors sputtered like a car with water in the gas tank. First, they claimed "administrative oversight." Then they suggested Emir's interview had been "informal" and therefore "non-material." Finally, in a last desperate ploy, they implied the document might have been fabricated after the fact—a theory Chisholm shredded in one blistering reply backed by chain-of-custody records and timestamps from 1997.

It was a bloodbath.

Even the appeals judges, seasoned career officers with plenty of reason to protect the system's dignity, couldn't ignore the stink rising from the case.

On 12 May 1999, the ruling came down.

The air inside the visiting room felt different that day. Sharper. Charged.

Chisholm came in late, a thick envelope tucked under his arm. His usual cocky grin was nowhere in sight. Instead, he dropped into the chair across from Shane and laid the envelope on the table with a soft thud.

"Congratulations, brother," he said simply.

Shane stared.

Chisholm opened the envelope, sliding out the typed order with a flourish. "Court's granting you a new trial. Official language is 'based on newly discovered exculpatory evidence, material to the outcome, improperly withheld from the defense.'" He grinned. "That's fancy talk for 'we got their asses dead to rights.'"

Shane didn't touch the paper at first. Didn't speak. He just sat there, breathing hard through his nose, shoulders rigid.

He should've felt triumphant. Should've jumped up and whooped like some of the other guys did when they won appeals.

Instead, he felt...cautious. Wary. Like a man stepping onto a frozen pond, waiting for the crack under his boots.

"They're ordering your transfer back to Fort Bragg for proceedings," Chisholm said after a second. "Prep meetings. New defense team, though I'm staying on. Maybe a real shot this time."

Shane finally leaned forward, picking up the paper, feeling the fine texture of it under his fingertips. He forced himself to ask, voice low, "How bad are they gonna fight it?"

"They'll fight," Chisholm said. "Every inch. But the tide's turned, Shane. They can't bury this anymore. You're getting another bite at the apple."

Another battle. Another set of lawyers and judges and uniforms who would look at him like a problem they didn't want to deal with.

But it was something. It was a crack in the wall.

They were packing up when Shane, still gripping the edge of the table like it might vanish, finally asked: "Mike...what if they try to say Emir's lying? That he's confused, or wrong?"

Chisholm shrugged like he'd been waiting for it.

"Well, if it comes to that..." he said, voice casual, "Milo promised me a real trump card."

Shane blinked. "Trump card?"

Chisholm grinned. "Got a few of his medic buddies to make sure it's under legal and court-admissible 'evidences' rules."

"What the hell is it?" Shane asked, half-exasperated, half-hopeful.

Chisholm just chuckled, slapping the file closed with a crisp thwack. "Let's just say...you better not mind toddlers at your trial."

Shane stared. "Toddlers?"

"Yep."

He clapped Shane on the shoulder as he passed, whistling a little tune under his breath like a man without a care in the world.

***

The appeals court ruling trembled a little in his hand, the weight of it starting to settle across his shoulders.

A new trial.

A real shot.

However, he also knew it wasn't over. Not by a damn sight. They weren't gonna welcome him back with parades and medals. Hell, they might even come after him harder this time, angrier for being embarrassed.

Still.

He tucked the ruling into the waistband of his pants, under the cheap prison shirt, where no one else could touch it. It wasn't freedom yet.

But it was *close enough to taste.*

And for the first time in too damn long, Specialist Shane Alexander let himself believe that God willing, he was gonna walk out of this nightmare standing tall.

That night, he had another task cut out for him. For the first time in over a year, Shane sat cross-legged on the thin mattress in his cell, surrounded by a scatter of letters.

He hadn't touched them before. Not really. Christmas, he'd ripped open a card from his parents, stared at it for a long time, then stuffed it under the mattress like it burned. The rest had piled up. Mail call came twice a week, and he'd ignored it, told himself it didn't matter.

But now, with the court ruling tucked safely into his waistband and a future cracking open just an inch in front of him, he let himself reach.

He sorted the envelopes with a slow, mechanical hand.

Some were neat, carefully addressed in looping cursive. Some were scrawled in angry block letters. A few were postmarked overseas—Germany, England, even one from Sarajevo that he turned over twice before setting it aside.

The first letter he opened was short. Kind words, mostly. Some woman in Minnesota thanking him for "doing your duty, whatever the cost." Another from a schoolteacher in Texas: "My class says thank you. We pray for you."

He set those aside carefully, a little stunned. Civilians. Regular people. Some of them still saw him as more than a headline.

A kid from Kentucky had sent him a drawing—stick figures holding American flags. A woman from Vermont wrote a rambling letter about her brother, who served in Korea, and said she knew what it was like to have a good man railroaded.

One international letter, typed neatly in French, simply read:

"Nous savons. Courage."

We know. Courage.

Another letter came from Pakistan, neatly handwritten, no wasted words. It was from a military analyst at a think tank in Islamabad. A man who'd seen wars come and go, governments rise and fall.

"In every country, at every time, there are people whose honor outlives their governments.

Politics erases the living, but history remembers the dead.

Hold fast. Truth is not owned by borders.

— A Friend."

Shane didn't know what to make of it exactly, but he folded it and set it carefully atop the French letter. Something about it settled heavy and sure in his gut, like an anchor.

There was another from Australia—barely legible handwriting on rough brown paper.

"Brother in arms,

Heard about the stitch-up from our news down here. Bastards love their scapegoats.

You stood your ground when it counted. That's all that matters, mate.

Don't let 'em take your soul with the rest of it.

— Danny, 1RAR, retired."

(He had to think a moment before remembering 1RAR was 1st Battalion, Royal Australian Regiment. Good infantrymen. Tough sons of bitches.)

The letter from an ANZAC engineer was more straightforward.

"Your truth will not be buried. The earth doesn't contain foul for too long.

-A Sister in Unifrom"

Similarly, the small envelope from the Philippines, written in careful English, was simple:

"To the American soldier:

You are not forgotten. Men of honor have brothers across oceans.

Fight your battle with dignity."

No signature. Just a small, hand-drawn sun, like the one on their national flag.

From Thailand came a bright, almost childlike postcard — an old Buddhist temple painted in gold.

On the back, someone had written:

"Even in the deepest night, the lotus blooms.

Courage, brother.

— With Respect."

Shane turned the card over a few times. Simple words. But somehow it hit harder than most of the long speeches. He sat there, foreign stamps and broken English scattered all around him, a little stunned. The world had been reaching out all this time. Not governments. Not politicians.

People.

Veterans who understood. Civilians who still had a working heart in their chest. He thought about Chisholm, fighting every damn day without a paycheck worth mentioning. He thought about Rodriguez and Wilson sending word through the grapevine even when it wasn't safe for them to do so.

One was printed from a typewriter, all caps, no return address: "KILLER. YOU DISGRACE THE UNIFORM."

Another letter, thick with bad grammar and worse spelling, accused him of being a pawn of "military-industrial murderers." Someone had smeared red ink across the bottom like blood.

Shane shrugged and shoved those into the trash can by his bunk without reading further.

He didn't have time for people who wanted a villain more than they wanted the truth.

Some of the letters were from NGOs, advocacy groups, journalists—asking if he wanted to "tell his side," offering "resources for wrongfully convicted veterans."

Even a psychologist from Maine had written, saying she'd "help free your mind if you ever wanted to talk."

Shane smiled grimly.

If they'd cared enough, they'd have been here already—walked through the snow, sweated under the Kansas sun, sat through the endless, soul-grinding days like Chisholm had.

It was easy to send a letter. It was harder to stay.

One envelope was thicker than the others.

Different handwriting—blocky but strong, the ink pressed deep into the page. No return address beyond a scribbled "Tennessee."

Inside was a single sheet, written in the same rough hand. Words misspelled here and there, scratched out and fixed in the margins.

"Being in the army's standing for them that can't stand for themselves. Even if them bastards in suits forget it. Ain't no president or senator ever fought no real war, but they sure love sending boys off to bleed for 'em.

You remember this, son.

You don't fire on no kid, no woman, no good man. But if any of 'em stand up tryin' to rip away the dream of a better tomorrow—you damn well fire 'til you can't lift your arms no more.

That's the job. Ain't no medals in it. Ain't no clean victories.

But it's worth it.

Don't let 'em turn you mean, inside or out. Don't let 'em make you a monster wearin' a good man's skin.

America's still got a place for you, soldier.

We'll be waitin'.

— Joshua and Lana Laughlin,

<u>Proud</u> American Parents."

At the bottom, a heavy underline under "proud," like they wanted to hammer the word straight into his bones.

The name made Shane blink.

Laughlin.

It twisted something deep in his chest.

Staff Sergeant Laughlin. Maybe they were related or maybe not; perhaps these Laughlins had served too—probably knew the same bitter truths—that wars were just rich men's games played with poor boys' blood.

He reread it twice before folding the letter carefully, smoothing out the creases like it was something holy.

It didn't fix anything. Didn't make the walls disappear. But it…eased something sharp inside him. Just a little.

By the end, the pile was thinner. The light outside his cell door had faded to soft gray, the guards switching shifts. He sat there a long time, the best letters laid out like stepping stones in front of him.

Proof that not everybody had gone blind.

Proof that maybe—maybe—he wasn't alone after all.

He closed his eyes and breathed deep, the rough paper smell filling his lungs.

Let them come.

Let the bastards in suits rage and lie and claw.

He wasn't backing down.

Not this time.

Twenty One

Return Fire

June 1999 Fort Bragg, North Carolina

The sun hung high, thick with Carolina heat, as the transport bus hissed to a stop outside the Fort Bragg JAG offices. Shane Alexander stepped off second in the line. He didn't look around. No stolen glances at the base signs or the trees. No breath held like he was home. Because he wasn't.

He was harder now—leaner, face tighter, jaw always set like something inside had broken but welded itself back shut. His Class A uniform still fit, but the drape wasn't the same. Prison had sanded off the shine. Even his shoes, freshly polished, looked wrong under the green.

Chisholm waited near the steps, sleeves rolled, tie loosened, flipping through a binder like it owed him money. When he saw Shane, he gave a small nod.

"Welcome back to the land of bureaucratic warfare."

Shane gave a grunt that might've been a greeting. "They make you dress like that for court now?"

"Figured I'd match the circus," Chisholm said, flipping a page. "We start tomorrow. Pretrial motions. And the prosecution's already sweating. I've filed for discovery violations, evidentiary suppression, and just for fun—an affidavit from a very irritated goat herder named Emir Begović."

Shane exhaled through his nose. "What are they saying?"

"That he couldn't possibly see what he saw. Visibility, elevation, direction of wind—I mean, we're one step away from them blaming the moon."

"They using Article 36 to keep it under wraps?"

"For now," Chisholm muttered. "But they're running out of clean corners to hide the dirt. Court's ordered them to produce the full files. Including every 'miscellaneous' document they never turned over."

They walked into the courthouse in silence.

The hearing room smelled like coffee and copier toner. A military panel, three officers in dress greens, sat on the bench. No jury—this was pretrial, just the law being hammered into shape before the show began.

Prosecutors spoke first—Major Kilburn, lean and sharp, delivered an icy defense of procedure. They hadn't "withheld" Begović's statement, he claimed. They'd "omitted it based on questions of credibility." After all, he was a civilian, standing nearly four hundred meters away. No military training. No way to verify line of sight.

Chisholm stood slow, calm.

"Permission to play a recording."

He didn't wait. A scratchy audio clip played. An older male voice, speaking deliberate English. "I saw them run from the market. I saw the soldiers take cover. One soldier stood, the tall one with the black vest. He fired. The others, the attackers—they were not retreating. They turned back, firing over the carts. He shot last, yes. But he shot at men who were still trying to kill. There was no pause."

Silence.

"That's Mr. Begović," Chisholm said. "Interviewed in 1998. Never disclosed to the defense. Never included in trial evidence."

The panel shifted. The legal officer scribbled something.

Kilburn cleared his throat. "Objection to admissibility—this interview was not verified through NATO intelligence protocols, and—"

"He was interviewed *by* your own team," Chisholm snapped. "And conveniently discarded when he didn't match the story your office chose to prosecute."

No one moved.

Chisholm straightened. "Your Honors, this is not a question of credibility. This is about *access*. My client has the right to confront *all* evidence. Not just the bits the government found useful."

That stuck.

The judges recessed. When they returned an hour later, the ruling was unanimous: Begović's testimony was admissible. The prosecution was ordered to release *everything* from the initial CID investigation. No redactions. No excuses.

By week's end, the whispers on base had grown louder.

To some, Shane was a lit fuse. A bad precedent. A soldier who broke protocol and still might walk free. But to others—especially the combat vets—he was exactly the kind of guy they *wanted* in a firefight. Orders or no, he'd fired last because the threat hadn't stopped. That counted for something.

In the chow hall, in the motor pool, at the range—soldiers talked.

One NCO put it plain: "Hell, if Alexander's guilty, then I'm guilty ten times over for Fallujah."

Another leaned across the table: "He didn't shoot civvies. He shot back."

***

Shane found Laughlin by accident.

Late Friday, he was walking past the old gym when he spotted him—Staff Sergeant Laughlin, outside the back lot, smoking, wearing civvies, head shaved tighter than before.

Shane stopped cold.

Laughlin looked over. Blinked once. "Alexander?" He then nodded and flicked ash. "Figured you'd look taller coming back from Leavenworth."

Shane didn't smile. Just walked over, stood a few feet away.

They didn't speak for a while. The smoke drifted sideways in the heavy air.

"I read the affidavits," Laughlin finally said. "Begović. That woman—Na'ada, right?"

Shane nodded.

"They put a few of them in front of me. Back then. I never got full names. Just photos. She wasn't one of 'em."

"You ever tell 'em what you really saw?" Shane asked, quietly.

Laughlin looked off. "Mostly. Enough. But not all of it."

Shane waited.

Laughlin sighed. "They had me meet with a couple higher-ups from NATO command. Day before my testimony. Colonel Jervis. Some guy from CJTF-HQ. They didn't tell me to lie. Not directly. But they said if I gave the impression that things got *too* chaotic, it'd raise questions. They wanted it clean. Neat."

"Because of the Rules of Engagement."

"I mean, I'd said it in front of the jury, so did Fitz, but," Laughlin sighed. "We were losing the hearts and minds game. Too many reports of friendly fire. Too many gray zones."

"So you shaded it behind the scenes?"

"I shaded it," Laughlin said. Then looked him dead in the eye. "But I never said you fired on unarmed people. I never said you were reckless. I just... let the room assume there might've been a moment where you didn't have to shoot. And that's what they ran with."

Shane's jaw flexed. "You know that last guy was still armed."

"I do now."

Shane looked down. "Why didn't you say it?"

Laughlin didn't answer for a long time. Then: "I was tired, son. Tired of seeing the mission get screwed, tired of CID, tired of lawyers asking me what fear *looks like*. I figured—hell, maybe it was just easier to let 'em have their scapegoat. One guy. Neat."

They stood there. Then Shane said, "Still easier now?"

Laughlin crushed the cigarette out on the pavement. "No."

They didn't say goodbye.

Later that night, Chisholm found Shane at the barracks.

"Laughlin talked?" he asked.

Shane didn't look up. "Yeah. Didn't lie. Just played dumb."

"Fits the pattern."

Shane gave him a long look. "This going anywhere? Really?"

Chisholm nodded. "With the Begović file found and the court's ruling, yeah. I'd say it is. But it's not done."

He leaned against the bunk frame. "If we win this motion, we get a new trial. No guarantee of acquittal. Just the chance to try again. But this time—with *everything*."

Shane leaned back, arms crossed. "And if we lose?"

"We appeal again," Chisholm said. "Or we go to Congress. Hell, I'll throw it on the front page of *Stars and Stripes* if I have to."

Shane grunted. "You really believe in this."

Chisholm gave a slow smile. "Enough to carry through."

***

Fort Bragg – JAG Office, East Wing

A week had passed. Shane sat alone in the corner of Chisholm's cramped temporary office—bare cinderblock walls, a dying ficus in the corner, and files stacked like sandbags on every surface. The overhead light buzzed faintly. The room smelled faintly of toner, must, and old floor polish.

He sat with elbows on his knees, reading a yellow legal pad. Chisholm's notes were in a kind of looping shorthand that looked part-military, part-cursive chaos. Shane read slow. Prison had made him patient.

The door opened without a knock.

Private Rodriguez leaned in, uniform faded and soft from wear. "Sir?"

Shane blinked. For a second, he didn't move. Then he stood, slowly.

Behind Rodriguez, Specialist Wilson stepped in, carrying a manila envelope and looking more awkward than a boot in a promotion board.

Rodriguez nodded. "We heard you were back. Thought maybe we'd check in."

Shane didn't say anything for a beat.

"Didn't think I'd see either of you again."

Rodriguez gave a crooked smile. "Yeah. Me neither."

Wilson cleared his throat and held out the envelope. "We... uh, came to turn this over. It's my personal notes from that day. I wasn't sure if it'd help, but I wrote it all down back when it happened. Stuff I saw. But I sure as hell said all of it when I was asked."

Chisholm's head popped into the doorway behind them. "I was wondering when you two were going to show up. You sit out the first trial, I figured you had something to get off your chests."

"We didn't sit out. We were told to do so. We did get inter-viewed...and we answered. All of it." Rodriguez sat down uninvited. "We did what they told us. CID said stick to the facts and don't spec-ulate. But when they started twisting it to make it sound like Shane went off-book, we got quiet. Too quiet cause we'd told 'em that it wasn't the case, but I guess our words all twisted made perfect sense to them during trial."

Wilson stood there, shifting on his feet. "I didn't want to tank my career by arguing after the trial...seemed pointless."

Chisholm took the envelope. "You're saying you'll testify this time?"

Wilson looked at Shane. "If they let me. I'll tell it clean again. I re-member the second they opened fire. I remember the kid crying. I re-member Taylor bleeding out in the corner."

Rodriguez leaned forward. "And I remember you didn't fire until we were already pinned. You didn't panic. You waited."

Shane rubbed his jaw. Chisholm nodded. "Good. I'll need you both in prep by Tuesday."

As they left, Rodriguez looked back once. "You look different, man."

Shane didn't respond. The door closed behind them.

***

Judge's Quarters, Fort Bragg Command HQ

The next morning, news came fast—an administrative bulletin posted outside the courtroom door like it was a notice for fire drills or base closures.

Brigadier General Nolan had filed for recusal.

In the interest of maintaining the integrity of military judicial proceedings, and to prevent any perception of bias...

The language was clinical. Distant. But it meant everything.

Chisholm stared at the bulletin. Then, slowly, he smiled. "Bastard blinked."

Shane stood beside him, unreadable. "Who replaces him?"

"Colonel Edward Matthews. Judge Advocate since Desert Storm. Three years in Kosovo command rotation. Known for being *annoyingly* impartial. Exactly the kind of guy you want when you're holding a loaded case and you're the underdog."

Shane narrowed his eyes. "That help us?"

"Oh, it doesn't just help us," Chisholm said. "It means the prosecution doesn't get a friend on the bench anymore. No more leading questions slipped past the gavel. No more conveniently timed recesses. Matthews plays it clean."

He folded the bulletin and handed it to Shane.

"Our fight just got fairer."

Shane read the name again.

Matthews.

Then he folded the paper and slid it into his jacket pocket like a letter from the front. Chisholm watched him for a moment, then tipped his head toward the hallway. "Walk with me."

They moved through the corridor in step, past offices still quiet at that hour. Chisholm stuffed his hands into his coat pockets and said, "Look, I know you're carrying a boulder uphill. But don't drag chains with it."

Shane gave a faint grunt, not quite in agreement.

"I'm not telling you to forgive anybody. You got a right to be pissed. Hell, if I were in your boots, I'd be halfway to burning this whole goddamn place down."

They rounded the stairwell, heels echoing on the concrete.

"But you can't afford to burn hot when they're watching. Not in front of the panel. Not in uniform. You want to be mad? Be mad on your own time. In court, I need a soldier. Calm. Cold."

Shane didn't stop walking, but he turned slightly. "You think I'm gonna snap?"

"No," Chisholm said flatly. "But I think you're still punishing yourself more than anyone else is. And that ain't helping the case."

They passed the old water fountain near the briefing room, the same one Shane remembered from pre-deployment briefings. A ghost of who he was stared back in the metal reflection.

"You saw Wilson and Rodriguez," Chisholm continued. "They tried. Maybe late, maybe soft—but they came. That counts for something. Let 'em do the right thing now."

Shane said nothing for a while. Then: "They ain't come for me. Not the way I woulda."

Chisholm stopped, waiting. Shane faced him, voice quiet but edged. "They came because they're scared of their conscience, or their careers, or both. But they ain't showed up when it coulda changed a damn thing. You're the only one who did."

That caught Chisholm off guard. Especially given how he'd noticed that Shane reverted to a different accent whenever he was raw. He looked away, jaw working. Then he chuckled softly. "Well. That might be the nicest backhanded compliment I've ever gotten from a young man facing forty-three years."

Shane didn't smile, but something in his posture loosened—just slightly.

Chisholm clapped him on the shoulder. "Just keep your shoes under you and your hands out of your pockets. I'll take care of the rest."

They turned the corner and headed toward the prep room. The real fight was still ahead. But finally, Shane Alexander wasn't walking into it alone.

Twenty Two

Across Borders

Fort Bragg, July 12, 1999

The courtroom was packed well before 0800. Rows of pressed uniforms filled the benches—majors, captains, MPs in berets. The media huddled like birds on wire in the gallery's corner, notebooks primed, miniature recorders clutched like relics of an age that still trusted tape. Shane's parents sat in the front row behind the defense table, stiff with quiet resolve. Mary clutched her husband's forearm like a lifeline; Timothy's jaw hadn't unclenched since he entered the room.

The panel—six junior enlisted soldiers and one senior NCO——wore their Class As, stiff collars and ribbons in place, the solemnity of the occasion weighing every uniform. Combat boots scuffed beneath navy slacks. One juror, a female Corporal and from the 82nd airborne, had her hair in a tight bun so sharp it could cut glass. The rest sat poker-faced, flipping through the thin folders placed before them.

The prosecution opened with markedly less fire than they had during Shane's first trial. Captain Leland, younger than his predecessor but just as sharp, stood behind the lectern with his notes neatly bound.

"Members of the panel," he began, "this case is not about heroism, nor is it about politics. It is about discipline under fire and the laws that govern our conduct in combat. The accused—Specialist Shane Alexander—fired his weapon during a peacekeeping operation in violation of established Rules of Engagement. Our position is not that Specialist Alexander acted out of malice, but rather that he allowed emotion, fear, and confusion to override his training, leading to the unnecessary deaths of individuals who no longer posed a threat."

He walked slowly past the jury box. "War is chaotic. That is understood. But chaos does not absolve accountability. We will present evidence that shows a pause in hostile fire prior to the final shots, that the situation had de-escalated, and that Specialist Alexander—whether knowingly or not—continued to engage targets outside the scope of lawful self-defense."

There were no dramatics. No high-handed moralizing. Just measured certainty. Calculated restraint.

Chisholm watched from his seat, arms folded.

When it came time to rise, he did so with the quiet deliberation of someone winding a spring—not flashy, not loud. But ready.

"Members of the panel," he began. "You will hear many things over the course of this trial. You'll hear about protocols, timelines, ROEs printed in black ink, and then interpreted through red mist. But I want to start with one word. One. *Reaction.*"

He let it hang.

"In firefights—real ones, not the ones on range day—there are no pauses. There are bursts. Surges. Screams. Misdirection. Fear. And through that, soldiers have to make choices—split-second, muscle-memory choices that decide who lives and who dies."

Chisholm reached for the clicker and nodded to the screen.

A video began to play. The room darkened. Subtitled footage of Emir Begović, seated in his small home in Sarajevo, filled the projection wall. His voice came through clearly in translation.

"There was *no* pause," Begović said. "There were bullets. Grenades. Screaming. People running. I ducked behind my market cart and heard the shots—three, maybe four. And before I stood again, it was over. But there was no pause. No silence. It did not stop and then start again. It was constant."

The tape ended. Chisholm paused.

"This man was not contacted in the first trial. Why? Because his name was buried in untranslated documents in the original investigation files held by Major Davis. We have those logs now. And they show that Begović was interviewed—twice. But neither translation nor summary made it into the court record."

He placed another sheet on the evidence display. A memo from Milo, dated six months earlier.

"This is former NATO translator, Milo Jovanović's written statement confirming he interviewed Begović while attached to the investigation. His notes—gone. Vanished. But this memo was saved to a separate folder that hadn't been scrubbed. You'll notice on-duty supervisor, Colonel Harrison's signature authorizing deletion of duplicate reports 'for clarity.' There's nothing clear about erasing a man's testimony."

The prosecution objected.

"Sir, unless the defense is accusing a superior officer of deliberate suppression, this line of argument is speculative—"

"It's not speculative," Chisholm fired back. "It's *documented.* We'll call Milo to testify after recess. For now, I'll move on."

He flipped to the next file.

"Next, we'll hear from Lubov Maarijen, a civilian witness, female, aged 37 at the time of the incident; whose husband, Stratimir, gave us a sworn affidavit stating that days after her initial statements—ones that described the final shooter as *armed*—she was called in again for 'follow-up.' After that, she returned dazed, exhausted. 'My head hurts,' she told him. 'I just want to sleep.' Days later, a military liaison told him she'd been diagnosed with *neurological instability.* Disqualified as a witness. Not because she lied. But because she couldn't be relied on."

He stepped forward. "Tell me—what does that sound like to you?"

The prosecution stood. "Even if this account is accurate, the defense is implying coercion without evidence. There are ethics here. If witnesses were dismissed on psychological grounds, it was for their protection, not some cloak-and-dagger cover-up."

Chisholm didn't flinch. "I don't doubt the system wanted her *protected.* But from what? From the truth?"

He held up her translated statement from Bosnia: *'The man who fired last had a rifle. I saw it. He was not surrendering.'*

"And yet she was not present in the first trial. You want ethics? Where were they when her voice was silenced?"

The courtroom was quiet. Even the scratch of reporters' pens had gone still.

Chisholm turned back to the jury. "I'm not here to paint Shane Alexander as a saint. He's not. He's a soldier. One who acted under fire, with the noise of war in his ears, and saved the lives of the people around him. This is not about rules on paper. This is about how war *actually* works."

He returned to his seat and leaned toward Shane.

"Hold steady," he muttered. "We just made contact."

Shane sat motionless, but his jaw ticked once. Then again.

He didn't nod.

But he didn't flinch, either.

The room quieted as Specialist Shane Alexander took the stand.

He raised his right hand, swore the oath, and sat—back straight, hands clasped lightly in front of him. His dress uniform was crisp. Collar starched, dress shoes mirror-shined. The only irregularity was the look in his eyes—something worn in, like a man who'd walked out of a storm still soaked to the bone.

Chisholm approached slowly.

"Specialist Alexander, for the benefit of the panel—walk us through the events of May 4th, 1997. The moment you opened fire. Start from what you saw."

Shane nodded once.

"We were at the market checkpoint in Kiseljak. Rotation was nearly done. I remember that. It was cold, not cloudy but cold—like, the kind that settles on you. I was posted on Post One, operating under sector Bravo, with Specialist Jeremiah Wilson, Private Miguel Rodriguez, and Specialist Loran Taylor," he paused, sighing, "my best friend."

He looked down for a second. Cleared his throat.

"There was chatter on the local net about a group of Serbs moving toward the area. Not confirmed hostile. Just movement. Staff Sergeant Laughlin had checked in earlier. We stayed alert, but nothing out of the ordinary until I saw two of them come through the vendor stalls—moving weird. Not browsing. Just... watching."

"Did you make a call?" Chisholm asked.

"I gave a quiet heads-up to Staff Sergeant on the radio when I noticed separate movement uphill. The rest were around in person. Staff Sergeant mentioned it in his interviews, too. Anyway, we shifted. Didn't draw rifles up yet. Then everything happened at once."

"Go on, Soldier."

"There was no warning. No alert. We were watching vendors pack up. Kids chasing a soccer ball. A woman was haggling over tomatoes. Some guy trying to sew clothes in his booth. Then a shot went off. Just cracked through the air like that. Hit a civilian. Then came two more—snaps from the alley near the butcher stall."

"Did you make a call?" Chisholm asked.

"There wasn't time. We were turning carts and objects over to create cover and barriers. Taylor shouted something, moved to pull a woman out of the way. That's when he was hit. Right in the neck. Dropped like his knees gave out. I was already moving—returning fire. I saw muzzle flashes behind a kiosk, at least three shooters, maybe four."

His hands closed slightly.

"They weren't yelling anything. No warning. No demands. Just shooting into the crowd. People ran. Screamed. I got behind a crate and laid down suppressive fire. One attacker dropped. Then another ran and left behind a van."

Chisholm asked, "And the final shot?"

Shane's eyes darkened.

"That last guy moved again. Not fast. Just a shift. His shoulders squared like he was lining something up, and a strap on the side of his shoulder. I *knew* he was armed. I didn't wait. I fired. Two shots center mass."

Chisholm leaned in. "Why?"

"Because Taylor was bleeding out. Because the crowd wasn't clear. Because I didn't know if the man behind that van had a rifle, or if another burst was coming. There was no pause. No ceasefire. I wasn't counting seconds—I was trying to keep people alive."

Shane looked at the panel.

"They say I should've waited. That the threat had passed. But it hadn't. Not in my eyes. You don't stop in the middle of an ambush and ask for a status report."

A pause.

"I didn't fire out of rage. I fired because no one else could."

Chisholm stepped back. "No further questions at this time."

Leland from the prosecution rose slowly. "Specialist, you seem very clear on the events. More so than in your original testimony. Why is that?"

"Because I've had over a year to live inside that moment. *Every day.*"

Leland raised an eyebrow. "And yet at the first trial, your account was emotional, inconsistent. This time, it's methodical. Some might say rehearsed."

Shane's voice didn't change. "It's not rehearsed, sir. It's just been lived."

Leland pressed, "You understand that according to ROE, the use of force must be proportional and based on an immediate threat?"

"Yes, sir."

"So how could you be certain the final individual posed an immediate threat?"
Shane looked him dead in the eye.

"I couldn't. That's the truth. I wasn't certain. But I *believed* he did. And in combat, sometimes that belief is the difference between getting home alive or in a flag-draped box."

He shifted in his seat. "We're trained to assess, to verify—but no one trains you for the moment your best friend's lying dead six feet from you, and someone's still moving with a rifle-length shadow behind a van. I made a call. Not a perfect one. But a professional one."

Leland tried again. "So you admit you weren't sure?"

"I admit I didn't have the luxury of being sure."

Silence settled again. And with it, something new. Not sympathy. Not agreement. But understanding. When the cross ended, Chisholm leaned across the table and whispered, "You just bought us something better than mercy, Shane."

Shane raised an eyebrow.

"Respect."

Shane had barely finished his last sentence when one of the panel members—a captain with a reddish buzz cut and a sharp brow—leaned forward.

"Colonel, I believe a brief recess would be appropriate," he said, glancing down the table.

Colonel Edward Matthews, presiding over the Article 32 hearing, gave Shane a look that wasn't quite concern, but close. His fingers tapped once on the table. "Granted. Twenty-minute recess."

The gavel didn't bang, but the tension dropped all the same.

Shane stayed seated for a beat too long. His breathing had thinned out, chest rising faster than it should've. The room was cold, but sweat had beaded under his collar. He stood without a word, following Chisholm and the others to the adjoining room they'd been given as defense prep.

Inside, the small space buzzed with energy.

One of Chisholm's assistants, a tall, tubby fellow in a wrinkled blue button-up, was flipping through a file like he'd lost a winning lottery ticket in it. The other—a much shorter man, thin as a flagpole and twitchy—was hunched over a legal pad marking something rapid-fire in red pen. Neither stopped talking.

"Jury's following. You saw the second guy from the left, nodding? If even one is engaged, the rest will lean," the tall one said.

"Yeah, but if the prosecutor leans on the ROE clause again, we need to tie it back to actual field conditions. Need that—what's the term you used, the 'mud math' argument."

Chisholm stood in the corner near the open window, rubbing his temples like they hurt worse than anything in Bosnia ever had. A cigarette hung from his lip, barely clinging on. He hadn't lit it, just chewed the filter like a man trying to smoke a thought.

Shane opened his mouth to say something, but a voice beat him to it—accented and oddly cheerful.

"Mike!"

They all turned.

In the doorway stood a lanky man with the build of a hero in a business meeting—tall, narrow shoulders, and long arms that made his sleeves look perpetually too short. His dress shirt was blindingly white and tucked into dark slacks held up by a pair of suspenders, like he was trying out for a courtroom drama set in 1954. Thin-rimmed glasses sat on a long nose, and a sweep of blond hair, more gold than yellow, flopped across his forehead.

Slavic features. High cheekbones, narrow chin. Somehow, both sharp and soft. He might've been handsome in that lean, rakish way—if he hadn't smelled like he'd gargled with spoiled milk and ashtrays.

Shane instinctively turned his face away. Chisholm was downplaying it; Milo's breath was like a chemical fire.

"Milo," Chisholm said, straightening, sliding the cigarette behind his ear. "You get everything lined up?"

"Of course," Milo said brightly, stepping inside. "All things in place. Transcripts reviewed. Letters notarized. You will have them if judge makes fuss."

Chisholm nodded. "Appreciate it. Just keep it simple. You're up first, hopefully. Confirm you translated for NATO, show them your official appointment. That's all we need."

Milo beamed like someone had complimented his shoes. "Yes. Of course. They will see. I made it all—how do you say—clean."

He tapped the folder tucked under his arm, as if that settled everything.

"You wanna know what's the feel inside?" Chisholm asked, rubbing his jaw.

"I think from your look," Milo shrugged one shoulder. "They are quiet. Listening. That is already good, yes?"

He smiled wider, too wide.

Shane watched him closely. Milo moved like a man always three seconds ahead of the room, like he already knew how the conversation would land. There was something rehearsed in his casualness.

Chisholm motioned toward the table. "And the trump card? Got her dressed for the American people?"

Milo's eyes lit up like a kid on Christmas. "Oh, yes. Skirt below knee, she insisted *ankle length*, scarf—not silk, but looks like it. Little heels. Very... palatable. Shoes from Germany. Expensive. She looks like someone's sad cousin who just wants justice."

Everyone was quiet while Chisholm gave a slow nod. "Good. People find their humanity when the other person looks like them or at least *tries* to." He handed Milo a cigarette, which one of his assistants had pulled out of his pocket.

Milo's brows knotted. "That's harsh, is it not?"

"Harsh or not, it's the truth, pal." He replied and lit it up before Milo could protest, and told him to take a deep inhale.

Shane, on the other hand, didn't say anything. He had no idea who they were talking about. Some witness, he guessed. Probably civilian. Maybe one of the women from the market.

Then, Chisholm's tone dropped just low enough that the assistants stopped talking. "Alexander," he said.

Shane looked up.

Chisholm squinted at him like he was gauging wind direction. "I need you to hold together a little longer. Just a bit. You did what needed doing in there. Don't let it crack now."

Shane nodded once. Not stiff, not slow—just steady. They didn't speak again as they reentered the courtroom. The panel was already returning to their seats. Colonel Matthews gave a nod toward Chisholm.

"Defense, call your next witness."

Chisholm rose. "The defense calls Mr. Milo Jovanović."

Milo walked to the stand like a man arriving late to his own dinner party—cordial, upright, and mildly amused. His suspenders didn't shift an inch as he raised his hand for the oath, his round glasses catching the light.

Once sworn in, Chisholm moved toward the table with a small stack of documents.

"State your name and occupation."

"Milo Jovanović. I am a certified translator and linguist. Formerly attached to NATO Civil Affairs, Kiseljak Sector, from 1997 to 1998. I translated and filed civilian testimonies—Bosnian, Croatian, Serbian, Arabic, even Turkic—whatever came in."

He spoke perfect English, but slipped between registers like gears in an old truck. "I have the papers. All official. No... how do you say... made in garage."

Light chuckle from one of the civilian observers.

Chisholm gestured to the exhibit table, where three original translated statements had been placed: Emir Begović, Lubov Maarijen, and Na'ada Hussein.

"Mr. Jovanović, are these documents familiar to you?"

"Of course. I typed them. I remember Madam Lubov Maarijen had very large handwriting—loop like onion. Mr. Emir Begović was literate in both Serbian and Bosnian, clearly properly educated. Very nervous man, however. Miss Na'ada..." He paused. "She was the closest. She saw everything. Her hands were... shaking. She had a baby."

Chisholm didn't interrupt. Milo went on, adjusting his collar with one hand.

"In my records—my supervisor at the time, Major Keane, signed authorization—I have all three documents logged. Proper ID numbers, case designations. Not guesswork. This was a job. I didn't just ask people questions in a parking lot. I filed under the NATO system—digital and paper. I have records, yes?"

He produced a stamped NATO Civil-Military Cooperation document showing his role and the registration of all three witness statements.

Chisholm took it and handed it to the clerk to mark as Defense Exhibit 14.

The prosecution attorney, Leland, stood. His expression was all politeness, but the tone had a lean edge.

"Mr. Jovanović, these witnesses... particularly this one, Na'ada Hussein. According to the original trial file, her name is listed, yes. But there's no photograph. No personal file. No corroborating material. Nothing except a line of text—just a name."

Milo shrugged, but it wasn't dismissive—it was structured.

"Is not strange," he said. "This was post-war zone. We didn't get... passports and headshots. Some people gave their name, some refused. But she came back three days in a row. I spoke with her each time. I know what she saw. She did not invent gunfire or explosion."

"But you understand," Leland continued, "that in a post-conflict region, there were many false reports, impersonations, even fabricated statements. The court has no way of verifying this woman exists."

That got Milo's attention. He smiled slowly, almost like he was sad.

"She exists," he said softly. Then, more formally, "I brought her with me."

Leland blinked. "You what?"

"She is here. In America. I arranged a passport. Visa. Plane ticket. She is outside this building." He reached into his satchel and produced a small folder. "I have a passport copy. Visa stamp. Travel itinerary. You may inspect."

There was a murmur around the room—not loud, but enough that Matthews tapped the desk. Leland glanced at Chisholm, then back at Milo. "Why wasn't the prosecution notified in advance?"

Chisholm rose with both palms up. "We notified the court of our intent to introduce witness testimony as part of the defense's rebuttal phase. No rules violated. In fact, we even urged for prosecution to arrange for their own translator if they wanted to prove that Milo was impartial."

"And have they?" Matthews asked, not looking up, as he took the passport copy from the bailiff, scanned it, and then passed it back.

"Yes, sir," came Leland's response as he handed the ID for another linguistics expert, this time, court-appointed and not a witness. Mehmed Eleyas. "He will remain present to ensure fidelity during testimony."

Matthews nodded at that, too, focusing on the man seated on one of the back benches. Reddish hair and a common suit. Then he turned his head to Milo. "Mr. Jovanović, we may need to hear from this woman directly. For now, you're dismissed. You may remain in the gallery."

Milo stood, nodded once, and walked off like he'd just delivered a weather report. Behind the defense table, Chisholm allowed himself one sharp exhale. He didn't smile—but he came close. Shane didn't move, but a flicker of something lit in his chest.

Colonel Matthews adjusted his glasses and gave a curt nod.

"Per prior arrangement, the defense may now present the civilian witness. A court-appointed translator, Mr. Mehmed Eleyas, will remain present to monitor translation accuracy. Mr. Jovanović will act as intermediary translator for the witness."

He glanced toward the gallery.

"Bring her in."

The double doors eased open.

Na'ada Hussein stepped in slowly, her hand gripped around that of a small child who clung to her side. The boy couldn't have been more than three—he waddled beside her in little canvas shoes, his free hand dragging a toy truck along the floor.

The young woman looked presentable but visibly uneasy. She wore a soft pink blouse with long sleeves and a matching ankle-length skirt. Her scarf, a lighter shade of milky white, was pinned loosely at one shoulder and hung gently around her neck. Her light tan complexion had drained slightly with nerves, and her large, dark eyes shifted anxiously across the courtroom. The lower curve of her full lips trembled, as if she were trying not to cry.

At the threshold, she leaned down and whispered to the boy. He blinked up at her, then allowed one of the interpreter staffers to take his hand and lead him gently to a seat at the back. He went without fuss, too small to understand the weight of the room.

Na'ada moved forward alone. Milo Jovanović rose to meet her at the stand. Mehmed Eleyas took his seat off to the side, already holding a pen and notepad, prepared to monitor every word.

Colonel Matthews addressed her directly. "You are now under oath, Miss Hussein. Mr. Jovanović will translate your responses. Mr. Eleyas will verify the accuracy of the translation for the record. Please answer only what you saw and experienced. Nothing more."

Milo translated briefly, and Na'ada nodded. She responded in a soft voice. "Er, yes."

Chisholm rose from the defense table and approached carefully, posture easy, tone measured.

"Miss, could you tell the court where you were when the shooting began at the Kiseljak market?"

Milo translated down to matching Chisholm's tone for her. When she answered carefully, he did the same for the room.

"I was walking with my son and friend, Diniella Georgeiva. My son was just a baby then. There were gunshots. Someone shouted, then grabbed me, pushed me down behind a cart. There were more gunshots. I fell on my knees, but I held onto my son. The man who helped us—he... he was shot."

"And after that?"

"I stayed down. My son was crying. I was afraid to look. But I saw the Americans, some of them. One was firing. I remember he kept his head low and shouted at others. I didn't understand the words."

"You're saying you saw him fire his weapon?" Chisholm asked.

"Yes," she answered through Milo. "I did. I know that he did. But not at people in the market. He was firing toward the back, where the noise was loudest."

"Back? Where exactly were you?"

She paused, thought for a moment, then used her hands to gesture while speaking to Milo. He nodded, then explained, "She means from *behind the cart*. She was behind the cart, used as a barricade closest to Post One, she is pointing out that the shots came from the opposite, so that would be the market place."

"Objection, that could've been Specialist Alexander's fire!"

"No, because as per your own placements, Specialist Alexander was standing *by* the checkpoint," Chisholm answered Leland. "He can't fire from the market's side. His position was opposite."

"Overruled," Matthews called. "Continue."

Chisholm's brow furrowed slightly. "You saw the man fall?"

"Objection, unnecessarily connecting witnesses to the case creates bias."

Chisholm sighed. "She was close enough to smell his blood; there's already a close connection."

"Overruled."

After Milo translated, Na'ada nodded. Her eyes seemed to focus on a spot beyond the wall behind the judge. "He fell very near. Almost beside us. He didn't move. I touched his face. I—" Her voice cracked slightly before she continued. "I closed his eyes."

Chisholm nodded once. "Do you know who that man was?"

Na'ada shook her head slowly. "No names. But they showed me pictures before, in questioning. I pointed to his face. He was a very young man."

Chisholm held up an official headshot of Specialist Loran Taylor. He didn't name him, showed the room the picture, and asked Na'ada if she knew who this was. Her eyes almost welled with tears. She muttered something shakily to Milo, who urged her to speak up because Mehmed looked at them with suspicion. She repeated it louder, and Milo affirmed it.

"She says that's him. The dead one."

Chisholm stepped aside. "No further questions for now."

Leland stood almost immediately.

"Miss Hussein," he began with polite skepticism, "you say you were there, holding a child. Yet no photograph or full record of your testimony existed in the official trial files. Only your name. No ID card. No date of birth. Just a handwritten note."

Milo translated, and Na'ada, wiping her eyes, actually frowned. "I gave my name. I was there three times. They took notes. That's all I knew. No one asked for a photo."

Leland stepped forward, slowly.

"Do you expect this court to believe that in a chaotic firefight, while protecting a child and hiding behind an overturned cart, you could observe specific behavior? Such as who was firing where, or what their intent was?"

Na'ada's reply, after a steady pause, came low and level. "I know what I saw. I remember the face of the one who saved me. And I remember the face of the one who kept firing. He was not firing at us. He was trying to stop it."

Eleyas didn't interrupt. The translation had been fair. He merely made a note and nodded once toward the bench.

Leland's tone sharpened. "You say you saw this man's face and that he protected people. But again, no complete record of this identification exists. Why should we believe *you're* even who you claim to be?"

Na'ada's jaw clenched when Milo told her what was implied. Then Milo added something in English—not translated, but spoken directly to the court, his voice suddenly crisp.

"She is who she says she is. I brought her here myself. Her passport, visa, and entry documents are available. I arranged them through the U.S. Embassy in Sarajevo. She's not a name on a paper. She's in this room."

Na'ada spoke again, looking at Milo, who added, "And she was also allowed entry into the marketplace using the same ID earlier on the same day. The same checkpoint alongside Diniella and her son. The soldier who died, she claims, is one of those who'd checked her in after asking questions."

Chisholm, true to his nature, held up a document, stating it contained marked passages from both new and initial interviews conducted by MP Harrison. Specialist Wilson and Private Rodriguez both mention a woman, distinctly with Na'ada's features, and an infant. The list of entered civilians recorded that day by the Bravo squad also included her. He offered it to the bailiff.

There was a pause. Colonel Matthews looked over his glasses toward the prosecution table. Then, at the papers presented. "Mr. Leland, the documentation will be reviewed. The witness will remain seated."

Leland gave a short, clipped nod and returned to his seat.

Matthews turned back toward the translators. "Proceed. The court will continue to observe."

Na'ada shifted in her seat, visibly holding herself together. She blinked once toward the rear, where her son sat, sucking on his thumb. Then she faced forward again, hands folded tightly in her lap. Leland adjusted his tie and stepped back toward the witness box, pivoting just slightly to ensure both Na'ada and the jury could see him. He let the silence sit a moment too long before speaking.

"You said you saw the American soldier fire during the event. And that you later identified him from a photograph. But you're not a soldier or a trained observer. So I ask again: how can you be certain Specialist Alexander," he gestured to Shane at the defense table, "wasn't firing at civilians in that market?"

Milo translated without pause. Na'ada didn't answer right away. Her hands tightened in her lap, and she exhaled slowly before speaking.

"I was still there when it ended. I saw him afterwards too, helping in the tents. I spoke to others. My neighbors. People come together after tragedies...the war had brought whatever was left closer. They were hurt—some bleeding, some hiding. But no one said the Americans shot at them."

Milo's voice dropped slightly as he translated, respectful but clear. "They didn't know seconds or angles. They didn't count bullets. But they knew who helped and who didn't. They knew the young man in uniform did not harm them."

Leland tilted his head and pounced on a word.

"Helped? That sounds like opinion, not evidence."

"She is speaking to the environment of the aftermath," Chisholm cut in calmly, "and the collective memory of the locals. That's admissible under the context of general reputation evidence in a community."

Colonel Matthews nodded. "Sustained. The answer stands."

Leland hesitated, regrouping.

"And you expect this court to believe, with all due respect, that in a post-war region where facts are elusive and records missing, no one-no one at all—would've blamed the soldier if he had fired wildly? You think people would say nothing?"

Na'ada's reply, when it came, was razor-steady.

"In a war town, we have to put everything aside—religion, past grudges, even pain. We are family. We watch for one another...aside from those who wish to watch everything still burn. Even when we hate it. If a soldier had hurt someone, we would have known. We would have remembered. We do not forget that kind of thing."

Milo had paused briefly in translation but did not embellish it. Mehmed Eleyas gave no indication of error. Leland narrowed his eyes, shifting now, not to the witness but toward the child sitting in the rear. The little boy had fallen asleep sideways on the bench, drooling slightly. His fair skin was flushed pink around the cheeks and nose, and his light hair slightly tousled.

"And how do we even know that child is hers?" Leland asked suddenly. "He doesn't look anything like her. Not even close."

There was an audible shift in the room, low murmurs. Shane didn't move, but his jaw flexed once. Milo stared at Leland. He blinked once and said nothing. No translation.

Chisholm didn't rise—he only sighed, pinching the bridge of his nose. "Objection," he said flatly. "The prosecution appears to misunderstand how genetics work."

The courtroom laughed—low, restrained—but real. Matthews banged the gavel once and gave Leland a sharp look. "Watch your line of questioning."

Milo finally turned to Na'ada and translated the gist of it. She blinked, clearly insulted, and muttered something curt. "He takes after his dead father," Milo translated coldly. "You can check the IDs."

Chisholm stood slowly. "No further questions for the witness."

Leland, smart enough not to press further, gave a stiff nod and sat down.

Colonel Matthews leaned forward. "The witness may step down. Mr. Jovanović, thank you. Mr. Eleyas, your oversight is noted in the record."

Na'ada exited quietly, pausing only to scoop her sleeping child into her arms. Shane turned in his seat to look at her as she walked, her son's cheek pressed against her shoulder.

Matthews exhaled through his nose, then gestured.

"Closing arguments. Defense first."

Chisholm stood and walked forward with deliberate calm, hands clasped behind his back. He faced the jury squarely as Shane turned his attention forward.

"Ladies and gentlemen. This is not just a case about Specialist Alexander. This is a case about what we owe every soldier we send into harm's way. A presumption of innocence. A full review of facts. Not just fragments of paperwork. Not just assumptions. And certainly not silence passed off as truth."

He paused briefly, scanning their eyes.

"What you have now—what you did not have before—is the whole picture. Witnesses. Translations verified by the court. Civilian testimonies that were left out of the original trial, intentionally or otherwise. And a young man, barely in his twenties, who has sat in a cell every day knowing that his life was nearly destroyed by half a story."

He walked once along the rail, slow and steady.

"You have the full story now. The truth has waited long enough."

He nodded once and returned to his seat.

Leland rose next. He tried to echo authority, but his rhythm faltered.

"Members of the court, no one questions the chaos of war. Or the tragedy of loss. But clarity, even now, is in short supply. The defense wants you to believe the original trial was incomplete. But what was heard then—and what you've heard now—does not fully exonerate Specialist Alexander. It cannot explain all of his actions."

He glanced once at Shane, but it didn't land.

"You have a duty to evaluate not just the emotions here, but the law. We ask that you do so."

He sat down. There was no applause, no movement. Just silence.

Colonel Matthews looked out across the courtroom, his expression unreadable.

"We will recess. The jury will deliberate. All rise."

Twenty Three

Bullet for my Brother

Outside the courtroom, the hallway smelled faintly of old paper, floor polish, and tension too long held. The jury had retired behind closed doors. The rest of them were left to wait.

Chisholm's two assistant attorneys had already carved out a corner by the water cooler. Backs against the wall, jackets off, they tore into a post-mortem of the proceedings with all the sharpness of a blade drawn for the third time. A few paces away, Chisholm stood beside Shane, who had taken up a spot near the corridor benches. The older man had one hand on his hip, the other gesturing occasionally—not sharp, but steady, grounding.

"You'll hear some noise when they come back," he was saying lowly. "Chairs scraping. Feet shifting. Don't watch them first. Watch the judge. Always watch the judge. That'll tell you everything before the words do."

Shane didn't answer. His eyes had drifted, lazily, to the end of the corridor where the benches sat quietly in a streak of dust-lit light.

Na'ada was there. Her scarf had shifted slightly, exposing a few dark strands at the nape of her neck. She sat on the bench like she was waiting for a bus that might not come—not tense, not relaxed either. Just still.

Her toddler was curled beside her, asleep with his back to the corridor, one chubby fist tucked beneath his cheek. Her arm lay along the edge of the bench, palm facing out like a barrier, ready to stop him from rolling off without thinking about it.

Chisholm followed Shane's eyes, then let out a slow breath.

"Kid's cute, huh?" he asked quietly.

Then, for the first time in weeks, his tone softened—not tactical, not clipped. Just...normal. Like he was speaking to someone who hadn't spent the last year buried in iron and accusations.

"You're just a kid, Alexander," he said. "Hell of a thing to be caught up in. No shame in being scared right now. Doesn't make you less of a man."

Shane blinked slowly. His face didn't change, but his shoulders settled back just a notch, as if hearing it aloud gave permission to let a little air in.

He didn't say anything in return. He didn't need to.

Across the hallway, Milo leaned against the windowsill and exhaled a soft stream of smoke through his nose. The two attorneys had gone quiet now, too, both watching the corridor like a theater curtain might lift at any moment.

The whole hall had stilled. Just boots on tile. Breaths held in waiting.

***

Four hours.

That's all it had taken. Four hours of deliberation after weeks of argument and testimony. A far cry from the first trial—a slow, churning ordeal that dragged on for days, like they'd been afraid of what the truth might cost them.

Now, not even a full afternoon.

The room was packed but hushed. No shifting. No whispering. Just breathing—the kind that filled your throat like gravel.

Specialist Shane Alexander stood at attention, his boots locked in place on the polished courtroom floor, his uniform pressed so stiff the seams might've sliced open his arms if he shifted wrong. His jaw clenched. Shoulders squared. Not a single muscle flinched.

Colonel Matthews gave the nod, his face as carved as ever, one hand folded over the other.

"Specialist Alexander, remain standing for the reading of the verdict."

Shane didn't blink.

The jury foreperson, a woman in her late forties with iron-grey hair and a calm face, rose with a single sheet in hand. Her voice didn't shake, didn't rise. It landed with the weight of a gavel.

"On the charge of violation of Article 118, Murder—this court-martial finds Specialist Shane Alexander: not guilty."

Silence cracked. Not relief yet. Not until the next words.

"On the charge of Article 92, Failure to Obey a Lawful Order—Specialist Alexander: not guilty."

Shane's hand flexed once at his side, fingers curling tight, then straightening again.

"And on the charge of Article 134—Conduct Unbecoming—Specialist Alexander: not guilty."

It didn't feel real.

For a second, no one moved. No one breathed. Shane's chest rose once, slow and unsteady, and his eyes locked on some point in the far corner of the room like he needed distance to stay upright.

Then the noise broke.

His mother was first—shoving past the rope barrier like protocol didn't matter anymore. His father wasn't far behind, slower but steady, eyes glistening behind thick-rimmed glasses. They were at his side in an instant, arms around him, pulling him into the kind of embrace that shook apart whatever walls he had left.

Shane didn't resist. He couldn't.

His knees buckled a little as he sank into them, head falling forward. The tears came hot and fast, no use trying to stop them. Not this time. Not anymore.

Chisholm stood a step behind, hands still folded, mouth a firm line—but his eyes said what his voice didn't. He waited until Shane straightened, still pressed between his parents, then stepped forward and laid a hand on the back of Shane's shoulder. Firm. Measured. Like closing a book.

"Good soldier," he said, just loud enough for Shane to hear. "You held the damn line."

Around them, the courtroom was shifting again—reporters, officers, observers. But inside that tight circle—Shane, his parents, Chisholm—there was only the sound of breath returning to lungs that hadn't dared draw deep in over a year.

No shackles this time. No guards flanking him. Just a free man standing in the same uniform they'd tried to shame, now bearing the truth on his chest like a stripe earned.

And outside the courthouse doors, the sun was still rising on the rest of his life.

***

The minute the verdict was read, the press surged. Even behind the courtroom's roped boundaries, a dozen local and national media reps came alive—cameras slung from necks, microphones angled like bayonets, voices rising in a scatter of rapid-fire questions.

"Specialist Alexander—how do you feel right now?"

"Will you pursue reenlistment?"

"What do you say to the families of the civilians?"

Shane didn't even look their way. He followed Chisholm's back, steady and unhurried, through the restricted side corridor off the courtroom. Media weren't allowed in this wing. No cameras, no press. Just Army personnel, legal staff, and a few cleared civilians. The echo of their footsteps filled the plain concrete hallway.

Behind him, his parents stayed close. His mother's hand hadn't let go of the fabric at the back of his uniform jacket since she grabbed it in the courtroom. She wasn't crying anymore, but her grip hadn't softened.

The two assistant defense attorneys walked a few paces behind. One of them, McKinney—lean and sharp-eyed—was still muttering about the prosecutor's last-minute attempt to cast doubt with the child's appearance.

"Genetics," he scoffed, lighting a cigarette before Milo even asked. "You'd think the man never saw a Punnett square in his life."

"Or the damn father's picture on IDs. But it *did* help landing them flat on their asses." The other assistant, Jacobs, a dry-tongued, round fellow, added flatly, "Thanks to Jovanović."

Milo gave a sheepish, pink-cheeked smile. "I didn't do—"

"Shut up," Jacobs said, stuffing a cigarette into Milo's hand and waving him on toward the door. "Go make yourself useful. Keep them off the girl."

Milo blinked, took the hint, and broke off toward the end of the hallway where one of the interpreter staffers stood, quietly gesturing toward the front entrance. She leaned in, said something low. Milo's face changed.

"She said to get her out of here," he reported back to the attorneys. "The press are hounding her. They're already saying she's political."

No one had to ask who "she" was.

Outside, in the courtyard area reserved for legal personnel and family, Chisholm finally stopped. The air was humid, July pressing down like a soaked flak vest. The brick perimeter wall offered no privacy, but it was quiet here. No press, no officers. Just an open patch of concrete and an Army-issued bench bolted into the ground.

Shane stood off to one side, his parents following Chisholm a few feet ahead, already deep into talk.

"We're pushing for full expungement," Chisholm said, tone still clipped and professional, but slower now. "If that clears, reenlistment could be an option. But no guarantees. He'll need to decide if that's even what he wants."

His mother clutched her handbag like a weapon, having finally let go of Shane's uniform. "We're just glad you got him back to us," she said with a tight smile. "You gave our boy back."

"No, ma'am," Chisholm said, glancing back at Shane. "He did that himself."

A few feet away, Shane stood in the sunlight near the perimeter wall, gaze drifting. Not watching anything in particular. Just being outside. Just breathing. Na'ada had strode before standing beside him. Her toddler had moved a few steps off, sitting on the warm concrete, spinning the plastic wheels of his beat-up truck. She kept one eye on the boy, the other on Milo, who was speaking with the interpreter staffer.

Then, without warning, she turned—spoke something loud, clipped, and fast in her language. Milo flinched, answered with equal speed and tone, then walked over to one of the defense assistants and borrowed a pen and a sheet of legal pad paper. He handed them to her without question. She pressed the paper flat against the low stone wall and began drawing.

Shane didn't notice.

He wasn't in Fayetteville anymore.

He was in Oklahoma, back in the half-cracked tiles of his junior high math class. Loran was sitting in front of him, spinning around in his seat with a shit-eating grin and freshly installed braces.

"Check this out," he said, holding up a dog-eared issue of *Superman.* "Corner store still had a few. Grabbed it when I was pickin' up smokes for my pa. You believe that?"

Tinsel Teeth, that's what they'd called him for a while. The memory stung—pure and untouched. Loran laughing with his face still whole. No blood. No shock. No goddamn war.

Then—

A hand was shaking his arm.

Shane blinked hard, pulled in a sharp breath. The yard came back into focus. The wall. The concrete. Na'ada. She was holding out the sheet of paper.

He took it slowly, eyes narrowed. The sketch was loose. Ballpoint ink-smudged lines, not realistic—but the details were unmistakable. Buzzcut hair. Wide-set, kind eyes. A cleft chin. And that slight crook in the nose he'd gotten during that eighth-grade dodgeball game when Marcus Alvarez cracked him with a blindside throw.

It was Loran.

The features weren't exact, but they were there. Captured not in realism but in memory.

Na'ada said something. English—halting but clear.

"I...remember him...I see him, in my, uh," she paused, pointing to her head. "I thank. I pray...for him, you also."

Shane didn't say anything. Couldn't.

His throat worked, eyes locked on the paper. No expression. Just the steady fall of tears down his face—silent, mechanical. He hadn't realized he'd been standing like that for minutes. Maybe ten. Maybe more.

Chisholm's voice finally cut through.

"Alexander. Let's go. Your folks want to discuss next steps—get your ass over here."

Shane blinked once, twice, then nodded. He didn't fold the drawing. Just carried it with him, one hand locked around the edges like he was afraid it'd disappear if he let go. He crossed the yard in silence, the sketch still in his hand. Chisholm stood with his parents near one of the concrete benches, one foot propped on the seat as he leaned forward, speaking low.

"...depends on Personnel Command," he was saying, "but the gears are already in motion."

Chisholm straightened when Shane approached, nodding toward the man who had just arrived from the building. He was in uniform—colonel, light bird, no nonsense. His nametape read **Morgan**. Not someone Shane had met before.

The colonel came to a stop in front of Shane, eyes level, tone all business.

"Specialist Alexander."

"Sir."

"You're to be advised that, pursuant to your full acquittal, Personnel Command has authorized reinstatement to active duty status. Effective immediately."

Shane stood straighter without thinking.

"You'll be restored to your previous rank of Specialist E-4," Morgan continued. "With all associated entitlements—back pay, benefits, service time, and clearance. Administrative processing will begin within seventy-two hours."

Shane didn't blink.

The colonel's tone shifted, only slightly—professional still, but measured.

"Additionally, due to the findings and recommendations from the Article 15-6 investigation and subsequent board review, you're being placed under assignment control pending transfer to Special Operations Command. You'll report to the 1st Special Warfare Training Group at Fort Bragg—initially for assessment."

Shane's mother made a sound—half gasp, half breath—but didn't speak. His father's hand landed silently on her shoulder.

"They'll determine whether you'll continue through selection or be reassigned. That will depend on readiness, medical clearance, and your own willingness to continue service," Morgan said. "But the door's open."

He reached into the folder under his arm and held out a sheet of paper—orders, typewritten and stamped.

Shane took them slowly, eyes flicking over the bold header. **ASSIGNMENT CONTROL ORDER — USASOC REVIEW PENDING.**

The colonel didn't shake hands. Just gave a crisp nod and turned away.

They were alone again.

Chisholm looked at Shane, then down at the paper in his hand.

"That's the Army's way of saying they want you back," he said. "Even if they're not sure how."

Shane's fingers curled slightly around the edges of the paper. The other hand still held the sketch Na'ada had drawn. He glanced down at it again—Loran's animated smile staring up from the page, eyes too kind for war.

Behind him, the toddler's toy truck clacked against the stone wall as he played.

Chisholm stepped aside, giving him space.

His mother's voice finally broke the quiet. "We thought you were gone. We thought—"

"I *was*," Shane said, voice low. "We both were. One by a bullet." He looked at the drawing again. "The other...for shooting it."

Na'ada watched them from her spot but said nothing. She didn't understand the words, but she understood the weight. Anyone could at this point.

The sun was high now. Too bright.

The Army had handed him back his future. Rank. Pay. Assignment. It was all there in ink and officialese. But what came next—what he could be, after all this—none of that could be found on the page.

Chisholm finally called to him again, voice steady but insistent.

"Alexander. You've got decisions to make. Come on."

Shane tucked the orders under his arm and followed.

Epilogue

The sky was gray enough to sweat rain, but hadn't made up its mind yet. Humid, too, like Oklahoma always got in August—air heavy enough to chew.

Shane squatted in front of the headstone like it was the foot of a bunk bed, arms draped over his knees, a bunch of daisies sticking out of a plastic wrapping beside him. The stems were already browning. He didn't care.

"Mama sent these. Said you liked 'em. I think she just didn't want me showin' up empty-handed," he muttered. "They're a little bent up. Like us." He set them down just under the chiseled marble.

"I was tryin' to explain the internet to you the other day in that dumb dream," he went on, voice quiet, like he wasn't sure if he was talking to the air or not. "MSN, dial-up, all that mess. You kept thinkin' it was a fax machine with colors."

He chuckled once through his nose. It didn't last.

"You ain't around to check your Top Eights. Or your Yahoo chain emails, or whatever dumb shit we were all doing. Don't worry—I'm keepin' it all up on your behalf."

Shane leaned back on his hands, stretching out his legs, letting his boot heels scuff the base of the stone.

"You shoulda met Chisholm. You'd've liked him. He's a pain in the ass. Can't keep it in his pants either. You'd respect that."

A breeze kicked dust across the grass.

"I saw Wilson and Rodriguez again. Wilson's got that look like he wants to say somethin' all the time and never does. Rodriguez, he said he tells his wife about you. Yeah, shitbag got married to his girl."

Shane paused, jaw tightening briefly. He scratched the side of his face, suddenly self-conscious for no reason at all.

"The girl with the baby? The one you dragged outta the blast?" Shane said, watching his fingertips drift along the edge of the headstone. "Yeah. She came. Her name's Na'ada. Spoke maybe eight words total. But she drew you. Like, actually stood there and drew you."

He reached into the manila folder beside him and pulled out the folded page—creased and worn now from how many times he'd opened it.

"All cartoon like Superman. Got your stupid nose right too. Kinda proud of that." He hummed before folding it back and putting it in his breast pocket. "They dressed her up real nice that day. Looked like she was goin' to church. Guess somebody told her what it meant to show up for a soldier."

The wind picked up again. This time, the sky looked serious about opening up. "I got orders," Shane muttered, looking down at his shoes. "They want me to re-enlist. With SOC. Special Warfare."

He gave a bitter smile that didn't quite reach his eyes.

"Feels like they want me more now that I'm broken in."

Silence stretched between him and the stone. He let it hang a second longer, then whispered: "So. What do I do?"

A long pause. Then—

He smiled. Small. Real.

"Yeah," Shane nodded, standing up, brushing the back of his jeans with one hand. "Yeah, you got it, dumbass."

He started to walk off, folder under his arm.

Stopped.

Turned back around, gave the headstone a second look. **Specialist Loran J. Taylor**. The flowers lay on the earth below it. Shane cleared his throat.

"Also," he added, casual as you please, "you were right."

He shrugged his shoulders. "Young moms *are* kinda hot."

He turned away again—this time for real—and walked off without a backward glance.

BOSNIA AND HERZEGOVINA
CROATIA
SERBIA
VOJVODINA
MONTENEGRO
ALBANIA
REPUBLIKA SRPSKA
BOSNIAC-CROAT FEDERATION
ADRIATIC SEA

N. Gradiška
V. Kladuša
Stušic
Varoška-Rijeka
Trzac
Bosanska Dubica
Bosanska Gradiška
Previc
Derventa
Odzak
Brcko
Bijeljina
Bogatic
Šid
Sremska Metrovica
Vinkovci
Bač. Palanka
Prijedor
Ivanjska
Prnjavor
Doboj
Gradačac
Vučkovci
Gračanica
Srebrenik
Sabac
Bihać
Bosanska Krupa
Sl. Rijeka
Piskavica
Sanski Most
Banja Luka
Vošavka
Miljanovci
Teslic
Raduša
Maglaj
Tuzla
Ugljevik
Krstac
Loznica
Banja Koviljača
Bos. Petrovac
Sanica
Ključ
Krupa-na-Vrbasu
Mašidvare
Skender-Vakuf
Mladikovine
Zavidoviđi
Zepce
Banovici
Kladanj
Cerska
Zvornik
Kamenica
Konjevic
SERBIA
Titov Drvar
Bos. Grahovo
Mrkonjić-Grad
Sipovo
Jajce
Oranovačko Polje
Travnik
Zenica
Vareš
Olovo
Vlasenica
Bratunac
Srebrenica
Gracac
Ervenik
Knin
Glamoc
Pucarevo
Vitez
Busovača
Breza
Vogosta
Sokolac
Žepa
Banja Bašta
REPUBLIKA SRPSKA
Drnis
Kupres
Gornji Vakuf
Fojnica
Kiseljak
Sarajevo
Pale
Rogatica
Višegrad
CROATIA
Šibenik
Sinj
Livno
Rumboci
Prozor
Tarčin
Hrasnca
Gorazde
Čajnice
Priboj
Trogir
Divolje
Vinica
Prisoje
Duvno
Jablanica
Konji
Foča
Split
Omis
Imotski
Rasko Polje
Meshovina
G. Dreznica
Jasenjani
Kalinovik
Pljevja
Kočerin
Letica
Mostar
Postire
Brač
Hvar
Makarska
Vrgorac
Ljubuški
Blaga
Medugorje
Stolac
Nevesinje
Gacko
Avtovac
Metkovic
Blato
Korčula
Pelešac Peninsula
Opuzen
Bleca
MONTENEGRO
Niksic
Sutar
Lastovo
Vis
Biševo
Mjet
Sipan
Trebinje
Dubrovnik
Herceg-Novi
Kotor
Cetinje
Podgorica
Budva
Bar

BOSNIA AND HERZEGOVINA

National capital
Town, village
Airport
International boundary
Inter-entity boundary line
Republic boundary
Autonomous province boundary
Main road
Secondary road
Railroad

0 10 20 30 40 50 km
0 10 20 30 mi

Eric brings the weight of lived experience to every story he tells. With nearly two decades of military service—including time in both the U.S. Army and the U.S. Coast Guard—Eric writes with the rare authority of someone who's been there. His deep understanding of duty, sacrifice, and the moral complexities of life in uniform shapes every page he pens.

After retiring from active service due to medical reasons, Eric turned to writing not just as a creative outlet, but as a mission. His stories are grounded in gritty realism and emotional truth, capturing the honor, tension, and brotherhood that define life in and out of combat. Readers come for the action—but stay for the heart, the humanity, and the unflinching honesty behind each character.

When he's not crafting page-turning military thrillers, Eric enjoys time with his wife, four daughters, and grandson. Whether he's out exploring new places or following political developments, he brings a storyteller's curiosity to everything he does.

His writing isn't just entertaining—it's lived-in, powerful, and unforgettable.

www.ingramcontent.com/pod-product-compliance
Lightning Source LLC
Chambersburg PA
CBHW071146100726
47908CB00002B/260